DARK TIES

DARK
TIES

A NOVEL

MARK DAME

FutureLine Press

Printed in the United States of America

Print: 978-1-946298-10-2
ePub: 978-1-946298-11-9
MOBI: 978-1-946298-12-6

First Edition

For Tracie

*For encouraging me in the beginning and
sticking with me through all of it.*

CHAPTER ONE

I N THE MIDDLE of the Monongahela National Forest, not far from the more famous Snowshoe Mountain ski resort, Murphy Creek was an unremarkable speck on the map. Travelers on West Virginia Route 28 usually passed through without noticing it. Except, that is, for Labor Day weekend.

That weekend, Murphy Creek was the home to the Pocahontas County Fall Festival. The carnival rides, games, food, and live music drew crowds from all over the county and beyond, making Murphy Creek, with its official population of forty-two, the largest town in the county for three days every year. People came from as far as Beckley and Charlottesville. The Fall Festival even attracted hardcore fair and festival enthusiasts from Ohio and Pennsylvania, much to the delight of the bed and breakfast owners in Murphy Creek and the surrounding towns.

Most everybody in the area looked forward to the festival. Those who had never wandered far from home imagined it was what New York City must be like. For the kids, the festival was the highlight of the year, even if it did mark the end of summer freedom and the return to school. They would spend the entire weekend running all over the fairgrounds, squandering their hard-earned allowances on rides and junk food. Young couples wandered the grounds hand in hand, the boys trying to impress their dates by winning stuffed animals in the carnival games. Older couples and families set up blankets and picnic baskets in the grass field in front of the main stage. While the kids ran around the festival, the parents would listen to the live music, enjoying one last weekend of summer. This year, the big Saturday Night Concert featured The Frog Mountain Trio, a regional bluegrass band that had even recorded a few albums in Nashville.

But for Ken Simmons, the Fall Festival was overwhelming. He felt dizzy just walking through the main gates. Blinking lights were everywhere. The air was thick with the late summer humidity and the scents of the carnival: the stench of hot cooking oil from the fryers and griddles, the sickly sweet smell of cotton candy, the musty scent of the straw that covered the ground, the hot stuffy odor of the crowd. Bells and whistles, clacking carnival rides and their screaming riders. The music from the concert added to the cacophony.

Ken stopped to catch his breath. Sara, his wife, was next to him, grinning ear to ear. She loved this kind of shit. She tried to drag him to every carnival, festival, and county fair within a hundred miles. Ken found large crowds to be annoying, and, since almost being killed by a deranged fan a few years earlier, a little frightening. He absently reached up and touched the scar on his face where the doctors had rebuilt his cheekbone and jaw.

Someone bumped into him from behind.

"Nice place to stop, asshole!" The man pushed his way around them and moved on.

"Are you okay?" Sara asked Ken, ignoring the man. "We can leave if you want."

Ken took a deep breath to steady himself. "I'll be fine."

"You sure?"

"Yeah. Just feeling a little claustrophobic." He flashed her a quick smile, trying to hide his anxiety.

"Okay. Let's get a funnel cake. Deep-fried dough sprinkled with powdered sugar can fix anything." Sara grabbed his hand and pulled him through the crowd to one of the booths.

The funnel cake didn't cure Ken's anxiety, but it was awfully good.

They wandered around the fairgrounds, watching people play the rigged carnival games as they pulled off pieces of deep-fried goodness and licked sticky sugar off their fingers. They stopped at another booth to buy beer coupons, then traded a couple at the beer booth for red plastic cups of tasteless amber liquid. Certainly not the Sam Adams Ken preferred.

Ken, a bestselling crime fiction writer, had moved to Murphy Creek with his wife almost ten years ago. They had grown tired of fans constantly knocking on their door and peeking in the windows of their house in Upper St. Clair, an upper middle class neighborhood just outside of Pittsburgh. The *price of fame*, his mother had told him. Ken didn't quite understand why so many people were interested in the life of a man who told lies for a living. So, while he was grateful for his fans, he just didn't like people. At least not in large numbers.

Ken had reached the national spotlight after one of those TV evangelists had picked *Roadside Stalker*, his first book, as an example of what was wrong with the country. The novel was about a serial killer who kidnapped a woman involved in a terrorist plot. The killer had to decide whether or not to expose the plot, risking his freedom. Ken had written it so the reader could empathize with the killer, even root for him, long before Jeff Lindsay's Dexter character became a cultural phenomenon.

Roadside Stalker hadn't sold very well until Reverend Ernest Funk held it up on his weekly television show and denounced it as a work of Satan. Sales skyrocketed and K. Elliot Simmons had become a household name almost overnight.

Nearly twenty years later, his latest novel, *Terror in Suburbia*, was becoming his biggest hit since *Roadside Stalker*, maybe even bigger. But unlike his first book, his second foray into the life of a serial killer wasn't a feel-good tale of redemption. It was the first time Ken had published a story that he wished he hadn't. He wasn't able to put his finger on why, but he suspected it had to do with Cory Rivers, the killer in the book. Nobody, not even Ken, could empathize with Cory, much less root for him.

Whatever doubts Ken had, his fans loved the book. They had shown up in record numbers at every stop in the publicity tour. After the five-week, fifteen-stop tour that crossed the country from Boston to San Diego, Ken was looking forward to starting a new project and putting Cory Rivers behind him. Even Sara, his biggest fan and an eternal optimist, was happy to be done with the book.

Drawn by the music, Ken and Sara found themselves watching The Frog Mountain Trio on the main stage. Neither of them was particularly into bluegrass, but the band was pretty good and Ken found himself tapping his foot to the music. Sara seemed to be equally engrossed. He smiled at her, noticing some powdered sugar above her lip. He reached over to wipe it off, startling her. She smiled back at him.

"Feeling better?" she asked him.

"I'll be fine," he replied. He didn't feel fine, but he didn't want Sara to have a bad time worrying about his issues. Besides, maybe being in the crowds could help him get over his crowd phobia.

Immersion therapy. Wasn't that what they called it?

The band started playing another tune that Ken recognized. It was a bluegrass interpretation of CCR's "Proud Mary." So maybe bluegrass wasn't so bad after all. He pulled her close and she leaned against him, wrapping her arms around his waist. With her head on his chest, he could feel her humming. When the band reached the chorus, she sang out loud, along with the rest of the crowd. Ken couldn't help but join in. He glanced down at Sara and saw she was watching him. He bent down and kissed her, then pulled her closer. She squeezed him back. Maybe he was starting to feel a little better.

Between songs, the bandleader started talking about the finger-picking skills of the banjo player. From where they stood near the back of the seating area, Ken and Sara couldn't make out much of what he said. Without speaking to each other, they started walking back to the main aisle, stopping at the beer booth for a refill.

"I think maybe—"

A loud scream interrupted Ken. He spun around to find the source. Cheering erupted around a booth across the aisle. A teenage girl was jumping up and down, clapping her hands. Apparently her boyfriend had just won her a large stuffed pink elephant. She jumped on him, wrapping her arms and legs around him, nearly knocking him over.

"Hell yeah!" the girl's boyfriend yelled. "Who's your daddy!"

The other teenagers gathered around them hooted and hollered in response.

"We were never that obnoxious, were we?" Ken asked his wife.

"No, sweetie, you were much worse." She grinned at him. "And that's the way I liked it."

Ken shook his head and turned way. He could barely remember being that young, much less acting like an idiot. At least not in public.

They continued down the aisle, stopping occasionally to play a game or buy a deep-fried pickle or pork on a stick. Ken liked watching people try to win the games, though winning was usually more about luck than skill. His writer's brain was busy taking notes, especially of the more interesting characters in the crowd. Ken could people watch all night, but Sara started to get bored.

"Come on," she said after a while. "Let's go ride the Ferris wheel."

"I don't think so."

Ken wasn't big on amusement park rides. He had a mild fear of heights and didn't feel the urge for adrenaline-inducing activities. He had decided a long time ago that being a writer made him a coward. His mind was tuned to coming up with crazy shit, so he tended to look at most things in life from that perspective. Amusement park rides designed to fling people around in seemingly death-defying ways were ripe for his imagination, especially the rickety, portable rides at a traveling carnival. Even the Ferris wheel scared him. He had a wild image of it breaking loose from its supports and rolling away. He had never heard of one doing that, but there was a first time for everything.

Sara, on the other hand, loved amusement park rides and could occasionally talk him into riding one with her. She would use her puppy dog look and the next thing he knew, he was strapped into some diabolical killing machine.

Looking up at him now, she stuck out her lower lip in an exaggerated pout and threw in a couple of Disneyesque eyelash flutters. Game over.

Ken sighed. "Okay, fine. But just one ride."

Sara smiled in victory and led him to the other side of the fairgrounds where the rides had been set up. They were bathed in the tangy smell of grease as they walked down the row of spinning and whirling machines toward the Ferris wheel at the far end. Each one seemed to have its own unique way of killing you.

A miniature roller coaster ran along the outside edge of the fairgrounds. It didn't take much of Ken's imagination to see where that could go wrong. In his mind, the kids riding it weren't screaming with excitement but rather with terror as the train broke free from its track and went hurtling through the air. *Twelve Killed in Freak Roller Coaster Accident* the papers would say.

Opposite the roller coaster was a tamer ride for the little kids. Cars painted like happy, smiling ladybugs moved around an undulating, circular track. Scary enough for a four-year-old, though the teenagers all thought it was boring. For Ken, it was a disaster waiting to happen. He imagined whatever speed limiter it had breaking, the cars hurtling around faster and faster until they flew off the track. He could almost see the toddlers flying out of the cars like bug parts.

Shaking his head to get that image out of his mind, he looked at the next death trap, which didn't help. It was a horizontal wheel on top of a twenty-five-foot tall post. Seats hung from the outer edge of the wheel on thin wires. People voluntarily strapped themselves into this device, which then proceeded to spin fast enough to make the seats swing out almost forty-five degrees. Ken's imagination jumped right past breaking cables sending the passengers flying across the fairgrounds. Instead, he imagined the wheel detaching from the tower and rolling down the aisle, dragging and flopping the riders into the people who hadn't risked their lives on Death Wheel 3000.

By the time they made it to the Ferris wheel, Ken was convinced they were going to die. It wasn't a matter of probabilities. It was a simple fact of life: the Ferris wheel was going to break loose and roll through the Fall Festival crowd, crushing people as it went. He turned to Sara to tell her there was no way she was going to drag him to his certain death.

Like she was reading his mind, she looked up at him and smiled.

"It's not going to break. You're not going to fall out. The ride operator can't make it spin so fast your head pops off."

Ken looked down at his feet. She was right. It was all in his head. At least the bit about the Ferris wheel. He still wasn't sure about the Death Wheel down the way.

"One ride. That's all I can take tonight," he said, playing his

sympathy card. He knew he probably wouldn't get to use it again, but he wasn't about to get on one of the other death machines.

"Okay. After this, we'll do what you want to do."

"What if what I want to do involves you and me at home, naked?"

Sara rolled her eyes and turned to give two tickets to the ride operator. She let him help her into the car. Ken followed, noticing the operator didn't help him in.

"Keep your hands and feet inside the car at all times, folks. No standing until the ride is over."

He must think we're stupid, Ken thought, but he kept it to himself. No point in upsetting the guy who was about to be in control of their lives. Instead, he grabbed the lap bar in one hand and Sara's hand in the other. He hoped she would take the gesture as being romantic rather than being scared. Looking at her, he guessed she knew exactly what it was, but she was being nice and didn't say anything. At least while there were other people around.

The big wheel turned enough so the next car was in position to swap riders. This first stop was only a few feet off the ground, but the car was swinging with residual momentum from the short move, which made Ken grip the bar tighter. His rational mind told him that gripping the bar tighter wouldn't keep the car from falling and the emotional side of his brain told the rational side to fuck off. Then the wheel rotated a little more, moving their car higher, and the rational side of his brain went quiet.

By the time they reached the top, Ken was a mess. Sara actually looked like she might be feeling bad about making him ride. She looked like she was about to say something when the Ferris wheel began moving again. This time, it didn't stop. They were hurtling toward the ground and Ken felt the funnel cake flip in his stomach. He instinctively pulled his legs up before the car smashed into the ground.

Then suddenly, they were traveling backward. Their car flew through the loading station and back up the other side. Ken broke out in a cold sweat and a pit formed in his stomach. Before he could come to grips with that, they were hurled over the top and back to the ground again. His vision blurred, his head slowly spinning. He tried to look at Sara, to tell her he wasn't feeling so hot. As he turned his head, his vision closed in and went dark.

*

A sliver of light spilled in under the door. He waited until he heard the shower running before opening the closet door and walking into the bedroom. A short skirt and a white button-up blouse were sitting on the bed, along with a pair of lacy thong panties. He ran his fingers over the soft lace and licked his lips.

He knew her Saturday night ritual better than she did. Home from work at the Hy-Vee by 9:00. Shower and a microwave dinner. Then she would get dressed up in her slutty clothes and go meet her fuck buddy at The Ranch, the local country and western bar. Afterward, they'd go eat at some all-night diner before coming home.

She wasn't going to make it tonight.

Her singing drifted from the bathroom. Some country song he heard on the radio all the time. The bathroom door was open and he could see her silhouette on the shower curtain. He watched while she washed herself, thinking about the game that was coming. His pulse raced in anticipation. He had waited a long time for this ride.

When she turned off the shower, he moved to the living room. Her cell phone had been *dinging* with incoming text messages and he needed to give her time to answer them to avoid raising anyone's suspicions. He hid in the shadows where he could see down the hallway into her bedroom. She walked out of the bathroom, wrapped in a towel. She had another one wrapped around her hair. Her cell phone *dinged* again. She picked it up and read the messages while she walked toward the kitchen.

He slid along the wall to get a better view. She was pulling a frozen meal out of the freezer. He watched and waited for the right opportunity. She opened the box and put the meal in the microwave. Another *ding* from her phone. She smiled as she replied.

He moved closer.

She put the cell phone on the table, then turned her back to him and opened the refrigerator. He stepped forward silently as she bent over to search for something. She stood up, a bottle of flavored water in her hand. He reached around her, clasping one hand over her mouth and nose, the other around her waist.

The plastic bottle fell, thudding on the floor and bouncing away. She struggled against his grasp. Strong as a snake, this one. He gripped tighter, lifting her off the ground as he hauled her back through the kitchen.

Her muffled screams turned into hitching gasps, sucking his hand tighter to her face. She reached up and grabbed his arm, desperately ripping and tearing, trying to free her mouth. He pulled back harder, squeezing her head against his chest. The suffocating stench of flowers from whatever god-awful soap or shampoo she had used in the shower made him turn his head away.

He half carried, half dragged her down the hallway toward the bedroom. She struggled and kicked, anything to try to break free. Strength was fading from her body. It wouldn't be long now. In one final effort to escape, she pushed off the floor with both feet, trying to knock him off balance. He grinned at the attempt, but his grip never faltered. This wasn't the first time he'd played this game. He had captured much more challenging prey than this skinny bitch.

He heard a *ding* from the kitchen. He paused. The microwave. Her supper was ready. Too bad she would never get to eat it.

He continued to drag her down the hall. By the time he reached the bedroom, she had gone limp. He uncovered her mouth. He didn't want her to die yet. That would be a waste of all of his time and planning.

He switched his hold on her, grabbing her under her arms so he could drag her the rest of the way to the bed. They always seemed heavier when they were unconscious. Not too heavy for him to handle, though. He kept in shape. That was important for his hobby.

Her towel fell to the floor as he lifted her onto the bed. Looking at her, he frowned. The other towel was still on her head. Lying there naked with just that towel on her head, she looked silly. He pulled it off and tossed it aside.

Much better. Smiling, he knelt next to the bed and stroked her soft skin. His heart raced, his hands trembled. He had waited so long for her. Everything he had dreamed about for the past three years, fantasized about, was about to become reality.

His tool bag was under the bed where he had stashed it earlier. It had everything he needed, including rope, which he pulled out. He felt a shiver of excitement as he climbed onto the bed and straddled his toy.

He licked his lips. She was so peaceful. That would change. He propped her up on pillows so she was half sitting.

She needed to be able to watch him play.

He tied her wrists to the headboard, making sure there was no slack, then moved to her feet and secured her ankles to the legs at the foot of the bed. He stored the rest of the rope in the tool bag. He would dispose of it later. He was good at covering his tracks and that included not keeping any of the extra rope.

One final touch. He picked up the underwear from the bed and stuffed it in her mouth. Then he cut a strip from the blouse and tied it around her head to keep the gag in place.

His catch secured, he went back to the kitchen to fetch her cell phone. He didn't want to chance her fuck buddy coming home before he was finished.

He read through the text messages. The guy was already drunk. A quick follow-up text, telling the asshole to stay out as long as he wanted, should ensure a few hours to play. He put the phone in his pocket, then picked up the towels and the remains of her clothes. They would just get in the way, so he threw them into the closet with the rest of her dirty clothes.

Everything was ready.

He checked the ropes one last time to make sure they were secure, then went into the bathroom to splash some water on his face. He was sweating from the struggle and he didn't want to risk leaving any DNA evidence. He had shaved all the hair off his body, even his eyebrows, and wore gloves to avoid leaving fingerprints. He would rinse off in the shower before he left to avoid tracking her blood out with him. He would burn his clothes and dispose of his tools in random dumpsters around town.

Chances of leaving any physical evidence or taking any with him were low, which was why he had never been caught.

Just because he hadn't played in a long time was no excuse to get sloppy.

He heard a moan from the bedroom. His toy was waking up.

He turned off the water and dried his gloved hands. Standing in the doorway, he watched her regain consciousness. She tried to move, pulling against her restraints. She tried to scream through her gag. Her panicked breathing whistled through her nostrils as she turned her head from side to side, looking around the room. She apparently didn't see him standing in the doorway, which wasn't surprising. The only light came from a lamp on the nightstand, leaving much of the room in shadow.

Besides, panicked people tend to not be very observant. Dumber than a caged rat.

He watched awhile longer, enjoying the transition from panic and fear to anger and frustration, knowing soon fear would return and consume her for the rest of her short life. It was all part of the game.

He smiled as she tried to calm herself with deep breaths. He followed her eyes as she looked at her alarm clock on the dresser across the room. 10:18.

Time to get started. He guessed he had at most four hours, assuming cockboy stayed at the bar until close like he usually did.

"Wakey, wakey, bitch."

She jumped at the sound of his voice, straining against the ropes. She turned her head toward him. Adrenaline flowed through his body, his heartbeat quickening and his skin tingling with excitement as surprise washed over her face and turned to fear. Her eyes widened so much they looked like they might pop right out of her head. He knew he was intimidating in his dark coveralls, gloves, and shaved head, but he still enjoyed the confirmation. Their reaction when they first saw him gave him a charge that made the rest of the game even sweeter.

Ding!

He pulled her cell phone from his pocket and checked the message. It was from her cockboy.

Goood mite bsbe liv u

He replied: *Good night. Have fun! Love you!*

"Your cockboy says, 'Good night,'" he said, putting the phone back in his pocket. "Let's make a surprise for him when he gets home."

He laughed as she began to realize what was going to happen to her. She was wrong, of course. At least, in the details. The end result would be the same, but she had no clue what he had in store.

She tried to scream again, struggling against her bonds. He stepped up to the bed and pulled his Bowie knife from its sheath on his belt. He held it up so she could see it. Her eyes opened even wider. His stomach fluttered and his skin prickled with new goose bumps. She looked a little pale. The wait had been worth it.

He took his time, basking in the moment. He watched her face as he lowered the knife to her chest, lightly touching her breast with the tip of the blade. Gently, slowly he dragged the blade down her body, leaving a light, white scratch on her skin. Her muscles twitched and trembled in response. He held the blade lightly on her quivering stomach.

"We're going to play a game. You like games, slut? I'll bet you play games with your cockboy all the time. Do you like to play with his friends too?"

She turned her head away from him. A hot flash of anger rose in him like bile.

"Look at me when I'm talking to you, bitch!" He grabbed the hair at the back of her head and turned her face back toward him. "We've got a lot to do and you're gonna watch it all. You'll like this game." He laughed. "Well, maybe you won't, but I will."

He pulled a lighter from his pocket and grinned as he lit it. He held up the knife so she could watch as he heated up the tip of the blade.

"This is a game you've never played before. It's my favorite game. You wanna play?"

She tried to shake her head without taking her glistening eyes off of him. The tears were coming soon. He laughed again and continued to heat the tip of the knife. A lighter wouldn't get it glowing red, but it would suffice. To test it, he touched the tip to her cheek. Her skin made a satisfying sizzle sound, like a juicy steak on a grill, before she pulled her face away. She sucked in her breath and tried to scream again, but no sound came from her. Pain sometimes did that.

He inhaled the sharp charcoal aroma of her burnt skin. Yes, the lighter would do nicely.

But she wasn't watching. She had closed her eyes again.

"Open your fucking eyes, bitch, or I'll open them for you!"

He lit the lighter again to reheat the knife. The mark on her cheek was already blistered with a small black line of charred flesh. Soon she would have more to match it. Later, there would be some cuts, the red blood and the black burns forming beautiful patterns on her skin.

This was all foreplay. The main event would come later.

He glanced at the clock: 10:29. Plenty of time.

He lowered the knife, contemplating where to place the next mark. She tried to scream again.

It wouldn't be long before she gave up.

*

"Ken! Ken, wake up!"

Ken's vision began to clear, but the spinning in his head hadn't stopped. A yawning sensation filled his stomach as the Ferris wheel flung them over the top and down the front side again. One more trip through the loading station, then he shared his partially digested funnel cake and beer with the riders in the car below them as they rose up the back side of the wheel.

Now Ken *really* felt sick. It was bad enough being afraid of riding a Ferris wheel, but then to actually puke on it? And worse, puke on other riders. The embarrassment was a new low for him. Sara was looking at him, her eyes wide. The passengers in the car behind them were screaming profanities at him. Below, the ride operator was laughing.

The wheel stopped to let Ken and Sara off. Ken struggled to climb out of the car, his head still spinning. Sara helped him down. He leaned on her as they moved off the loading platform. The Ferris wheel stopped again to let off the unfortunate recipients of Ken's stomach contents. The couple glared at him as they got off. They were dressed in jeans and T-shirts with leather motorcycle vests and chaps. They both had hair well past their shoulders that was now filled with sticky funnel cake remnants. If Ken hadn't been so scared, he might have laughed.

The man was several inches taller than Ken. Several inches wider too.

"I'm so sorry." Ken braced himself for the blow that had to be coming. He turned his head a little to protect the side of his face that had already been through reconstructive surgery once.

"What the fuck!" the woman screamed at him. She lunged at Ken, fists clenched. Ken flinched, but the guy grabbed her shoulders and held her back.

They continued to scream at Ken. He couldn't really understand what they were saying, but he supposed it didn't matter. They were obviously upset about getting puked on.

"I don't know what happened," Ken said. "I think I'm getting sick or something. Let me buy you guys a beer."

"It's gonna cost me a hundred bucks to get this cleaned!" He didn't seem to be listening to Ken.

"Everything okay here, folks?"

Ken turned and saw a sheriff's deputy standing next to him. He recognized him, but couldn't remember the name. He looked like he couldn't be older than sixteen, but he was just as big as the guy threatening Ken's well-being.

"This asshole puked on me and my old lady!" the guy screamed.

"What kind of pussy-ass motherfucker pukes on a fucking Ferris wheel?" his *old lady* added.

"I'm sure he didn't do it on purpose," the deputy said. "Getting arrested for assault won't make your night any better."

"We were trying to offer them some beer tickets to make up for it," Sara said.

"Will that be good with you folks?" the deputy asked the couple.

"Whatever," the man replied.

Sara held out their last four beer tickets, apologizing again.

The man ripped them from her hand and sneered at Ken. "I ought to fuck you up, but I don't want to embarrass you in front of your mom."

Still grumbling, the guy and his girlfriend turned and stormed off.

"You okay, Mr. Simmons?" the deputy asked.

Ken looked at him and remembered his name: Mitch Armstrong. The last time Ken had seen him, Mitch had been talking about becoming a cop. Now here he was in uniform, coming to the rescue.

"I'm good. Thanks, Mitch."

"Yes, thank you so much," Sara added. "I don't think they would have actually started a fight, but I'm glad we didn't have to find out."

"No problem, Mrs. Simmons," Mitch said. "Well, you folks have a safe evening."

Mitch turned to walk off when Ken remembered something.

"Hey, Mitch!" Ken called after him. Mitch turned back. "You still interested in helping me out with a book?"

Mitch's eyes lit up. When Mitch had still been in high school, he had told Ken that once he became a cop he could help Ken out with the "inside scoop." Ken had never had trouble getting the inside scoop from various police departments, so he had never followed up with Mitch. After tonight, though, maybe he owed the kid a little.

"Sure, Mr. Simmons!" he said, losing his professional law enforcement officer demeanor. "That'd be awesome! You want to do a ride along?"

"Absolutely. You have an email address?"

Mitch reached into his shirt pocket and pulled out a business card. "You can email me at work."

"Great. I'll take you up on it."

Mitch smiled and waved to them before continuing his patrol.

"Are you okay?" Sara asked when Mitch had moved out of earshot.

Ken gave her a weak nod.

"I'm sorry I made you ride."

"It's okay. I've never puked on a Ferris wheel before."

"Well you have now." She grinned at him, trying to cheer him up. "Are you sure you're okay? You actually passed out."

Ken remembered the dream. "It was strange. I started to feel dizzy, then I was dreaming about Cory Rivers. I think it was where he killed Sydney Wilson in my book. Only it was different somehow." Ken shuddered. "I don't know. Anyway, it was just a dream. The real nightmare was waking up and puking on Biker Bob and his babe." He tried to laugh, but only managed a hoarse grunt.

"Yeah, that could have gone real bad."

"I guess we can thank Mitch for coming along at the right time." Ken shuddered again at the thought of what might have happened. "I think I'm done for the night."

"Okay, let's go home. I'll drive."

Sara squeezed his hand and kissed him on the cheek.

CHAPTER TWO

SHERIFF ALLEN JAMES leaned back in his chair, twirling a pen and staring at the case files on his desk. Specifically, the stack on the right side that went back ten years, from even before he had taken office as the sheriff back in 2008. The cases involved unsolved murders. Not just any murders, though. These were particularly heinous. Allen had suspected they were the work of a serial killer after they had found the second body. The stack had grown in the last couple of months with the discovery of similar cold cases from neighboring counties.

"You ever going to clean your desk?"

Deputy Phil Crawford had been his best friend since grade school. Sometimes Allen felt like Phil took advantage of that. Allen knew his desk looked disorganized. The case files regarding the serial killer he was looking for weren't the only files on his desk.

"I know where everything is. Besides, I have better things to do with my time than cleaning my damn desk."

Phil laughed like he always did. Allen supposed they would have this same conversation another hundred times before they traded their badges and guns for fishing hats and rods.

Phil picked up a requisition form for 9mm pistol ammunition. "You're falling behind on your paperwork." It had been sitting in his *In* basket for over a week, along with a dozen or so other forms he needed to review and sign.

"When the good citizens of Woodford County elect you sheriff, you can do it your way. As long as this is my office, I'll do it my way." The fact was he knew he was behind on paperwork. He had been spending too much time on the serial killer case the past few months. "Was there something you wanted, or did you just come in here to give me shit?"

"You called me, Boss."

Allen sighed. He had asked Phil to stick around after his shift. At three o'clock in the morning, they should both be home—Allen to his wife and kids and Phil to his dog.

Allen put the pen he had been playing with back in the penholder his son had gotten him for Father's Day a few years ago. It was shaped like a revolver cylinder with a plaque that read *The World's Best Dad.* Lately, he didn't feel like he had been living up to the title.

"Come on. Let's get some coffee," Allen said. He picked up his coffee-stained mug and followed Phil out of his office.

The rest of the building was dark, and had been since the last of the office personnel left at six o'clock the evening before. The third-shift deputy on duty was out on patrol. Their holding cell was empty, as it always was after six. They moved all overnight detainees to the Ashford Police Station, which also served as the county jail, to avoid the need to hire an additional deputy to babysit a normally empty cell.

"What's bugging you, Allen?" Phil said. "I've been off duty for three hours and you still haven't told me why you wanted me to stick around. I enjoy your company and all, but what gives?"

"How long have we known each other?" He hoped he didn't sound as tired as he felt.

"Shit, I don't know. Thirty-five years? Maybe more. Why? You ain't dying, are you?"

"No, not yet," Allen said, trying to smile.

"Then what's up?"

"Do I strike you as somebody who believes in witches or ghosts or little green men?"

Phil laughed, but stopped when he realized Allen wasn't. "You're serious."

"Yeah, I'm serious. Do I look like the kind of guy who falls for bullshit stories?"

"You're about the most skeptical asshole I know. You remember that surprise party Ginnie tried to throw for your fortieth birthday? You remember how you totally screwed that up because you thought she was stepping out on you?"

"Don't you ever tell her that or I'll castrate you with a fork!" They had been married for over ten years at the time of the party. Allen had suspected all the private phone conversations and mysterious "trips to the store" were because she was cheating on him. He had followed her around and caught her buying decorations for the party. He had managed to play it off as coincidence that he had just happened to be at the same store. Only Phil knew the truth. He still felt bad about it, but at least Ginnie never found out that his suspicion was what blew the surprise.

"I won't say nothing to her," Phil said, refilling his coffee cup. "You know I wouldn't do that. I'm just saying that if your own wife can't even pull off a surprise party for you, even doing it a month early just to throw you off, I don't see how anybody else could bullshit you without you figuring it out."

Allen filled his own cup, but didn't reply.

"But that's what makes you a good cop, Boss."

"Kissing my ass ain't gonna get you nothing," Allen said.

"Hey, you're the one who asked." Phil furrowed his brow. "What the hell's going on? Somebody trying to scam you or something?"

"It's that goddamn book you gave me."

Phil liked reading crime fiction novels, especially those by his favorite author, K. Elliot Simmons. Several months ago, he had read Simmons' latest book, *Terror in Suburbia*. When he had noticed the murders in the novel were suspiciously like the real murders, he brought the book to Allen. Phil had been working the cases since the beginning and knew them almost as well as Allen.

"So I was right? There is something to it?" Phil asked.

"I'm not sure what to think about it. Every one of our cases is described in the book. After I read it, I called every sheriff's office in two hundred miles. Even the ones across the border in Minnesota. I asked them to send me any cases they had involving murders with our guy's MO. You know what I got?"

"A headache?"

"I got more unsolved cases. That makes one for damn near every murder in the book. The only one we don't have a match for is the last one."

Back in his office, they sat down at his desk again.

"What about the one that got away? You know. At the end?"

"A lot of case files from the area could fit that one. Or maybe none at all. Maybe he just added that one so he could have an ending."

"That's possible," Phil said, nodding. "And don't forget the cop in the book is practically named after you."

"Yeah, I noticed that too." The cop in the book was named Alan St. James. Although he was a detective and not a sheriff, that seemed like a distinction without a difference.

"You don't think Simmons is our killer, do you?"

"It doesn't look like it," Allen replied. "The thing about public figures is they tend to be easier to track than most folks. According to stories I found on the Internet, when Sandra Bell was killed, he was in New York at the opening for a movie made from one of his books. And he was in Los Angeles doing a book signing or some shit during the Jordan Rosenbaum murder. I didn't find out where he was for the others, but I suspect if I dig deep enough, he'd have alibis for those too."

"So what then? Did he figure out who the guy is and interview him?"

Allen shook his head. "I don't know. That seems pretty unlikely. Do you think some jackass from West Virginia could find this guy when we've been looking for him for ten years? Besides, even the goddamn newspapers haven't picked up on it, so how would Simmons know about it?"

Phil nodded again.

"Hell, until a couple of months ago, the State boys didn't even think there was a serial killer. Goddamn politics. Nobody wanted to accept we had our very own BTK Killer."

"Well, it's not like South Dakota has a big serial killer problem," Phil said. "Besides, he's been pretty slick about it. Only killing once a year and then in different counties. Not too surprising that nobody put it all together until you started asking around."

Allen grunted. "For all the good it's done."

"Irregardless, Simmons had to talk to somebody," Phil said.

"Yeah, but who? Who knew about all the cases before us?"

"Maybe our guy went to Simmons? Trying to get his story out without getting caught?"

"I don't think so. You really think a guy who's managed to go this long without getting caught would do that?"

"They say these guys like the spotlight. I read an article about it by an ex-FBI guy. He said that some of them even leave clues at the crime scenes trying to get caught 'cause they want everybody to know who they are. Besides, what other explanation is there? It can't just be a coincidence. How many cases are we up to now? Since you got the new ones?"

"Seven. One a year from 2005 to 2011."

"Jesus," Phil said, shaking his head. "And the new ones are like the others? All the details the same as to book?"

"Yeah."

"So seven cases where he got the all details right, even stuff that wasn't made public."

"Seems so."

Phil shrugged. "I suppose that's why I gave you the book in the first place, but damn."

"I know. Ginnie probably wishes you hadn't." Allen had been spending almost all of his free time working on the case since he read the Simmons book. His wife hadn't said anything to him about it yet, but he could tell it was bugging her.

"Maybe Simmons is a psychic or something."

Allen just looked back at Phil without answering.

"Shit, Allen. You can't really be thinking that?"

Allen threw his hands up. "No, but how else do you explain it?"

"Have you tried calling the guy?"

"Apparently he doesn't have a home phone and his publisher won't give out his cell phone number without a warrant. I'm thinking about taking a trip out to West Virginia to talk to him in person."

"Really?" Phil asked, perking up. "Need some company?"

Allen smiled. "I don't think so. I don't need a fanboy slobbering all over him while I'm trying to interrogate him. Besides, this trip isn't in my budget for just me, much less two of us."

"I'll pay for it myself then. Come on, Boss."

"Not this time."

"You're a real asshole, you know that?"

"Maybe, but you work for this asshole."

"Just 'cause you went around sucking up to everybody to get your job doesn't make you a better cop. It just makes you a damn politician."

"Kiss my ass, Crawford."

"Why would I do that? You just told me it wouldn't get me nothing." Phil laughed.

Allen smiled, but he wasn't in the mood to laugh.

"Well, at least get his autograph for me," Phil said.

"I'll see what I can do."

"So what's the deal with the new cases?"

Allen picked up the top file from the stack.

"Rachel Pierce. Twenty-four years old. Lived in Colman with her roommate, Amanda Burroughs. Worked at Walmart in Sioux Falls. Killed late June 13 or early June 14, 2009. Her roommate was spending the night with her boyfriend in Madison and discovered the body in the afternoon of June 14 when she got home. No witnesses. The victim was bound to the bed using generic nylon rope, gagged with a pair of women's underwear, presumably her own. Multiple contusions and abrasions indicating prolonged torture. Cause of death: exsanguination due to stab/cutting wounds to chest and abdomen. Victim's heart was removed postmortem. The crime scene investigation yielded no fingerprints, no DNA."

Allen tossed the file onto the desk and picked up the next one.

"Alexis Morrison. Twenty-six years old. Lived in Clear Lake with her parents, Pat and Lennor Morrison, and her cousin, Drina Burton. Worked at Country Inn as a housekeeper. Killed August 6 or 7, 2011. Her parents had rented a cabin on the lake for the weekend. They discovered her body the next afternoon when they got home. No witnesses. Victim bound to her bed—" He closed the file and tossed it on top of the Pierce file. "You get the point."

"So just like the others. The guy ties them up with rope you can get from any hardware store and gags them with whatever happens to be available. He tortures them by cutting and beating, eventually cutting them open and taking their heart."

"And we aren't any closer to catching him than we were in 2005 when we walked into Sandra Bell's bedroom." Allen leaned back, stretched, and rubbed his eyes. "I've been a cop for almost twenty-five years and haven't seen anything like what this guy does. You remember what I told you when we found Jenna Hampton the next winter?"

"Yeah, I remember. You said you were going to make it your life's mission to catch him."

"I'm starting to wonder if that isn't what it turned into."

"Maybe you need to let it go, Boss. Hell, we haven't had a new case in five years."

"Four years," Allen corrected. "Alexis Morrison was 2011."

"Whatever, it's been a long time. Maybe we got lucky and he's locked up for something else and we'll never hear about him again."

"You want to tell their families that?" Allen asked, waving his hand at the stack of case files.

Phil didn't answer. He just looked down at his coffee.

"Me either. So we need to follow up every lead. Even if it seems outrageous, like a writer in West Virginia who somehow knows the details of seven unsolved murders."

Allen's phone buzzed on his hip before Phil could answer. He checked the caller ID and saw it was Gus Norris, his deputy on duty tonight.

"Hey, Gus," Allen said. "What's going on?"

"Hey, Sheriff. Sorry to bug you so late, but I think you need to see this one." The deputy's voice was unsteady.

"That's okay, I'm still at the office with Phil. What do you have?"

"We have a dead girl, but I think it would just be simpler for you to see it for yourself."

"Why, what's wrong?"

"It's bad. I've never seen anything like it."

*

Allen and Phil pulled up to the apartment building on Euclid Avenue. Gus' car was in front of the building, blue and white lights flashing. An ambulance was parked behind the deputy's car, its own red lights flashing, the EMTs leaning against the side, smoking. The mass of red, white, and blue flashing lights from the three vehicles bounced off the buildings and the small crowd that had gathered on the sidewalk.

Gus Norris was standing by the entrance to the apartment building trying to calm another man who was yelling and waving his arms around. Allen radioed the dispatcher his location, then got out of his car. Gus was asking the man if he had any place he could stay. The man seemed incapable of understanding the question. The deputy waved when he saw Allen and Phil, then turned back to the distraught man.

"Mr. Buchanan, why don't you have a seat on the steps for a few minutes and we'll see what we can do to help you out this evening?" Gus turned to Allen and said, "Thanks for coming out so late. This is a mess."

"It's okay. Phil and I were just sitting at the station going over some...stuff." Allen led him out of earshot of Mr. Buchanan. "Tell me what you have."

Gus wiped his forehead with his sleeve. "I don't know, Boss. I've never seen anything like it. It's..."

"Just relax. Start from the beginning."

The deputy's face was especially pale in the flashing emergency lights. He swallowed before continuing. "I got a call from dispatch around a quarter to three. I was over by the highway. That's the best place to catch drunks trying to drive home. Nothing else going on and all. It's been a quiet night."

"Come on, Gus. Focus. You got a call."

"Sorry. Yeah, dispatch called with a ten fifty-four. It only took me about five minutes or so to get here. I found Mr. Buchanan there standing outside the door. He was freaked out. It took me a couple of minutes to calm him down enough to figure out what was going on. He's drunk as a skunk, which didn't help, but I finally got out of him that he had been out with some friends and when he got home, he found his girlfriend dead in their bedroom. He ran out of the apartment and called 9-1-1. He said he waited outside and hadn't been back into the apartment. I told him to sit down while I checked it out, then I went up to the apartment."

Gus paused to wipe his face again.

"It's okay." Allen put his hand on the deputy's shoulder to try to calm him down. "Take a deep breath, and just tell me what happened."

He nodded and took a few deep breaths before continuing.

"The door was open, I guess from Mr. Buchanan running out. I went straight to the bedroom and saw…"

He stopped again, clenching his jaw. He looked like he might lose his dinner.

"You found the body," Allen said. "Then what?"

"The EMTs showed up while I was still in the bedroom. I checked the other rooms to make sure there wasn't anyone else in the apartment, then cleared them to check the body, but there really wasn't any point. She's dead."

"Just take it easy. You did your job. Is that Pete's car over there?" Allen asked, pointing to a plain dark sedan parked across the street. Peter Greene was the Chief Medical Examiner for Woodford County.

"Yeah. I called him right after I called you. He's in there with the body right now."

"Okay, you hang here. Why don't you see if you can get anything else out of Mr. Buchanan? Phil and I'll find the bedroom on our own."

"Thanks, Boss."

Allen and Phil walked through the main door to the apartment building and up the central stairwell to the second floor. The door to apartment 2B was open. Phil hesitated.

"Wishing you hadn't taken up my offer for a late-night coffee?" Allen asked.

"You mean that was a request?" Phil rolled his eyes, then followed Allen inside.

The apartment was cluttered, shoes on the floor in the entryway, jackets and mail piled on a table just inside the door. In the living room, a heap of clothes filled one end of the couch. He couldn't tell if they were clean or not. Dirty dishes, DVD cases, and video game controllers were scattered on the coffee table. An ashtray overflowing with cigarette butts and some empty beer cans sat on an end table between the couch and a recliner. The place reeked of stale beer and cigarettes. And something else.

Allen pretended to look around the apartment. He was in no hurry to see the body. If his suspicions were right, it would be just like the other four he had seen.

He watched Phil cross the living room toward the balcony door. Apparently, he was in no hurry either.

Allen moved to the kitchen instead. The sink was full of dishes and the countertop between the sink and the stove was littered with old fast-food bags and frozen-dinner boxes. The microwave was flashing *END*. A bottle of flavored water on the floor and an overturned chair were the only indications of a struggle.

"Hey, Boss!" Phil called. Allen walked back to the living room.

"What'd you find?"

Phil was standing by the sliding door to the balcony. "Looks like he busted the lock on the patio door," he said. He shined his flashlight on the side of the sliding door where the latch was supposed to be. It had been broken open, probably with a pry bar.

"That wouldn't have been quiet," Allen said. "It looks like he surprised her in the kitchen, so he must have broken in before she got home and waited for her."

"That's what I was thinking."

Allen and Phil examined the busted lock for another minute, then Phil turned to Allen.

"Could have been the boyfriend."

"Only if my luck's changed."

Phil smirked, but didn't reply.

"Guess we have to go see the body," Allen said.

Phil nodded. They turned back into the apartment and headed down the hallway. Flashes from the medical examiner's camera came from the bedroom. Allen led the way, using his flashlight to scan the floor and walls for any small bit of evidence. He would have to get the crime scene unit to do a formal search, but with the foot traffic that had already been through, he didn't expect to find anything.

Approaching the end of the hall, he smelled the death coming from the bedroom.

Bodies of people who die from trauma almost always have a strong smell. Even before decomposition sets in, bladders and bowels release. In cases like this, where the victim had been tortured and beaten, there was the chance of ruptured organs. If the body cavity was opened, like when cutting out a heart, the odors from the ruptured organs could quite literally smell like shit. Allen was familiar with the scent, having field dressed plenty of wild game in his life. Something about the smell coming from a human made it worse.

They turned the corner into the bedroom. As soon as Allen saw what was lying on the bed, he had to turn his head to keep from losing his supper.

"Oh, God!" Phil said and ran out of the room.

The medical examiner turned at the sound.

"Hey, Allen," he said. "Hope you haven't had breakfast yet."

"Hey, Pete," Allen replied. Pete had worked all of the "Cory Rivers" cases in one capacity or another. "What can you tell me?"

"Well, exact cause of death is obviously going to be a little hard to determine, but it's safe to say manner of death isn't natural, accidental, or suicide."

"You know, Pete: I like you. You're an all right guy, for somebody who makes a living playing with dead bodies, but I'm never going to get your sense of humor."

Pete smiled. "That's the only way you can stay sane in this job."

Allen grunted. "You call yourself sane?"

"Somebody has to do this shit. I don't see you volunteering."

"You got that right. So what else can you tell me, besides she didn't stab herself a hundred and fifty times?"

"Look for yourself. It's pretty straightforward. Be careful where you step!"

Something crunched under Allen's foot. He looked to see what he had stepped on.

"Is that what I think it is?"

"Yeah. It's a tooth. He pulled out every single one. From the ones

I've been able to find and examine, I'd guess he used a standard pair of pliers."

Allen shook his head and continued to the bed, watching where he stepped this time.

Shelby's body, what was left of it, was lying in a massive pool of blood and bodily fluids. Her abdomen looked like it had exploded from the inside. Like the other victims, she was bound to the bed by her wrists and ankles. Her eye sockets were just bloody holes. Her mouth hung open, with no gag this time, blood still oozing from her gums where her teeth had been. Both ears had been cut off. Both arms and both legs were covered with bruises, cuts, and what looked like burns. Most of the body seemed to be covered with bruising, but it was hard to tell from all the blood. Only her hands and feet seemed to be unscathed…until closer examination revealed more burns on her palms and the soles of her feet.

"Jesus," Allen said. "This is worse than the other ones."

"So you're thinking it's the same guy." It was a statement, not a question.

"Don't you? I mean, I hope to God there isn't another one out there."

"I'm just the pathologist, but it sure looks like the work of the same guy to me."

"Did you check for her heart?"

Pete nodded. "It's gone."

"Okay, I'll get out of your way. I want to see the full report as soon as you're done."

"You got it." Pete picked up his camera and started clicking away again.

Allen walked back to the living room where Phil was waiting for him. At least the color had come back to Phil's face.

"Still think he's locked up?" Allen asked Phil.

"No, but where the hell's he been for the last four years?"

"No clue. Come on. I need to bum a smoke off one of the EMTs."

CHAPTER THREE

SARA STOOD IN the doorway to the back deck, looking at Ken. He was sitting in a lounge chair, drinking coffee, watching the sunrise, and listening to the woods wake up. He often told her it was one of his favorite things about living in the mountains of West Virginia. A thick layer of fog filled the valley below the Simmons' house where the Greenbrier River flowed south to join the New River. A whip-poor-will called out from the valley. A few minutes later, a woodpecker started up with its *ratta-tat-tat*, which set off the crows. A mourning dove called out somewhere in the distance.

The house had been a hunting lodge built in the 1960s by a man named Elmo Rawley. They had bought it from the Rawley Estate a few years ago when they decided to escape the city. Rawley had built it as a private hunting resort that he and his buddies could use to get away from whatever business they had been in. The locals still liked to talk about all the illegal deals that had been struck inside the walls of the isolated lodge. Whether any of that was true or not, Ken seemed to like the story. He said it added to the house's character.

Another story Ken liked came from one of the old-timers in town. He had told them that the spot where their house stood had once been an observation post in the Civil War. They thought that might be possible; the spot had a magnificent view over a bend in the Greenbrier River, which she felt was its only real redeeming quality.

The only way to get to the house was what they called their "mile-long driveway." It was actually a mile and a half one-lane road named

Rawley Drive. "Road" was a bit of a euphemism. In reality, it was a gravel path barely wide enough to accommodate a car, having hardly been improved beyond the horse trail it had been since the 1800s. Apparently, the county had widened the path for Elmo Rawley so he could build his hunting lodge. There were rumors of payoffs to county officials to put the road under county responsibility, which was easy to believe, since the Rawley place had been the only thing the road was needed for. Over the years, there had been attempts to change the arrangement, but the road ran through state land for most of its distance, and getting the state to accept responsibility for maintenance was unlikely to happen.

That seclusion was what had attracted Ken to the property in the first place. The plot covered the entire top of the mountain, guaranteeing that they would never have neighbors close enough to see or hear. Unlike Sara, he liked the isolation. After so many years, she was starting think that dealing with Ken's fans trespassing was better than being alone all the time.

She did like the view, though. Especially in the morning.

"Good morning," she said walking up behind him.

"Morning," Ken replied as she sat down next to him. She shivered and pulled her robe tighter. Even in August the mornings were cool in the mountains.

"Any luck?" she asked after a few minutes. They had been home from the *Terror in Suburbia* tour for over a month and Ken was still trying to start a new project. So far he hadn't managed to start anything he liked. Before he had written *Terror*, he had spent almost a year suffering from writer's block while recovering from the shooting incident. He had gone into a deep depression until he had come up with the idea for the book. Sara was concerned that it might happen again.

"Not really."

"Still bothered by your dream the other night at the festival?"

"It was just a dream," Ken said, staring over the valley.

She picked up his hand. "I think you've been too wrapped up in *Terror in Suburbia*. Once you get going on a new story, you'll be fine."

"I wish it was that simple," he said. "I have plenty of ideas, but every time I start to write, I start thinking about Cory Rivers. Then I remember what I saw when I blacked out." He turned and looked at her. His jaw was clenched and his face had gone pale. "I know it was just a dream, but it felt like more. It was like I was there, almost like I actually was Cory, seeing what he saw, thinking what he thought." He shuddered.

"But it was just a dream. You're not Cory Rivers."

"I know, but I've never had a dream that…real."

They sat drinking their coffee and listening to the birds for a few minutes. Finally, Sara broke the silence and changed the subject.

"I'm going into town this morning to do some shopping. Do you need anything?"

"How about some apple pie?"

*

The Simmons' residence was not particularly far from Murphy Creek—about five miles as the crow flies, but about ten miles by the twisting mountain roads. The mile and a half Rawley Drive, rutted and pot-holed from years of neglect, took almost fifteen minutes to navigate and the rest of the drive to Route 28 wasn't much faster. Thirty minutes to town wasn't unusual. In poor weather, the drive could be downright treacherous.

But on a bright fall morning with the leaves just beginning to change, Sara found the trip to town to be serene. Fall in the mountains was prettier than anything she had known growing up. Since moving to West Virginia, she had gotten back into photography. When Ken was deep in a new book, she would go for a drive to find new places to photograph. She was even considering putting her photos together into a book of her own.

Unfortunately, today's excursion was a functional trip. Groceries for the week. And an apple pie for Ken.

Murphy Creek was located in the middle of the United States National Radio Quiet Zone, a large area covering parts of three states that the FCC had created in the fifties to protect some radio telescopes from human radio traffic. It was another thing Ken liked about the area.

The NRQZ meant no cell phones. Their only connection to the outside world was via the Internet; Ken had spent a small fortune getting a high-speed Internet line installed at the house.

In spite of the town's size, the population in the surrounding area was enough to support a few local businesses. That meant they didn't have to travel over an hour farther north to Elkins for standard necessities. Billy's General Store had basic tools and hardware, essential toiletries, and the fundamental foodstuffs to supplement the farmers' market at the other end of town. It was also the only gas station for miles, so Sara always made sure to fill up anytime she was in town. Running out of gas in an area with no cell phone coverage would make for a really bad day.

Pulling up to the pump, Sara saw Will Harper, Billy's grandson, coming out to meet her. Over the last few years, Billy had been leaving more of the operation of the store to Will and spending his days fishing. He wasn't getting around very well these days. "It's the miles, not the years that'll get ya!" he would tell anyone who asked him how he was doing.

"Hi, Mrs. Simmons!" Will was always cheerful and polite. She got the feeling on more than one occasion that he had a mild crush on her even though she was old enough to be his mother. She didn't mind. It made her feel good that she could still turn the heads of the young men, even if it was in a town with a population smaller than her high school graduating class.

"Hi, Will. How's your granddad?"

"He's good. Real good. Caught a whopper yesterday. He's been telling everybody about it all day. He's inside if you wanna see him. You want me to fill up the truck for ya?"

Sara's truck was a four-wheel-drive Nissan Armada with more in common with a luxury car than a truck, although not as much as Ken's QX80. But in the country, you either drove a car or a truck. SUV was apparently a city-slicker term.

"Sure, thanks, Will. I'll be inside picking up a few things." She got out of her truck and walked into the store, pretending not to notice Will staring at her rear end as she went. One thing she definitely liked about the small-town life was how friendly and helpful everyone was. She hadn't seen a full-service gas station in Pittsburgh since she'd been four years old. Will didn't charge extra for the service. He wouldn't even accept a tip if somebody offered it.

Inside the store was old and musty, but Billy kept it clean. "Cleanliness is next to godliness," he was fond of quoting, as if he had been the one to come up with the saying. The left side of the store had hardware and housewares. The right side had most everything else but food, which was in the back of the store. A row of coolers and freezers on the back wall stored the cold stuff.

Sara went straight to the back corner where Billy's wife, Marianne, ran the bakery. In spite of her age, she still made doughnuts every morning. Ken's favorite was the chocolate glazed. Sometimes, when Ken was working on a new novel, Sara would drive into town to get some for him. She often wondered if he appreciated how much she spoiled him.

Marianne was sitting in a chair reading when Sara walked up. Not one of Ken's books, Sara noticed.

"Good morning, Marianne," Sara said.

"Oh! Don't you look lovely this morning, Sara!"

"Thank you. Is that a new dress you're wearing? It looks wonderful on you."

"Bless your heart, child. Fibbing is a sin! I suppose the Good Lord will pardon you for trying to make an old bitty like me feel better." Marianne grinned from ear to ear. Even though she was probably ten years younger than Billy, she looked old enough to have taught Moses how to walk. Even so, she still got around better than some half her age.

"Say, do you happen to have any fresh apple pie? Kenny's been craving one."

"I'm so sorry, I don't. I have a nice blueberry and a peach, but no apple today."

"Well, thanks anyway. Just thought I'd ask."

"I tell you what I'll do. If you're going to be in town for a bit, I'll put one together for you and you can bake it at home. You can tell another one of those little fibs and tell Kenny you made it yourself.

He'll smell it cooking and he'll never know the difference!" Marianne smiled with the simple brilliance of her plan.

"I don't know. Last time I tried to bake something, we almost had to call the fire department." That was a bit of an exaggeration, but she knew that Ken hadn't married her for her cooking skills.

"Oh darling, it'll be just fine. You'll pop it in the oven for an hour and then set it on the counter to cool for another hour."

"Okay, but if the house burns down, we'll be moving in with you!"

They both laughed. Sara thanked her and promised to come back in an hour. Will was just coming in when she reached the front of the store.

"It's all filled up! I checked your oil too, just to be sure. Never can be too careful in the mountains."

"Thanks, Will. Just put it on my bill. I'll be back in a bit to finish my shopping. Your grandmother is making a pie for me."

"She makes the best pies in the county. If I only had one thing to eat in the whole world, it would be Nana's pie!"

"She does make good pies." Sara had never really experienced good home cooking until they moved to the county. What her mother had passed off as home cooked was only a step above frozen dinners. Before moving to Murphy Creek, she had never had soup beans and cornbread, homemade split pea soup, or baked cheese grits. And fried chicken had always been something you bought in a bucket from a colonel.

"Thanks again, Will. If you don't mind I'll leave my car here. I'm going down to the farmers' market. I'll be back in a bit to pick it up and finish my shopping."

"No problem, Mrs. Simmons!"

Sara walked outside and stood in the doorway for a moment, taking in the fresh air. With the gentle fall breeze and bright sunshine, how could anybody have a problem on a day like this?

Without thinking about where she was going to go, she started walking. Not that there was very much walking available. The town had its own post office and a small, one-truck volunteer firehouse, which sat next to Valley Baptist Church. The only restaurant in Murphy Creek, Mel's Diner—owned by a man named Frank Shaw—was conveniently located next to the only bar, the Dew Drop Inn, where many locals would spend Friday and Saturday night…and for some, Sunday through Thursday nights as well. An old farmhouse on the south end of town had been turned into The Stanley House Bed and Breakfast. The barn next to it was used for the farmers' market and the obligatory flea market/swap meet on the weekends. Past the barn was the fairgrounds where workers were still packing up from the Fall Festival. The newest building in town was Murphy Creek United Methodist Church, which had been built across from the old farmhouse in the '80s.

Sara's stomach began talking to her about the time she reached Mel's. She wasn't sure, but it sounded like it was saying, "Feed me." With time to kill, lunch sounded like a good plan. The diner didn't look very busy. The only cars in the parking lot were Frank's Ford Taurus and a Pocahontas County Sheriff's car.

The smell of country cooking overwhelmed her nostrils as she opened the door, making her stomach growl even louder. Frank was in the back washing dishes. He looked up in response to the tinkling bell.

"Morning, Sara! Be right with ya!"

"No rush, Frank," she replied.

It was too late in the morning for the breakfast crowd and too early for the lunch crowd. The only other customer was Mitch Armstrong.

"Good morning, Mrs. Simmons," Mitch said, holding up his coffee cup. "Mr. Simmons recovered from the other night?"

"Hey, Mitch." Sara waved. "Yeah, he's fine. He just had a bug or something. He felt fine the next day. Thank you again for your help."

"No problem. Glad I was there to help."

"How are your folks?" Sara asked. She had learned that in a small town everyone's business was everyone else's business.

"They're doing just fine, ma'am. Dad's fixing to retire and Ma's already making a list of stuff for him to do."

Sara smiled at Mitch. He was not much older than Will, but they couldn't be more different.

Will was a skinny kid with book smarts, but a little clueless about the world. He didn't have many friends, at least that Sara knew about. He spent most of his time at his grandfather's store.

Mitch, on the other hand, had played football in high school and it still showed. What he lacked in academic ability he more than made up for in street smarts. Sara guessed he still worked out every day and watched what he ate.

If she were twenty years younger and single…

Not that it would matter. She had heard that Mitch had a girlfriend who lived in Green Bank and that they were pretty serious.

Mitch stood up and grabbed his hat off the counter.

"I'll see you later, Mr. Shaw! I've gotta get back on patrol. Thanks for the coffee!"

"Any time, Mitch. Glad you stopped by."

Mitch smiled to Sara as he passed her on his way out. "You have a good day now, Mrs. Simmons."

"Thanks, Mitch. You too. Be careful out there." It seemed like the right thing to say to a cop on his way out to work.

Sara watched him walk out to his cruiser. The first time she had met Mitch, he had still been in high school. Seeing him in his uniform climbing into the cruiser suddenly made her feel old.

With Mitch gone, Sara was the only patron left. She sat down at the counter. She preferred sitting in a booth, but that seemed a little antisocial when no one else was there, especially in a small town where everyone knows everyone, and Sara and Ken were definitely known by everyone. Most of the town's residents were friendly and enjoyed having them. There were a few who didn't like the "rich city slickers" moving in to their town, but even most of those had softened over time. The business owners, on the other hand, all liked them. Ken and Sara weren't pretentious and always made sure to spend their money locally when they could, and that made them what Frank and Billy called "good people."

Frank came out from the back, drying his hands on his apron.

"What can I do you for this morning?" Frank asked.

"I think I'll just have a turkey sandwich and a coke."

"You want it toasted?"

"That sounds good. With just lettuce, tomato, and a little mayonnaise."

"How about some fresh cornbread? Just done pulled it out of the oven."

"Sure, why not?"

Frank fetched a big glass and filled it with ice and coke, then got busy fixing her sandwich.

"How y'all been? I heard Mitch asking about Kenny. He okay? I ain't seen him in a coon's age."

"He's fine. He just got sick the other night at the festival. Nothing serious."

"Well, that's good. No more problems from the accident?"

"The accident" was how the folks in Murphy Creek referred to Ken being shot. When he had come home from the hospital, the whole town had come together to bring them food. Sara hadn't had to cook for almost a month. She had been completely overwhelmed by it all, but Frank had told her "that's just what right folk do." Even after the first couple of weeks, Frank and his wife, the Harpers, and a few others had stopped by once or twice a week to check in on them and make sure they had everything they needed. It had been no secret that Ken had had trouble getting back to work after he recovered from the physical injuries.

"No, nothing like that." Sara hoped, at least. "His new book came out at the beginning of the summer. We spent a few weeks going all over the place to promote it. It was fun, but I'm glad to be home."

"Yeah, I heard you folks was out of town for a bit," Frank said. He pulled the bread out of the toaster and started assembling her sandwich. "By the way, one of them reporters came by last week asking about y'all. Wanted to know where your house was, but I wouldn't tell him."

"I appreciate that." It wasn't the first time someone had tried to find out where their house was from one of the locals.

"Yeah, I told the little weasel he'd have to kill me before I told him."

"You're a good man, Frank Shaw." Sara smiled at him.

"No matter what the old lady says, right?" Frank grinned back at her. "So, why didn't Kenny come down with you?"

"Oh, he's up there working. Sometimes I think I married a hermit."

"You tell him that if he doesn't come on down here to see us once in a while we're gonna have to go up there and drag him out!"

Sara laughed.

"You know I'm just joshing, but don't tell Kenny that." He pulled out a knife and cut Sara's sandwich in half diagonally—the fancy way, he called it—and scooped a big helping of coleslaw on the side. He carried the plate over to the counter and set it in front of her. The sandwich was so big Sara wasn't quite sure how she was going to fit it in her mouth.

"Let me go get the cornbread. It's sitting in the back." He hustled around the prep counter to the kitchen. "So no more problems for Kenny?" Frank called from the back.

"Yeah, I think so. It took a while, but he finally managed to get over whatever was bugging him. The doctors said it was PTSD. I think it was more than that. It was like part of him was missing, you know?"

"Uh, huh," Frank said, coming back with two extra large pieces of cornbread. He set one on Sara's plate and took the other piece to the prep counter. "I'll wrap this one up for Ken. You think he might want a samwich?"

"Sure. He likes turkey too, but put mustard on his instead of mayonnaise."

"Will do!" He set about making another turkey sandwich with even more turkey than he had put on hers. "The docs put him on that Viagra or whatever it's called?"

Sara laughed. "No, that would be for something else. But yeah, they tried a few medications. Ken didn't like how they made him feel so he stopped taking them. I guess in the end, it worked out okay. I think what finally made him start feeling better was when we went to the Mountain Fair up in Green Bank last year. It was like somebody flipped a switch."

"That's always a good time. I'll betcha getting outta the house was what did it. It don't do a body no good to stay shut up in the house all the time. It'll make you wrong in the head." Frank gave her a knowing nod.

"Maybe. You know, it's funny. They had one of those fortune tellers there. Ken thinks they're hokey, but I talked him into getting our fortune told. She said Ken was about to write his biggest bestseller. And she was right."

"I don't much care for them voodoo types," Frank said, shaking his head.

"Anyway, I'm just glad Ken got through it. Sometimes he doesn't seem quite the same though. He seems more serious these days." She honestly didn't think Ken was fully recovered, especially with his demeanor since they got home from the publicity tour. But there was no point in feeding more grist into the Murphy Creek gossip mill.

"That was a hell of a thing to go through. Getting shot and almost killed is bound to change a man."

"I suppose. But you remember how he was before. Did he ever tell you about when we met?"

"Not that I recall." He put Ken's sandwich and cornbread in a plastic bag and set it on the counter.

"He was a real goofball. We both worked at Walmart. I was a cashier and when it was busy and I was all stressed out he'd walk up behind the people standing in line and start making faces at me. Of course, the customers didn't see him, so if I laughed they would look at me like I was losing my mind."

"That sounds like Kenny, all right."

"Well, on our first date we went to the movies. I don't even remember what we saw, but it was horrible. Kenny started making up his own dialogue. We were laughing so hard I'm surprised we didn't get thrown out."

Frank was looking at her, being polite, but she knew he had no idea what she was talking about. He just nodded and said, "Uh, huh."

"He was always doing stuff like that. But he was charming, too. One night he drove me home and we sat in my parents' driveway talking for at least an hour, maybe longer. After a while, my dad came out on the porch. He pretended he was coming out to smoke a cigarette, but he never smoked on the front porch. He always went out back. I told Ken that I should probably call it a night and go inside, and do you know what he did?"

Frank just shook his head.

"He actually got out of the car, walked me to the front door, and introduced himself to my dad. My dad ended up being the one who was embarrassed instead of us!"

"That Ken's a good guy, all right. I hope my boy grows up with good manners like that."

"Yeah, that's Ken. He's the nicest man I've ever known, but he can be such a pain in the ass sometimes. He pretends like he's some kind of idiot."

"I think he just likes to make you laugh," Frank said. "You have a pretty laugh and if I was Ken, I'd want to see you laugh all day long."

Sara blushed a little. "I don't think it's all that."

"Sure it is. Every man likes to see his girl laugh."

She was about to say that it had been a long time since he had made her laugh like that, but she realized that she had been blabbering like she and Frank were a couple of school girls. Well, when you don't have a phone and the closest concentration of people is a thirty-minute drive…

"Anyway, I'm glad the book tour is over and we can get back to our normal lives."

"Don't be too hard on him. I'm sure he'll be all right. You know you 'uns ought to come down to the house for supper one night. The missus'd love to see y'all."

"We might just do that," Sara said. She took another bite of her sandwich. "Frank, I don't know what you do, but you make the best sandwiches."

"That's right kind of you, but I don't do nothing special," Frank said. "It just tastes better when someone else makes it, is all."

They continued to talk while she ate. She found out that Tammilynn Roder was about to find pups—hillbilly talk for being pregnant—and Gary Rodgers had been busted for cooking meth, which didn't surprise nobody, and old man Davenport was got by the cancer. All gossip passed through the town diner. When she finished eating, Frank took her plate and wiped the counter.

"Now we gonna see you and Kenny for supper?"

"I'll try, Frank, but no promises. You know how Ken is. How much do I owe you?"

"Two turkey samwiches and a coke. Let's call it nine fifty. The corn-bread's on me."

"You don't have to do that." Sara hated it when people didn't charge them for something, but she was getting used to it. Apparently that was just what "right folk do" in the country.

"If I had to do it, I wouldn't do it," Frank said, grinning at her.

She paid him fifteen dollars and told him to keep the change. She had learned long ago that there was a fine line between tipping well and tipping too much in a small town. When you had money, if you tipped too little they called you a cheap, greedy bastard; if you tipped too much, they called you a showoff or felt you thought you were better than the "workin' folk."

"Take care, Frank."

"You too. Thank ya again!" Frank waved as she walked out the door and headed toward the farmers' market.

CHAPTER FOUR

KEN AND SARA didn't have very many visitors, especially unexpected visitors. The whole point of moving to "Simmons' Mountain"—a name Sara used in sarcasm when she was feeling homesick for Pittsburgh—was to get away from that. Ken had even had an alarm system, complete with video, installed to let them know when someone was coming up Rawley Drive. The certainly weren't expecting anyone late Tuesday afternoon when the alarm dinged.

Ken got up from his desk and went to find Sara. He found her in the kitchen on her laptop.

"You expecting somebody?" he asked, looking over her shoulder at the video feed.

"No. Probably another lost tourist."

From time to time, sightseers would drive up to the house thinking the road led to a scenic overlook. Since the road was public, they couldn't mark it as a private drive until it crossed onto their property just below the tree line. By that point, there was nowhere for the curious traveler to turn around.

"I'll take care of it," Ken said and went out to the front porch to wait for the uninvited guest.

Gravel crunched under the car's tires as it slowly made its way through the trees. Ken suspected the driver would pull into the clearing, see him standing there, then turn around and drive back down the mountain. Occasionally someone would get out and ask where they were or for directions to the nearest interstate.

This car didn't stop and turn around. The driver didn't get out and ask for directions. Instead, the car pulled up and parked behind Ken's SUV. From the dust and dead bugs covering the car, Ken couldn't see inside the vehicle. Maybe waiting on the porch hadn't been a good idea.

The driver got out of the car and waved to Ken. He reached back into the car and pulled out a satchel before walking up to the house. Ken eased closer to the door.

"Can I help you?" he asked the stranger.

"Are you K. Elliot Simmons?" the man asked.

"You're on private property. Can I ask who you are?"

"You're a hard man to get hold of, Mr. Simmons," the man said, holding out his hand. "My name is Allen James. I'm the sheriff of Woodford County, South Dakota."

"Really? Allen James?" Ken asked.

"Yeah, it's a little weird for me too," the sheriff replied, putting his hand down.

"You'll excuse me if I don't accept that's your name just on your word."

"I understand." Allen pulled out his badge and ID and showed them to Ken.

"You're a long way from home, Mr. James," Ken said, after looking at the ID.

"Yeah, I am. I know this may sound a little strange, but I came here to talk to you about your new book."

Not really knowing what else to do, Ken invited him inside to talk. After introducing him to Sara, he showed the sheriff to his office.

Ken rarely had company in his office. He'd had it built, along with the equally oversized deck on the back of the house, when they bought the property. At the time, he had been proud of his private workspace. He thought of it as his fortress of solitude, or maybe his wizard's tower where the magic of his writing happened. Now he thought it was just ostentatious. Leading the sheriff through the door, he was a little embarrassed by the room.

A floor to ceiling picture window overlooking the valley to the north dominated the room. The bookcases and desk had been custom built by a local carpenter Billy Harper had recommended. Wood panels covered the vaulted ceiling, which was crowned by a giant ridge beam made from a single rough-hewn log. A leather reclining couch sat in front of the picture window. He and Sara would spend the mornings on the couch, watching the sun rise when it was too cold to sit outside. Another couch and several chairs provided seating around the center of the room. Ken had opted for end tables, rather than a coffee table, to keep the center of the room open so they could lie on the floor and watch movies on the huge LCD television that hung above the fireplace. He had even had a wet bar, complete with mini-fridge, built into the wall next to the fireplace.

"So, Sheriff," Ken said after they'd sat. "What is it about my book you want to talk about? It seems like a long way to come just for an autograph." Ken smiled, trying to hide his anxiety.

"Well, Mr. Simmons…"

"Ken."

"Ken? So why K. Elliot?"

"It's stupid, really. When I was trying to publish my first novel I didn't like the way Ken Simmons sounded, and Ken E. Simmons sounded too much like Kenny Simmons."

"What about Kenneth Simmons?" Allen asked with an amused smile.

Ken smirked. "I've never liked that name. Probably because that's what my mother used to call me when I was in trouble."

"I know what you mean," Allen said with a chuckle. "I got the 'Allen Nathaniel James' from my mother too."

"Allen James," Ken said. "Is that why you're here? Because your name sounds a lot like Alan St. James?"

"I suppose that's part of it."

Sara came in with a tray full of glasses, a pitcher of lemonade, and three slices of apple pie.

"What I really want to know is where you got the idea for your story," Allen said after everyone had poured a drink.

Ken smiled. "Usually I get pieces of ideas from all over. News stories, movies, other books. All kinds of things spark ideas. But you didn't come all this way to discuss writing craft."

"No, I didn't. But I do want to know about *Terror in Suburbia*. Where'd that story come from?"

Ken normally enjoyed talking about where he got the idea for a particular story. He found the whole creative process an interesting study in itself. How watching a leaf fall from a tree and land in a stream could lead to a story about a child growing up and leaving home, or how a woman hurrying to her car could lead to a story about a deranged stalker.

But he couldn't explain *Terror in Suburbia*.

"Honestly, I don't know. I didn't really come up with the idea for the book. At least, not in the usual sense."

"How do you mean?" Allen had pulled out a pen and a pocket notebook.

"Pretty much everything I write starts with some little nugget of an idea. Sometimes I just wonder how a book or movie would be different if I rewrote it, but changed a key point. Like how would *Fatal Attraction* have gone if Glenn Close's character had killed Michael Douglas' wife instead of boiling his daughter's pet bunny. Other times, some ordinary, inane event sparks an idea. Once, I came up with the premise for a book watching a guy walk down the street. *Terror in Suburbia* was different. I just started writing a random opening scene and it just came out from there."

"Mr. James, why are you really here?" Sara asked. "What is it about my husband's book that interests you?"

Ken was used to people accusing him of stealing their ideas or copying real crimes for his books. Of course, like many authors, he sometimes used real events for inspiration, but he tried hard to not blatantly copy actual cases. He certainly hadn't for *Terror*, though he suspected the sheriff was about to make that accusation.

Allen leaned forward, his eyes focused on Ken. "What I want to know is, who gave you the information."

And there it was. "And what information would that be?" Ken replied, already knowing the answer.

"Your book is obviously based on real cases. But there are things in your book that were never released to the public. My concern is that you've been talking to someone involved with the investigation. If it was one of my deputies or one of the officers from the Ashford Police Department, I'd like to know."

Ken smiled. "There's always another possibility."

"And what would that be?"

"That I'm the Suburban Stalker." *Suburban Stalker* was the nickname for the killer in *Terror in Suburbia.*

The first time Ken had been accused of copying a real case and the police had questioned him about it, he had been afraid he was going to be arrested or sued or something. Now it didn't bother him so much. Might as well have a little fun with it.

"Nice name, but I know you're not my guy. I checked. Your public travel schedule puts you well away from South Dakota for at least two of the…murders."

"Well, I'm glad that's established. Was there something else you wanted to discuss?"

"So you're not going to tell me your source? I know you writers are like reporters and like to hide behind the 'protecting your source' mantra, but this is a serious issue. If I have a leak in my department, I need to plug it. Leaks can hamper investigations or even lead to someone getting hurt. On the other hand, if you got the information from somebody else…" Allen trailed off, looking at Ken.

Ken laughed. "You can relax, Sheriff. You don't have a leak in your department. The story is completely made up. I didn't base it on anything. Sometimes fiction, especially crime fiction, seems to mirror reality. I mean, there's only so many ways to portray a serial killer."

Allen nodded. "I get that, and if it was just a book about a guy that stalked women in a small town, breaking into their homes to torture, rape, and kill them, then maybe I could chalk it up as an eerie similarity. Maybe you just saw it on the news and forgot about it, then it came out as a made-up story. But in this case there are too many details that aren't just close. They're dead on. And like I said, some of the details were things that we never released to the public."

"I think you're reaching. You have some unsolved murders and a book comes out that is remarkably similar, and, well you need something to grab on to."

"I wish it was that simple, but the details are just too specific. Let me ask you this. What was your first victim wearing? When Cory Rivers kills her?"

"She had just gotten out of the shower and was getting ready for bed, so she was wearing a nightgown."

"Yeah, but what color was it? What was the description?"

"I wrote that over a year ago. I don't remember every little detail of every scene."

Allen opened up his satchel and pulled out a copy of *Terror in Suburbia*. It had yellow and green sticky notes protruding from various places. The dust jacket was missing and the cover was scratched and dirty. Allen turned to the first sticky note.

"'He watched through the crack in the closet door as Sandy came out of the bathroom, her wet hair clinging to her bare shoulders. Her off-the-shoulder nightgown caused his pulse to race. The silky lavender fabric clung to her skin, still damp from her shower. White lacy trim framed her neck, shoulders, and thighs. Small decorative pearl buttons ran from the open neck to her waist. He licked his lips, watching the thin fabric brush against her legs as she made her way to the bed.'"

"It's a nightgown," Ken said. "They're pretty generic."

"Our first victim was Sandra Bell. She was killed in her bedroom wearing a lavender nightgown with white trim and decorative buttons down the front."

"Spooky," Ken said. "But it's just an interesting similarity. I'm sure lavender is a pretty common color for a nightgown."

"Okay, what about your second victim?"

"Like I said, I don't remember the details. She went out to the movies with some friends and Cory followed her home."

"Taylor Hamilton," Allen said turning to the next sticky note. "Our second victim was Jenna Taylor Hampton. She went by Taylor."

Ken raised his eyebrows, but said nothing.

"She was a college student home for the weekend. She was killed in her bedroom while her parents slept just down the hall. The crime scene you describe in the book is almost identical to what her parents found the next morning." Allen leaned toward Ken again. "There were several details of these murders that we didn't release, partly because they were too gruesome, but one in particular seemed like a signature. Even the victims' families don't know about it."

"Let me guess. He took their hearts."

Allen nodded, watching him, apparently looking for a reaction.

"I don't know what to tell you, Sheriff. The book is complete fiction."

Allen said nothing.

"Are there other similarities?" Ken asked. He was feeling uncomfortable under Allen's scrutiny.

Allen opened the book to another sticky note. "In your book, Katy Sanford worked nights at a twenty-four-hour diner by the highway. She was killed in the morning when she got home from work. The real Catherine Stafford was a waitress at a truck stop on I-29. Worked third shift, killed late morning or early afternoon." He turned to the next one. "Jordie Ross was a nurse. The real victim, Jordan Rosenbaum, was a doctor. Both were killed in their bedrooms. They were found tied to their beds, gagged, tortured, raped, and killed. Both had their hearts removed, just like Sandra Bell and Taylor Hampton." Allen closed the book and looked up at Ken again. "Frankly, Mr. Simmons, the only significant difference between the victims in your book and the real ones is that all of yours were single women living alone. Sandra Bell was the only one of the real victims who lived alone. Catherine Stafford was a divorced mother with two kids. She lived with her mother, who watched the kids at night while she was working. When she was killed, her kids were at school and her mother was at work. Jordan Rosenbaum lived with another doctor she worked with at Ashford Medical Center. The night she was killed, she and her roommate were working opposite shifts. They're all like that."

Ken glanced at Sara. He thought she looked a little pale. He felt a little queasy himself. "Doesn't that just help show that the story is made up?" he said, but he wasn't as confident as he had been at the beginning of their conversation.

It *had* to be made up. He hadn't heard of any of these women before he wrote about them.

"The important details are the same. Maybe you changed it so they didn't have roommates because you wanted to prey on the fears of young women living alone. And maybe some of the other minor points to make it more dramatic. I don't know. You're the writer."

"You make it sound like I'm the monster."

"I'm just trying to say that some minor differences don't prove you made it up. And I'm more convinced now that you didn't. You see, up until your book, we only knew about four victims. After reading it, I started wondering if maybe there were others. So I sent out requests to the counties around Woodford looking for any homicides where the victim's heart was removed and we got back cold cases matching most of the rest. As far as we can tell, this guy's been raping and mutilating women all the way back to 2005."

"Is this some kind of joke?" Sara asked. "Did Mandy put you up to this?"

Mandy Quinn was Ken's publicist. She was good at drumming up publicity for his books, although Sara didn't always care for some of her more unconventional approaches. She had once hired actors to do a mock interview as characters from *Billie Blue*. Another time, she had posted false news stories on the Internet about the death of Teri Chambers from *Forgotten*. Still, this seemed a little extreme even for Mandy.

"Ma'am, I don't know who that is, but I can assure you this is no joke."

Outside, the wind whistled through the trees on the mountaintop. Allen stared at Ken, waiting for a response. Finally, Ken broke the awkward silence.

"Okay, let's just say everything you told us is true. I don't know what I can do to help you. I didn't interview anybody for this book. Sure, I do that from time to time to get a better feel for a particular type of character or occupation or whatever, but for this one, I didn't even use the Internet. Everything just came to me. Anyway, I didn't get any of the information from one of your deputies or anybody else."

Allen looked at Ken, his brow furrowed and his lips pursed in a slight frown.

"That's unfortunate. I was hoping you would tell me you had talked to one of my deputies and he had given you the details. Then I could just go home and have a talk with whoever it was about releasing details on open cases, put a warning in his file, and go on back to work. If you didn't talk to one of the people working the case, things get a little more complicated."

"Why's that?" Ken's mouth was dry. He fumbled with his glass and took a drink.

Allen was watching Ken closely. "I think you know our killer."

"I'm sorry, I don't."

"Then how do you explain the similarities between your book and the real murders? I find it hard to believe that you could just make up the whole story and have it that close to the real thing. Hell, even the names of the victims are almost identical. Should I be looking for somebody with a name similar to Cory Rivers? Casey Pond? Coby Brooks?"

"I don't know how to explain that. All I can tell you is that I usually struggle to make up names for my characters. I keep an old phonebook in my desk. When I need a name, I just pull it out, flip to a random page, and point to a random name. For this book, the names just sort of popped into my head."

"So you're some kind of psychic then?" Allen scoffed.

"Kenny doesn't believe in that stuff," Sara chimed in. "Mr. James, should my husband be calling his lawyer?"

"Take it easy now. I'm not accusing your husband of breaking any laws. I'm just trying to find the son of a bitch that's killing people in my county. Pardon my language, ma'am, but my job is to keep the citizens of Woodford County safe, and this piece of shit is out there hunting them down. And I think your husband knows something about who it is."

Ken was staring off into space, only half listening.

"But how would he know anything about a serial killer in South Dakota? We've never even been to South Dakota."

"I don't know the answer to that. That's why I'm here."

"You said your cases go back to 2005?" Ken asked.

"That's right."

"Cory Rivers killed once a year, so that would put the last murder in 2012."

"Our guy seemed to kill every thirteen months until 2011."

"What happened in 2011?" Sara asked.

"Apparently he just stopped. At least until a few nights ago, when we found a young woman named Shelby Winston killed in her apartment just like the others."

Ken started. He opened his mouth, but couldn't make any sound come out.

"What night?" Sara said. Her voice was shaking.

"Saturday night. Why?"

Ken and Sara looked at each other.

"Is there something I should know?" Allen asked.

"I had a dream Saturday," Ken said, finding his voice. "It was about Cory Rivers. In my dream, he killed Sydney Wilson."

He recounted his dream. When he was done, Allen sat back, rubbing his chin, looking at Ken like he was trying to decide if he had just been fed a line of bullshit.

"Your dream is pretty close to what we think happened to Shelby," he said after a minute. "I don't know what to make of your dream though. Under other circumstances, I might just arrest you and sort it out later. But I'm sure this Deputy Armstrong will corroborate your story. At least as far as being in West Virginia Saturday night and not South Dakota. What time did you say you had this dream?"

"Maybe eleven o'clock. I don't know exactly what time it was."

"Hmph," Allen grunted, stroking his chin again. "That would make it about ten Central Time. That means you were probably dreaming about it right as it happened."

Ken stiffened, clenching his jaw. It had just been a dream, hadn't it?

"He did all of that and the neighbors didn't hear anything?" Sara asked. Ken hadn't told her the details of his dream. He reached over and squeezed her hand.

"Not a thing. That's one thing we can't explain. Nobody ever hears a thing. He gags them, but that wouldn't seem to be enough. We just don't know. I don't suppose you could shed any light on that?"

Ken shook his head. "I never really thought about it when I was writing the book. I just knew he managed to…do what he did without anybody hearing it. And nobody saw anybody sneaking around, I suppose."

"No. Shelby's apartment is in the back of the building and the security lights were busted out, probably by our guy. None of the neighbors saw or heard anything until my deputy showed up, lights and sirens. He's obviously very careful. There's a reason he hasn't been caught yet."

"But you think I can help you out somehow." Ken's voice sounded far off in his own ears. "I don't see how."

"Why don't you tell me about how you came up with the book," Allen said.

Ken finished his drink and stood up.

"I think I need something a little stronger than lemonade." He went to the bar to pour himself a drink. "Allen? Bourbon, whiskey, scotch?"

Allen looked like he was about to decline, then changed his mind. "You know, I think maybe a whiskey might be a good idea."

"Whiskey and coke," Sara said.

Ken went to the bar to fix the drinks.

"You know, there is one thing that's…" Allen paused, furrowing his brow. "Interesting, I guess you could say. All the murders in the book are virtually identical to the real ones. All of them except Shelby Winston. Why do you suppose that is? For that matter, how did you know he would kill her at all?"

Ken shook his head and replied without turning around. "I can't answer that any better than I can answer how the other ones are so close."

"Didn't you say all the other murders happened over four years ago?" Sara asked.

"Yeah, the last one before Shelby was in 2011."

"Well maybe this new one is different because it hadn't happened yet when Ken wrote about it."

"I suppose that makes about as much sense as any of the rest of this," Allen said, stroking his chin.

Ken handed out the drinks, then sat down and stared into his glass.

"You were going to tell me how you came up with the book?" Allen prompted.

"I suppose it all started about three years ago," Ken said, not looking up.

"Was that when you were shot?" Allen asked.

"Yeah. Some guy claiming to be a fan was under the delusion that if he killed me, I would write about him in my next book."

"How'd he expect you to write a book about him if you were dead?"

"He was insane." Ken shrugged. "Anyway, I had a lot of trouble getting back into writing after that. It took a long time, but when I finally started *Terror...* I don't know. It almost felt like somebody else was writing it."

Ken looked up. Allen was watching him, waiting for him to continue.

"Well, after I finished the manuscript and sent it off to my agent, I started having second thoughts about it. I was even debating whether or not I wanted to publish it, but once my agent read it and sent it off to my publisher, it took on a life of its own. They even fast-tracked it to get it out this last spring. Eventually, I just wrote off my concerns as jitters about getting back to work."

"I don't know what to make of that," Allen said. "It's interesting, but I don't think it helps me. What got you writing again?"

"Honestly, I don't know. I kept trying and nothing was working. Then one day, the dam burst and the story came pouring out."

"That's not the whole story," Sara said. "You left out the part about seeing the fortune teller."

"That gypsy at the fair?" Ken grunted. "What does that have to do with anything?"

"She said you were about to write a new book, then the next day you started *Terror in Suburbia*."

"That was just coincidence," Ken said. "Some stupid parlor trick didn't break my writer's block."

"What fortune teller?" Allen asked.

"Spring of last year, we went to the Mountain Fair up in Green Bank. There was some gypsy palm reader there and Sara talked me into getting our fortunes told. It had nothing to do with the book."

"Why don't you tell me about it anyway? You never know what little detail might be a clue. Maybe she said something that led you to our case."

Ken sighed and got up to get another drink.

"It was April. I was still trying to get started on a new project and I guess I was suffering from a little bit of depression, though I still think it was all the dope the doctor was pumping into me. One of the reasons why I stopped taking the crap. Anyway, Sara talked me into going to the Mountain Fair. I agreed because I tired of staring at the same walls every day. So we drove up to Green Bank on Saturday afternoon..."

*

The Mountain Fair was held every spring in Green Bank, a small town about half an hour north of Murphy Creek. The story was that the fair had been started by the first settlers in the region to celebrate the end of winter. Whether that was true or not, for the people of Pocahontas County, the Mountain Fair was the beginning of spring—a far more important event in the mountains than the symbolic beginning of summer on Memorial Day weekend.

A traveling carnival group had brought in the rides and carnival games. Ken had been watching a freak show while waiting for Sara to suffer through a porta-potty. The banner above the stage said "Frankie's Freaks: The Freakiest Freaks in the East!" On stage was a bald man covered in tattoos, body piercings, and horns—implants, Ken hoped. He was in the process of hammering a spike into his nose. The audience gasped and groaned with each hit of the mallet. A man wearing a black suit with a red shirt was narrating.

"Now comes the really dangerous part, folks. One wrong move here and he could drive that eight-inch spike right into his brain!"

The audience gasped again as he gave the spike another whack with the hammer, driving it completely into his nose, only the head of the nail showing.

"And there he is, folks! Let's give it up for Ramundo!"

Ramundo bowed and the audience erupted in applause, then louder as he pulled the spike—which was clearly shorter than eight inches—from his nose and bowed again.

"Don't go anywhere yet! Next on our stage is Elverna the Sword Swallower! You won't believe the size of the swords she can take down her throat!"

Sara walked up beside Ken before Elverna came out on stage.

"Ken, look! A fortune teller," she said, pointing to a small tent tucked away in the corner. In front of the tent was a sign advertising the mystical powers of Madam Drina. "Let's get our palms read."

"You don't really believe in that crap, do you?" Ken didn't believe in fortune tellers any more than he believed that the moon was made of cheese.

"Don't be a grump. It'll be fun!"

Ken rolled his eyes. "If you want to waste your money on it, go ahead. I'll stay here and watch this girl swallow long sticks."

"You're no fun," she said in a mock pout.

Ken tried to stifle a grin. "Nope, that's not going to work this time."

"Kenny is a grumpy cat," she chanted, dancing around him.

"Okay, fine I'll go with you," he said, laughing. "Just stop singing. You're embarrassing me."

She punched him in the arm. "Are you saying you don't like my singing?" she said, pretending to be upset.

"Ow, that hurt."

Sara smiled and reached up to kiss him on the cheek. "I'm sorry for beating you up. Come on!" She grabbed his hand and dragged him to the fortune teller's tent. There was no one waiting outside so she pulled back the flap and they looked in.

The inside was dimly lit by lanterns hanging in the corners and filled with the earthy scent of burning incense. The walls and ceiling were covered with red, blue, and purple silk that seemed to move and swirl in the flickering lantern light. In the center of the tent was a small round table covered with more silk, a glass fishbowl and an incense burner on one side. Two chairs sat in front of the table. Behind it waited Madam Drina.

Looking at her, Ken couldn't tell if she was young or old. Her eyes seemed ancient, but her skin was smooth with no signs of aging. Her

hair was hidden under a scarf trimmed with gold medallions that spar-
kled in the flickering lantern light like the gold choker she wore. Her
dress was closed at the neck and covered her arms all the way to her
wrists. It appeared to be made of layers of the same diaphanous silk that
covered everything else in the tent, swirling and flowing, making it hard
to tell where she stopped and the table began.

Ken was drawn back to her eyes. They seemed to glow, almost like
a cat's. He was sure it was the light that was playing tricks on him, but
they looked like they had flecks of green fire in them. He couldn't look
away. Those eyes seemed to look right into his soul.

"I've been expecting you," she said.

I'm sure you have, he thought.

"Please, sit," she said, motioning to the chairs in front of the table.

After they sat down, Madam Drina looked at the fishbowl, then back
to Ken. The bowl was half-filled with money, mostly tens and twenties.

"How much?" Ken asked.

"How much is your future worth?" she replied.

Ken glanced at Sara. She was staring at the fortune teller with a
blank look. Ken pulled out his wallet and found a twenty-dollar bill.
He looked back at Sara again, then dropped it in the bowl. Madam
Drina made no reaction, so he pulled out another twenty and added it
to the stash. It must have been enough because she smiled.

"Let us get started," she said. Her voice was soothing, hypnotic.
"You are a writer, yes?"

Ken nodded. *She must recognize me.*

The air was growing thicker. Her voice, the flickering lantern light,
the shifting colors, the incense. He was getting sleepy. He tried to look
at Sara, but found he couldn't move. His eyes were locked on the fortune teller's. She was waving her hands over the incense burner, sending
the smoke in long trails throughout the room.

"I know why you're here." Her voice seemed far away. "You are lost.
I can help. I can restore your spirit. I can help you and you can help me.
But you must enter into this pact willingly. I cannot force you to accept
my help. Do you understand?"

"Yes." Was that his voice?

"Then do you accept my help?"

Ken nodded again, not sure if he was making the decision or if she was making it for him. What kind of help did she think she could give him? Maybe an idea for a story…

"You must give me your hand and I will take a small drop of your blood."

Ken's head was spinning. Why did she need blood? Part of the charade? There was a buzzing sound in his ears. He watched his hand move across the table, but he wasn't sure if he was controlling it. Madam Drina took it and held it over a small wooden bowl that had seemingly appeared from nowhere. In her other hand was a large needle that looked like it was made of bone.

"Do you accept my help?" she asked again. Her voice was calm, soothing. Ken felt no fear, no pain. Only the floating peacefulness of her voice. He heard nothing but her voice and the constant buzzing.

The buzzing. It was almost deafening. His body was numb, except for the icy burn of her fingers. His vision narrowed. All he could see was his hand over the bowl with the medieval-looking needle poised over his thumb. Ken wondered if the needle was sanitized.

"Do you accept my help?"

He tried to speak. His lips moved, but no sound came out.

"You must accept my help."

He felt himself nod again. What was she saying? This was going too far.

He tried to pull his hand back, but he couldn't move. His muscles were frozen.

He felt a pinch on his thumb as she pricked it with her needle. A single drop of blood hung from his thumb for what seemed an eternity before falling toward the bowl. He watched it fall, so impossibly slow, almost like it was hovering in the stifling air. The lantern light reflected off the drop's surface, colors swirling, seeming to change to match the silk covering the table. It almost seemed alive, hovering above the dust in the bottom of the bowl.

The dust. He hadn't noticed that before. It was a fine powder. The color was hard to distinguish in the dim light. White, or maybe gray.

There were flecks of something darker mixed with it. The falling drop of his blood stood out against the paleness. The bowl filled his sight so that all he could see was the dust, the blood, slowly coming together.

The gypsy let go of his hand and used the bone needle to mix the contents of the bowl, chanting softly. Her voice faded into the buzzing. He watched as she stirred, the blood and the dust forming a paste. His vision continued to fade. She lit a long match and moved it toward the bowl, still chanting.

*

"The next thing I remember is standing outside the fortune teller's tent," Ken said.

"I think you're dreaming again," Sara said. "That's not at all what happened."

"That's exactly what happened. You sat there and watched the whole thing."

"What are you talking about? You were the one who sat there while I asked all of the questions."

Ken was confused. "Well, what do you remember?"

"After you paid, she started talking about our future. I asked her about your writing and she said you were on the verge of a breakthrough. She said we were getting ready to enter an exciting phase of our lives and new opportunities were in our future."

Ken stared at her. How could they have completely different memories of the same event?

Allen looked from Ken to Sara and back again.

"I don't know what I was expecting," he said, "but it sure wasn't that." He picked up his notepad and pen. "What'd you say the name of that fortune-teller lady was?"

"Madam Drina," Ken said. "Why?"

"I don't know. Something about that name sounds familiar." Allen made a couple of notes before continuing. "So after that, you started writing the book?"

"I woke up the next morning just like every other day. I didn't feel particularly inspired or anything. I just decided to write some random scene to try to get the juices flowing and the next thing I knew I had the first fifteen pages of the manuscript."

Allen nodded, stroking his chin.

"You don't believe that I was able to start writing just because she said I would, do you?"

"I wouldn't normally think that would be related, but after some of the other stuff you've told me, I'm not sure what to think."

"You two think what you want," Sara said. "I believe."

Allen smiled. "Regardless, I don't think it really helps me. But there is something else I've been wondering about. In your book, the detective catches Cory just before he kills the last victim. That almost never happens in real life. That's all TV and movie drama. With everything else in your book being so close to reality, why did you decide to do a Hollywood ending?"

"I'd like to say that's just the way it happened. Cory slipped up and Detective St. James tracked him down. But that wouldn't be true."

"Why's that?"

"In the first draft, Cory killed Alan. He was about to kill Tammy Knight when Alan came in. Cory heard him and hid in the closet. When Alan saw Tammy, he went to check to see if she was still alive and Cory snuck up behind him and killed him. Then he killed Tammy and drove off into the sunrise."

"You never told me that," Sara said. "You've never let the bad guy win in one of your books before."

"That's part of the reason I changed it, but mainly I felt like I just couldn't let him live. It was like letting him live would make me responsible for him."

"It's a character in a book," Sara said. "He's not real."

"I know. I'm just telling you how it felt."

"Tammy Knight," Allen said, seemingly to himself. "I wonder…"

"What about her?" Ken asked.

"Maybe it's nothing. All of Cory's victims have names similar to the ones of the real victims. We had a case a while back involving a Debbie Bishop. Knight, Bishop? Probably a stretch."

"Was she killed?" Sara asked.

"No. She was attacked in her home by a man back in 2007. We

think she may have been a victim that got away, but there's no way to know for sure. We don't get a lot of home invasions. The ones we do get are usually kids trying to steal small stuff they can sell to get money for drugs. Kids stealing for drugs aren't too bright, and there's only so many places around Woodford County where you can sell that kind of stuff, so we tend to be able to solve those without too much trouble. Occasionally, we'll get an ex-husband or boyfriend that breaks in, but they're obviously identified pretty quick."

"How'd she get away?" Ken asked.

"A nosy neighbor saw some commotion through the window when a lamp got knocked over. She went over and knocked on the door to see if everything was okay. The guy jumped out the back window and ran off. The only description we got was pretty useless. Average height, average build, bald, wearing a flannel shirt and jeans. He left a coat, but it didn't help. It was just a generic Carhartt work coat. Damn near everybody in rural South Dakota owns one."

"You couldn't get any DNA from hair or skin cells or something?" Sara asked.

Allen chuckled. "If only real life was like TV. We'd have had him locked up the next day. We sent the coat to the state forensics lab in Pierre. They found some trace evidence, but nothing particularly useful. Maybe if we get a suspect, it might lead to something, but even that's probably a long shot since it they didn't find any DNA." Allen finished his drink and stood up. "I suppose we're finished, unless there's something else you haven't told me."

"I wish we could have been of some help," Ken said. "But I'm just a fiction writer and the book is a figment of my imagination."

"You don't really still believe that, do you?"

"I don't know. I do know that I didn't talk to anybody about your case and I'm not a psychic. I'd never even heard of you or your case before today, so it has to be a coincidence."

Allen looked at Ken and raised an eyebrow. "A pretty amazing coincidence, don't you think?"

CHAPTER FIVE

"WELL, NOW WHAT?" Ken asked his computer.

The sheriff's visit had unnerved him. After dinner, he decided the best way to get his mind off it would be to work. He had been sitting at his computer staring at the blinking cursor for half an hour and was starting to question that logic.

He briefly considered writing something about Detective St. James. If he couldn't get *Terror in Suburbia* off his mind, maybe use it to his advantage. But he kept coming back to how his first draft of *Terror* had ended. Alan had died. He had no more tales to live, even if Ken had changed the ending for the final draft. That, and the way he had written the book, had made it feel like it hadn't been his story to begin with. While writing it, he almost felt like he had been in a trance. He remembered sitting in front of the computer with his hands on the keyboard, but it hadn't seemed like he was typing at all. It had seemed like someone else had been tapping the keys. Especially Cory's scenes.

Cory Rivers. Ken shuddered. Cory was evil. Not just a bad guy, or sick and twisted. He was real-life evil. Ken had read plenty about serial killers over the years—it was an occupational hazard. But nothing he had read about John Wayne Gacy or Jeffrey Dahmer approached the level of evil he felt oozing out of Cory. What he had read about most serial killers suggested they felt compelled to kill, that they had no real control over their actions—almost like they were puppets. Not Cory. He did it because it was fun. He was no more compelled to kill than a man was to play a game of pool. Killing was a passion, sure, but he never felt like someone else was pulling his strings. No, for Cory Rivers torture, rape, and murder was a game. A game he very much enjoyed to play.

Cory was thirty-four years old. He lived alone with his cat, Mittens. He had always liked cats, but most of them had ended up subjects for trying out his latest ideas. Mittens was the first animal he had actually kept as a pet. He had discovered the joy of watching her kill. He kept a cage of feeder mice that he bought from a local pet store—he told them the mice were for his pet python. Mittens got to kill one a week. She wouldn't kill it right away, of course. Cats like to play with their victims for a while. Cory understood that. It was fun. So he would make a bowl of popcorn and then sit on the couch and watch the party. It had been the only killing he had participated in since checking out of the Graybar Hotel. At least until Sydney...

Wait, her name was Shelby.

It didn't matter what her name was. She had been a fun ride. Four years between rides was a long time, but she made it worth it. Not that he wanted to wait another four years for his next project. He had learned a thing or two in the years between and he looked forward to trying out some new techniques. Some he had learned from Mittens, that cute little serial killer of mice. He had learned that to really play, to really have fun, they have to think that there's a way out, that they might survive playtime. Then, when they finally figure out that there is no escape, that hope had just been an illusion, when you see it drain out of them like pouring water from a bucket, that's when you make the last pounce.

He had been too quick with Shelby. He hadn't given her that hope. He supposed it was because it had been so long since his last ride. He had been too excited, anxious even. Premature exsanguination. Or maybe it was because he only had four hours to play. Or maybe it was because she owed him. Whatever the reason, he would do better next time.

And he would have to be more careful next time, too. He made a lot of mistakes he wouldn't normally make. Like ripping his shirt on the broken door lock. Sure, he was smart enough to check it to make sure he hadn't left any pieces, but if he had scratched his arm, he could have been fucked. And then the goddamn cell phone. He still couldn't believe he had left it in his pocket. He didn't know if they had been able to track it before he destroyed it, but it was another big mistake.

Well, even if it hadn't been perfect, the bitch got what was coming to her. With so little time to plan, things could have gone a lot worse. Tonight, he would just think about the fun part. He would sit on his couch and fantasize about her while he watched Mittens play with her own ride. Just thinking about how she had squirmed and jumped under his knife made him feel warm all over. He smiled as he drifted off to sleep.

*

Sara walked into the office to check on Ken. They had argued at dinner about what to do about what Sheriff James had told them. Ken had tried to tell her that everything was fine, but she knew better. After twenty years, he couldn't hide much of anything from her.

Sara knew her concern sounded irrational. Ken didn't believe in the paranormal, but she did. At least to an extent. She was a far more spiritual person than he was. She believed in ghosts and psychics and fate. Not to the extent that she thought she could talk to her dead Aunt Florence through a piece of lacquered pine board with letters and numbers printed on it—and sold by Hasbro—or that fortune cookies could help her win the lottery. She did, however, think that certain places were haunted and that things happened for a reason.

Even so, she couldn't explain how Ken could have known about what had happened all those poor girls. She was at least open to the idea that maybe something happened to him when he was shot. The doctors had said that he had technically been dead for almost a minute during the emergency surgery. She had read about severe trauma victims gaining various psychic abilities, though she was willing to admit that most of it was supermarket tabloid bunk.

But what other explanation was there?

Ken looked up at her when she opened the door to his office. His face was completely blank. He blinked, suddenly aware that she was standing in the doorway.

"How long have I been in here?" he asked.

"About an hour."

She saw that he had been writing. Ken looked back at the computer screen. The color drained from his face as he read what was on the screen.

"I don't remember writing any of this," he said.

"What is it? What's it say?"

"Cory Rivers has a cat named Mittens," Ken said. "He likes to give her mice to kill. He makes popcorn and watches from his couch while his cat plays with the mouse before killing it. He sees it as doing the same thing he does."

"Cory is seriously creepy." She shuddered. "How do you know if it's related to Allen's killer, though?"

"There's a bit about Shelby. He actually called her Shelby, although I suppose that could just be my mind imposing the name because we were talking about her."

Sara walked around the desk and read over his shoulder. She shivered as she read.

"And you don't remember writing this?" she asked when she finished.

"Not a word. I was thinking about maybe trying to write another story about Detective St. James and that led to thinking about Cory. The next thing I remember was you walking in."

"Ken? You're scaring me," Sara said. Her skin crawled with goose bumps and the hair was standing up on the back of her neck.

"Scaring you? I'm the one who wrote it."

"Do you think this is what Allen's killer is really like?"

"We've been through this before. This has nothing to do with a serial killer in South Dakota. It's just shit coming out of my head."

"This is me you're talking to. You don't believe that for a minute. You know there's something more to it."

"Come on, Sara. That psychic shit is a bunch of nonsense made up to scam people out of their money."

"I think maybe you're in denial."

"Denial? About what? Psychic connections to murderers?" Ken shook his head. "There has to be a more logical explanation."

Sara leaned down, put her arms around him, and held him tight. What she really wanted was for him to hold her, but he was too consumed with his own thoughts. She didn't know why, but she was genuinely scared. Why should she be scared? Even if Cory Rivers was real, he was a thousand miles away.

Then something occurred to her.

"Ken, what if the real killer finds out about your book?"

"What about it?"

"What if he decides to come after you?"

"Why would he do that?"

"Because you know about him. Maybe not his real name, but you know a lot about him."

"Now you're just being paranoid."

"I hope you're right." She stood up and rested her hands on his shoulders. She didn't want to think about it anymore. "Come on, Mr. Simmons. There's still a couple of pieces of pie left."

*

He had been looking forward to Saturday all week. Today he was going to start shopping for a new project. He was eager for his next ride, but he couldn't just go out and do it. He needed to shop for a while. Then, when he found something he liked, he would need to check it out—research, if you will—to make sure he'd made the right choice. It all led up to the big day, of course, but if he didn't take his time, he might end up making a mistake. And mistakes in his hobby could be disastrous. He had gotten lucky with the last one. So he took this part very seriously.

Not that looking for a new project was a chore. He looked forward to it. Sometimes he felt it was the most exciting part: the mystery of something new, not sure yet what it would be. He shivered with anticipation. The first day was the best. A clean slate. He would spend the day getting ready for tonight. He would go to town to buy a new batch of memory cards for his camera. He would need about fifty. He could buy them at the warehouse store in ten packs. He had a few left over from the last one, but better to start fresh.

And snacks. He had to have snacks and drinks. Chips or pretzels worked better than candy bars. And drinks in plastic bottles with a wide mouth and screw-on lids. Screw-on lids were important so his drink wouldn't spill. And when it was gone, the bottles could be used to avoid the distraction of finding a bathroom. That part was very important. He discovered that little gem a long time ago when he'd lost a prospect because he was in the bathroom at a fast-food joint. Public restrooms were disgusting anyway.

Standing at his own toilet, he yawned and stretched, absently scratching the stubble of hair that was growing back on his chest. His whole body itched. He always itched when the hair started to grow back. If it wasn't so much work, he would always keep his body shaved instead of doing it just once a year. This itching was different though. It was more of a tingling sensation that added to the overall strangeness he had felt since waking up. He flushed the toilet and moved to the sink to wash his hands and face. When he looked in the mirror, the odd claustrophobic delirium grew stronger.

This wasn't the first time he'd had this feeling. He had first experienced it over a year ago while he'd still been up state. It had happened every morning for several weeks. He had thought he was getting sick or something, which wouldn't have been surprising given where he had been living at the time. Then it had gone away and he had forgotten about it until a few nights ago. He had been sitting on his couch when he felt it, but he had been tired so he hadn't thought too much about it. This was the first time he had seen himself in the mirror while he was experiencing the sensation.

Now he was awake and the dreamlike feeling was stronger than ever. Looking at his face in the mirror, he felt like he was looking at someone else. Or maybe like he was seeing himself through someone else's eyes. Like he was being watched. There was someone there, he sensed it. Someone else was in his head, watching him with his own eyes.

"Get out of my head!" he yelled. He jammed the heels of his hands in his eyes, pressing harder and harder until they swam with color, trying to push out the intruder.

"Get out!"

*

Ken bolted upright in his chair, sweat dripping into his eyes, his hands shaking. He looked at his computer screen, hoping it had just been a bad dream, knowing it hadn't. That face still floated in his vision, like the afterglow of a camera flash. The cold, emotionless lizard eyes stared back at him, burrowing into his soul. He still felt the adrenaline that had been flowing through Cory's body as he'd thought about his next project. Ken's insides crawled from his bowels to the back of his throat.

He tried to stand, using his desk to steady himself. His knees gave out and he fell back into his chair. What the hell was happening to him? This time, he couldn't blow it off as some kind of dream or vision. This had been like he was sitting in the same room with Cory. No, that wasn't right. It was more like he had actually *become* Cory Rivers. He had been able to smell the air in Cory's apartment, feel the cold bathroom tiles under his feet, taste the garlic on his breath.

"It had to be just a dream, that's all," Ken said to himself, not believing it even as he said it. He was afraid. He didn't know what exactly he was afraid of, just that he was. Maybe he was afraid Cory Rivers might actually be real and everything he had written about Cory hadn't just been some dark tale from the depths of his imagination. Or maybe it was that Cory was out there, somewhere, planning another murder.

Or that maybe Cory could see into Ken's life just like Ken could see into his. Nietzsche's quote about staring into the abyss came to mind.

He wiped the cold sweat from his forehead and tried to swallow past the lump in his throat.

"Are you okay?" Sara's voice made Ken jump. "Sorry, I didn't mean to scare you. I heard you talking to someone."

"I'm fine," he lied. He was still having trouble breathing and his heart was still trying to jump out of his chest. "I was talking to myself."

"You don't look fine. You look like crap."

"I need a drink."

"Really? It's not even ten o'clock yet. What happened?"

Ken sighed. There was no point in trying to hide it from her. She knew him too well.

"I had another dream about Cory. Only it felt even more real than before. I can't explain the feeling. The closest thing I can come up with is it was like a dream where you don't have any control over your actions, and you know you don't have any control. Only it was more than that. With touch, and smell, and taste."

Sara looked at him, her eyes wide and jaw clenched.

"Ken, you have to stop," she said finally.

"How? I don't even know how it happens."

"I don't know, but I'm scared. And I think you are too."

"Scared of what? It was just a dream." He was trying to convince himself as much as her. How could he comfort her if she knew he how scared he was?

"Of what this means! Of what could happen. I don't know. What if he knows?"

"But it's not real! It can't be." He was lying to himself now too. "It's just a really vivid dream. I can't really be inside anyone's head. I'm just imagining things. There is no Cory Rivers."

"So explain how you could make up eight murder victims whose names are almost identical to real murder victims and the way they were killed was almost exactly the same? I'm not Sheriff James, trying to solve some murder cases. I'm your wife, and I'm scared of what's happening to you."

Ken sighed. He couldn't even explain it to himself. "A few months ago I would have said that the idea that anything in that book was based on something real was crazy. And that if you believed it was, then maybe you're the one who needs to see the shrink. Now... I don't know. I don't believe in ESP or any of that bullshit, but I can't explain it."

"Just because you don't believe in something doesn't mean it doesn't exist. You could be wrong. Why take the chance? Please, Ken? For me? Will you promise not to do it again?"

"But I don't know how to stop it. It's not like I'm doing it on purpose."

He looked at Sara, her dark eyes pleading with him, filling with tears. Her fear was as strong as his. Maybe she was being emotional and unreasonable—after all, he didn't even know how it was happening, much less how to stop it—but she was genuinely afraid of something. But then, so was he.

"Okay, I'll try. I don't know how, but I'll try."

"Thank you," she said, tears finally flowing down her cheeks. She smiled and put her arms around him and hugged him like she would never let go.

CHAPTER SIX

"WOULD YOU LIKE some more coffee, sir?"

He pushed his empty cup toward the waitress without speaking. The waitress frowned at him. She must have thought he wasn't looking. She filled his cup anyway. Stupid bitch. He should teach her a lesson about where she was in the pecking order. That would raise attention, though, and he wanted to stay anonymous in the back corner. She wasn't worth the trouble anyway. She was wearing a wedding ring, so she was somebody else's problem.

The waitress working the counter, on the other hand, showed some promise. She was young, probably in her twenties, which meant she was old enough to hang out at the whorehouses, spreading her diseases to the stupid drunk fucks who didn't know any better. A walking petri dish, like the other stupid bar bitches. If there was a God, he should have sent AIDS to take them out instead of the pillow biters. Just watching her made him feel like retching. She wore a cross on a chain around her neck, but he knew it was just for show. She was a lying whore just like the rest of them.

She had her blonde hair tied back in a ponytail. He imagined what it would feel like to wrap it around his fist and yank her head back. She would scream and he would smash her fucking teeth out. Probably make her swallow them and wash them down with blood from her busted face.

His hands were shaking enough to spill his coffee. He smiled as he set the cup down. She might be the one. He'd watched her for the last hour: walking around behind the counter, taking orders, delivering food, cleaning tables. Being a good little bitch, as his dad used to say.

He often thought of his dad when he was hunting. Dad had taught him how to hunt, although they had only hunted rabbits and deer. He supposed his dad would have enjoyed this kind of hunting too. Sometimes he wished his dad was still around so they could talk about his hobby. It was his dad who had taught him not to be a pussy or let some bitch walk all over him. Being a man meant being in charge—and that all started at home.

"A man's house is his castle, Charlie," his dad would tell him. Especially after he had to remind Charlie's mother about her place. "And a man has to be the king of his castle. You let some stupid bitch tell you what to do, especially in your own home, you might as well just cut off your fucking balls and feed 'em to the dog, 'cause you ain't no man."

Charlie had learned that lesson—not that he had ever had a wife, or even dated, for that matter. He tried once or twice when he'd still been in high school. He even had a crush on Gillian Lovell in tenth grade. He had thought she was the most beautiful thing in the world. He'd sat behind her in English class, and while Mr. Meade blabbered about the meaning behind *Moby-Dick* or the symbolism of the stupid fucking bird in *Slaughterhouse-Five*, Charlie had daydreamed about making out with Gillian under the bleachers in the gym. It took him all year to work up the courage to ask her to the movies.

She had been at her locker, gabbing with her group of bitch friends. Charlie had never liked them. They had all picked on him since third grade when he and his dad had moved to Ashford. They had called him names like "Charlie Bumpkin" and "Hillchucky." Gillian wasn't like the rest of them. Tenth grade had been her first year at Ashford High. He hadn't been able to understand why she would hang out with the mean clique.

Then he had gone up to her and asked her if she would want to go to the movies with him Friday night.

The whole group had stopped talking and stared at him. It had felt like they stood there staring at him forever. Then Gillian, that stupid fucking cunt, had burst out laughing. Then they were all laughing and pointing at him. Everybody in the hall had stopped and stared. That was when he knew that they were all a bunch of worthless cunts. He'd run down the hall and out the front door of the school and hadn't stopped until he got home.

That weekend, he'd killed her cat.

Charlie had thought about killing her too, but he hadn't had the balls to do it back then. He had thought about it since, but she had moved away after high school and he didn't know where she had gone. Some nights he fantasized that she would come back to town for a high school reunion and he would take her out to the cabin and work her over for days. Tie her up and make her watch while he cut off pieces of her and fed them to a stray dog. He was getting better at keeping them alive while he cut them. By the time he had his chance with her, he might be able to keep her alive for a few days. Maybe even a week.

What would Daddy think about that? Charlie liked to think his dad would be proud of him. He had learned his lessons well. He put all the whores in their place, just like Dad used to put his mother in her place, back when they'd lived in Tennessee. At least until she'd disappeared. Dad never talked about it, just telling Charlie that the whore had run off. He remembered his dad being arrested. The cops had asked him a lot of questions about his mother and how Dad had treated her. They never found her, so they had to let Dad go. His dad moved them to South Dakota not long after that because Uncle Bobby, Dad's brother, lived there.

Charlie imagined Dad had given her the final lesson. She probably deserved it, like all the rest of them. Charlie had never been able to bring himself to ask his dad about it, though. Then Dad had died of a heart attack and Charlie had lost his chance.

What was it the French said? *Say Lovey?* Whatever the fuck that meant.

As his daydream faded, he noticed the bitch behind the counter was looking at him. He must have been staring at her while he was reminiscing. He picked up his coffee and looked away. Out of the corner of his eye, he saw her talking to the guy working the grill. She pointed at him while she was talking.

Fuck.

A night of hunting shot to hell. If he killed her, the grill guy and the stuck-up troll serving him coffee would remember him. When the cops interviewed them they would give his description. They might even review the footage from the security cameras. Even though he doubted they would still have it by then, he wasn't going to take that chance. He had time. He still had three more weeks to find a target without getting off schedule.

Charlie finished his coffee and gathered up the newspaper he had been pretending to read. He threw a dollar on the table, not because he wanted to give any money to that skank monkey, but because not leaving a tip would make him more memorable and that wasn't good for his hobby.

"How was everything?" The grill guy took the check and his money. The two waitresses were watching him from the end of the counter.

The coffee sucked. The burger had been burnt and dry. The fries had been greasy and cold. The waitress needed an attitude adjustment.

"Fine." Complaining made you memorable too.

The grill guy was eyeballing him while he rang up the check. Maybe he needed an attitude adjustment too.

"Thank you and have a nice night," Grill Guy said, handing Charlie his change.

Charlie grunted. He pocketed the change and turned to walk out the door.

The turn made him feel dizzy. Only that wasn't quite it. It was *that* feeling again. That feeling that someone was watching him. Only they were watching him from inside his own head. Just like before.

He stumbled out of the restaurant and to his van. He had to use the door handle to keep himself from falling over.

"Go away," he hissed under his breath.

He fumbled with his keys, managing to open the door and climb into the van before he could fall. His eyes caught his reflection in the mirror. Looking back at him was the same stranger he had seen the previous morning.

"Get the fuck out of my head!"

He pounded his fists against his temples, the dizziness stronger than ever.

Then it was gone, leaving him slumped over his steering wheel, trying to catch his breath.

"What the fuck," he muttered. What was happening to him?

He looked up. The three restaurant workers behind the counter were looking at him through the window. So much for not being memorable. *Fuck.*

*

Ken woke dripping with sweat, his pulse pounding, flashbulbs going off in his head with every beat of his heart. The room was spinning, like he had been drinking too much.

His mouth tasted like coffee.

It was Cory Rivers. He had been in Cory's head again. Only this time, Ken had been sleeping. So it must have been a dream, right? There was no Cory Rivers. He was make believe, a monster in the closet, not real.

But it had seemed so real.

"What's happening to me?" he said.

Sara stirred beside him.

"What's wrong?" she asked, not quite awake.

"A bad dream. Go back to sleep," Ken replied.

Sara mumbled something, then rolled over and in less than a minute was breathing softly, asleep like nothing had happened. Ken watched the back of her head in the dark and knew he wouldn't be able to sleep for a long time.

*

"Did you wake up and say something to me last night?"

Ken jumped. He hadn't heard Sara walk in. He was sitting at the kitchen table, drinking coffee, thinking about his dream, or vision, or whatever it had been. He had almost convinced himself it had been a dream, even the part where he woke up. At least until Sara walked in and asked him about it.

"I'm sorry if I woke you up. I had a bad dream and must have said something."

Sara stopped pouring her coffee and looked at him.

"Was it about Cory?"

Ken turned away. He didn't want to say it out loud. Saying it out loud would make it real. If he just kept quiet, maybe it would go away.

"Ken? Tell me."

He sighed. "Yeah. He was at a diner. He was thinking about killing one of the waitresses."

"Oh, God." She sat down next to him at the table. "Kenny? What does it mean?"

That was a good question. He supposed if he knew the answer, he would be able to find a way to stop it. Or maybe even that was wishful thinking.

"Talk to me, Ken," she said, taking his hands in hers.

Ken looked down at his coffee and shook his head. "I don't know what it means or why it's happening."

"Maybe you should see somebody about it."

"Who? A psychiatrist? 'Hey, Doc, I'm having dreams about the serial killer from my book. Oh, and by the way, he's real and I'm dreaming about what he's doing.' They'd lock me up."

"You at least have to tell Allen."

"Oh, right. He'd have me committed too."

"Maybe not. He knows that you saw Cory kill that girl last week. Now that he's had more time to think about it, maybe he'll be willing to accept that it's real."

"I'm not even willing to accept that it's real." Ken pulled his hands away and rubbed his face.

"Yes, you are. You just don't want it to be real. You're easier to read than one of your books."

Maybe for Sara, that was true. Ken could read her just as easily. They couldn't hide anything from each other. The result of being together for so long, he supposed. He would occasionally wonder how people who cheated on their spouses got away with it. If he ever did something like that, Sara would know the minute he walked in the door.

"So what do I do then?"

"You mean what do *we* do. We're in this together, mister."

"Okay, fine. What do *we* do?"

They sat in silence, absorbed in their own thoughts. Suddenly, Ken thought of something.

"Charlie!" he said. Sara flinched, spilling her coffee.

"What?"

"I just remembered something from the dream! His name is Charlie!"

"Are you sure?"

"Positive." For the first time since the visions started, Ken felt some relief. If they knew his name, maybe Sheriff James could catch him.

"Then you definitely have to tell Allen." Sara must have been thinking the same thing. "If it helps him catch the guy, then maybe the dreams will stop. And even if they don't, at least you won't be dreaming about him killing people."

"I hope you're right."

"I am. Now go email him. While you do that, I'll make us some breakfast." She smiled at him, then hugged him.

"I think I would feel safer if *you* emailed Allen and *I* cooked breakfast."

"Screw you, Simmons," she shot back, punching him in the arm. "Go send your email or you'll end up eating cereal for breakfast."

Ken refilled his coffee cup and went to his office to find the sheriff's card. He wasn't sure exactly what he was going to say, but maybe Allen would just take his message at face value. After all, he had traveled all the way to the backwoods of West Virginia to find him, even knowing that Ken couldn't be their suspect.

But why would the sheriff believe he was psychically connected to the killer? Hell, Ken didn't want to believe it himself.

He sighed.

He supposed Sara could be right. Maybe it was true. Maybe he would have to accept it. And maybe Allen would accept it too.

Still, he wondered if any of this was going to help. Even if Charlie was really the guy's name, how many Charlies were living in Woodford County, South Dakota? And that was assuming he was even from the area. For all anybody knew, he could be from anywhere. Maybe he lived in Minnesota or Nebraska. For that matter, why not Tennessee? He only killed once a year, so maybe he just traveled there to go hunting.

Or what if he killed more than once a year, but only once a year in a given area? Ken shuddered. What if he lived in West Virginia and traveled all over the country to hunt? Maybe he lived in Murphy Creek and that was why Ken was connected to him.

Ken stopped himself. He knew Charlie didn't kill outside of South Dakota. He had seen, or rather felt, his method. He would stalk a target for a year before he killed her. It was some kind of ritual, although he thought Charlie probably saw it more as being careful. And he lived near his victims. There was no way he could stalk them like he did if he had to travel too far.

Ken didn't know how he knew that, but he did.

He turned on his computer to compose the message to Allen. He really hoped Sara was right about the dreams stopping. Even if Charlie never killed one more person, the experience of being in his mind was bad enough. If he kept having the visions, he really would go insane, and no amount of Phenelzine or Diazepam would fix it.

CHAPTER SEVEN

ALLEN WAS SITTING in his study when the email from West Virginia arrived. He was going over backlogged paperwork at home rather than the office, trying to appease his wife. She had been getting on him about the amount of time he was spending at work. He was well aware that working in the office at the house wasn't what she had in mind when she had suggested that he spend more time at home. The paperwork wasn't going to do itself, though, so he was hoping the compromise would buy him a little bit of good will with her.

Ken's email threw his plans out the window.

Allen wasn't sure whether or not to believe the information Ken sent him, but he was desperate. At this point, even if the information ended up being useless, at least it gave him something to do, which was better than sitting around with his thumb up his ass. If the information actually led to a suspect they could build a case around with physical evidence, then it would be a win for the home team. Even sports stars sometimes relied on silly superstitions to get out of a slump. Allen figured a ten-year slump justified stretching his views on the paranormal a little bit. Especially if it worked.

The two possible clues Allen pulled out of the email were that the guy's name was Charlie and that he had been in prison. How many people could there be named Charlie who had been released from prison in the last few months and who had been arrested after August of 2011? If he focused on arrests in Woodford and surrounding counties, the list couldn't be that long.

Allen sat down at his computer and logged into the state's law enforcement database. His search came back almost immediately. There were only three potential suspects: Charles Arthur Farmer (AKA Charlie), Charles Franklin Reese (AKA Charlie), and Charles William Ryder (AKA Chuck). For the moment, he disregarded Chuck. He was looking for a Charlie. That left Charlie Farmer and Charlie Reese.

Charlie Farmer had been arrested for third degree burglary in Woodford County in October 2012. Charlie Reese had also been arrested for third degree burglary, but in Lake County in September 2012. Not much to distinguish them from each other. He pulled up the cases for each one.

Charles Farmer had broken into the home of Frank and Marie Hanson on or about October 4, 2012. The couple came home from eating dinner out to find their back door had been forced open and the house had clearly been ransacked. Marie Hanson left the residence and called 9-1-1 on her cell phone while Frank Hanson retrieved a shotgun from his gun safe and searched the residence. He discovered Farmer hiding in an upstairs closet. Frank Hanson held Farmer at gunpoint until the police arrived taking Farmer into custody.

Charles Reese was observed by Francine Porter on or about September 12, 2012 peering in the windows of a neighbor's apartment while the neighbor, Shelby Winston, was at work. She called 9-1-1 and the responding officers discovered Reese in the bedroom, going through the dresser drawers, presumably looking for valuables.

Allen read it again. *Shelby Winston.*

Dammit. Why hadn't they found this before?

His mind spinning, he tried to convince himself that they would have found it eventually. After all, she had been killed less than two weeks ago and the arrest had happened in Lake County. He still mentally kicked himself for not finding it sooner. The only good thing was that the lead could have been found without any psychic nonsense, so he would have no problem justifying pulling Charles Reese in for questioning. And since he was on parole, Allen didn't even need a search warrant to search Reese's apartment.

He picked up the radio and called the deputy on duty to check out

Reese's last known address, and bring him in if he was there or wait for him if he wasn't. That done, he leaned back and put his hands behind his head.

For the first time in months, years really, they had a break. He was going to get this guy.

So why did he feel so uneasy?

*

Charlie Reese sat quietly in the interrogation room waiting for someone to come in. He was a patient man and had spent three years in prison, so it was no skin off his nose to sit here as long as the cops felt like dicking around. He supposed that if they took too long, he might have to find a new job, but he didn't much care about loading trucks anyway. Maybe road construction would be an interesting way to spend his days.

All he really cared about was getting to Roadside Diner by nine o'clock. He planned on spending the evening there scouting. Tomorrow night would be at Pump 'n Grub on I-29 and then (Eat At) Willie's the following night, if he still didn't have a prospect. Even though he had picked up targets at each before, it had been a long time, so he was probably safe to use them again. Besides, in this area, there were only so many places that dirty whores went to eat.

He knew he shouldn't be thinking about his new project while he was sitting in the cop station. That might just be tempting fate, though he wasn't too concerned. He was an expert at maintaining a poker face, even when pressed.

The interrogation room looked like any other he had been in. Compared to the cold, stark rooms shown on TV cop shows, the real thing was almost comfy. Instead of painted cinderblock walls, tile floors, and hard metal chairs on opposite sides of an equally harsh metal table, this room was carpeted, with acoustic tiles on the walls and ceiling, and a long, wood table in the corner. The chair he was sitting in at the end of the table was relatively comfortable. It even had padded armrests. Along the long edge of the table was a basic office chair with wheels and no armrests. He figured the cops gave the nice chair to the perp to try to soften them up.

Even so, the room was still plain. The walls were white, no pictures or signs. The floor was covered by ordinary dark gray industrial carpeting. Above him was a standard office drop ceiling with white, square tiles and two recessed fluorescent lights that gave the room an unflattering doctor's office feel. In one corner, a small camera was attached to the wall just below the ceiling. It was disguised as a smoke detector, like that was fooling anybody. The long wall opposite the table was mostly filled with a mirror, obviously one-way.

The cops must think people are stupid or something. Everybody knows there's somebody behind the mirror watching you. That prick sheriff is probably behind it right now, watching and waiting to see if I fuck up and give something away. I have better self-control than that. That pig fucker can watch all day and not get a clue.

Charlie took a drink of the coffee they had given him. He wasn't worried about giving them fingerprints or DNA. They had all that on him already, so he might as well drink it. Not that it was good coffee, but at least it was better than the piss water they served in the joint. That stuff wasn't even hot. Guess they were afraid you might try to throw hot coffee on one of the screws. They must not be worried about that when they interviewed suspects. Even ones on parole.

Charlie had known it would only be a matter of time before the police questioned him about that Shelby whore, but he wasn't worried about it. These stupid fucks couldn't figure out how to catch a dog on a leash taking a shit on the sidewalk. That thought almost made him smile. Almost.

He didn't care for dogs any more than he cared for cops. Dogs used to be his favorite target, a long time ago. His neighborhood never had a stray problem. He would take out the cats too—they just weren't as much of a challenge. Of course if he had known then what he learned from Greg Willis, he might have done things differently.

Greg had been his cellmate in the State Pen. He had been one crazy motherfucker. He would talk forever about his fucking cats. He said they were his only friends on the outside, the only ones who truly understood him. Charlie often wondered if Ole Greggie fucked his cats too, as much as he talked about them.

The one useful thing he got from Greg, before he had had enough of his blabbering and shanked him in the shower, was that cats were the ultimate killers. They would stalk their prey and attack like any other predator, but what made them different was they didn't kill right away—they played with their kills before eating them. Now Charlie wasn't about to eat whore-meat, but he respected their style. So when he'd gotten out, he'd decided to get himself a cat and find out.

He had found the ad for free kittens on the bulletin board at Pump 'n Grub. When he went to claim one, the little girl at the house had picked one up and handed it to him. She told him the cat's name was Mittens on account of her black paws. Charlie had no idea how you named a pet, having never owned one before, so he just called it Mittens until he could figure out something better. After a few weeks, he decided the name was as good as anything else, so he kept it.

At first, Mittens hadn't seemed to be much of a hunter and Charlie had been about to give up on her, when he remembered a kid in school who had owned a python. The kid—*was it Jerry? Jeremy? Who gives a fuck?*—told him that his snake ate mice that he bought at the pet store. So Charlie had gone to a pet store and told them he needed some mice for a python. After that, the weekly Mittens Play Time began.

He had learned so much watching her. So much so that he hadn't had enough time with Shelby to do all the things he'd learned. He was looking forward to the opportunity to expand. The next one would have better planning. Maybe even plan for a whole day. That would require a lot of work, but he wasn't worried about that. He had a year to figure it all out. He just needed to find a suitable prospect. With luck, this time next week he would be in tracking mode, finding out everything he could about number ten before October the following year.

He almost had the whole calendar done. In a few more years he would be back to January. Then what would he do? He supposed he could start a new calendar. Or maybe switch things up. Just as long as he gave himself enough time to prepare.

And Charlie enjoyed the tracking phase of a project almost as much as the scouting phase. Which was a good thing since it was the phase that took the longest. Scouting rarely took more than two or three weeks, and sometimes even less, if he got lucky. And planning for the Big Day was enjoyable in its own way, meticulously working out all the details. Still, that usually didn't take him more than a week or two. Of course, everything led up to the Big Day, the grand finale of the hunt, which was the best part of the project, obviously. It was what everything else was all about. But tracking had its own appeal. Sometimes relaxing, sometimes exciting, and always fun. He would take hours of video every night and review it every day. He would make notes that he would use during the planning phase. The notes would help him when he was reviewing a year's worth of video and condensing it down to a few hours. The review always brought back the memories and feelings of being out on the track.

At the end of a project, he always destroyed all of the original video, keeping just the condensed version. That always made him a little sad, but it was hard to hide that many memory cards. A handful could be hidden almost anywhere.

More than once, he had thought about videoing the Big Day. He had never done it though. To do it right would require too much equipment to get in and out quickly. So all he had were the edited videos from tracking his targets.

Well, that and their hearts. But those were out at the cabin so he couldn't pull them out to look at whenever he wanted to. He had actually planned on heading up to the cabin this coming weekend, but since the cops were being nosy, he decided it would be better to wait for a few weeks to take that trip. Eventually, they would get tired of watching him drink coffee and read the newspaper. Then he could go.

That thought did make him smile.

*

Allen drank a cup of coffee while he observed Reese through the one-way mirror. He liked to sit and watch for a while before interrogating a suspect. Sometimes a suspect would give away a lot of information before he even walked into the room. Besides, he was in no hurry to let this piece of shit go, which he'd have to do if the search of his apartment came up empty. When he saw Reese smiling to himself, he decided it was time. He poured himself another cup of coffee, picked up a notepad and pen, then headed into the interrogation room.

"Mr. Reese," Allen said as he walked in, "I'm Allen James." He extended his hand to Reese. Reese glanced at it, then back to Allen's face, but didn't accept the offer. Allen ignored the rebuke and sat down in the office chair, putting his notepad on the table. He rolled the chair closer to Reese, pretending to be friendly.

"Before we get started I just want to make sure we're on the same page. Deputy Crawford already informed you of your rights. I just want to remind you that you aren't under arrest, we just want to ask you a few questions about a case that we think you can help us out with. You do have the right to not help us and you have the right to have your lawyer here if you feel uncomfortable on your own. But it will be a lot easier if we can just have a nice friendly conversation rather than getting the damn lawyers involved. You know how bad a lawyer can screw things up. A lawyer could screw up your wet dream and then charge you for it. Am I right?"

Allen flashed a friendly smile. Reese just returned a blank stare.

"Okay, then, let's get started." Allen picked up his notepad and pen. "You remember Shelby Winston? The woman whose apartment you broke into?"

"What about it," Reese said.

"Well, there's been a complication. You see, someone broke into her apartment again, but this time she was there and got hurt."

"Too bad for her," Reese replied.

Allen couldn't read any emotional response coming from Reese. He decided to keep up the nice-guy routine for a while longer.

"I hate to ask this, but it's my job, you know. You were caught in her apartment, then just a few months after you get out of prison someone breaks into her home again. So people are asking: Did Charlie Reese break in again? Was there something he was looking for that he didn't get the first time? Maybe she owed you money? Or maybe you're just struggling to make ends meet working at the depot loading trucks. You figured you already knew her—maybe she would have the same routine, so you'd slip in and grab a few things to get you by until payday."

Playing the *we don't know shit routine* felt like a good approach for this one. Letting him know that they were looking at him as a serial killer wouldn't help. Better to get him to fess up to the easy one. Then they could press him on the rest. Besides, making him think they were clueless about the other women might stoke up his ego and get him to slip. But Reese just stared at him with eyes that were so blank they could have been made of glass.

"So what happened?" Allen asked. "Did she come home and find you there? I get it. It's hard to make a decent living when you first get out. And then Shelby comes home and you panicked. It happens. It's not your fault she came home early on a Friday night. She should have been out having a good time with her boyfriend. Then you could grab a few things and get out quick with no one getting hurt. You didn't want to hurt her, did you?"

"I don't know what you're talking about," Reese said, as deadpan as before.

"Okay, okay. We're just trying to find out what happened. My boss wants this case closed, so I'm willing to make a recommendation to the State's Attorney if you can help me out and just tell me what happened." Allen didn't have a boss—he had been elected. He hoped that Reese wouldn't pick up on that subtlety. But Reese just stared at him and said nothing.

"Okay, no problem. You don't have to talk to me, but I want to remind you that per South Dakota law, part of the parole agreement you signed allows us to search your residence without a warrant. My deputies are at your apartment right now with your parole officer and a representative from the State's Attorney's office. This is your chance to get out in front of this thing before it blows up."

"There's nothing to get in front of. You got the wrong guy. I haven't broken any laws since I got out. I haven't even driven over the speed limit. I learned my lesson in prison and I won't do anything that might put me back there. I make enough money to get by and even if I did need more money, breaking into her apartment again would be stupid. I'd be the first one you'd come after." Reese held out his hands and shrugged.

"That's true, you are the obvious choice, but that doesn't mean we're wrong. And it doesn't mean you're stupid. Desperate times call for desperate measures." Allen leaned toward Reese. "It's okay. You can tell me. I'll do everything I can to make sure you're treated fairly. All you need to do is be honest with me. You didn't know Shelby would come home and you panicked because you didn't want to go back to prison. You didn't mean to kill her, it just happened. Everybody will understand that. Sometimes shit happens and it's not your fault, right?"

Reese went back to staring at Allen and saying nothing. Allen sat back and stretched.

"I'm going for more coffee. You want some?"

Reese sat back as well and shook his head. Allen stood up and walked to the door.

"Hang tight," he said. As he closed the door behind him, a woman in a dark gray skirt suit walked out from the observation room.

"Hey, Kim," Allen said. "How much of that did you catch?"

"Didn't seem like there was much to catch," she replied.

Kimberly Barrett was the Woodford County State's Attorney. This was her second term, having been an Assistant State's Attorney in Minnehaha County for ten years, prior to moving to Ashford to be closer to her aging mother. Being in her forties and still single had some of the county's gossip hounds spreading baseless rumors about her. A forty-year-old woman should be married with kids, not trying to do a man's job. Allen didn't care about any of that. She seemed to be a good fit at the county courthouse in spite of her big-city background in Sioux Falls, and she was always an ally to his department. That was all Allen cared about. The fact that she had been elected twice told the real story anyway: most of the county had gotten over the good old boys' club of the past a long time ago.

"I'm just getting warmed up," Allen said as they walked.

"Well, you might as well cool down. He's going to walk."

Allen stopped and looked at her.

"We just got the report back on his ankle monitor. He was home the night Shelby Winston was killed. From the looks of it, he was asleep by ten o'clock and didn't move until after three thirty."

"How do you know that?"

"The log shows that from about eight o'clock until ten o'clock, he moved around a bit, probably between the kitchen, living room, and bathroom, but then stayed put for a while. Probably fell asleep on the couch watching TV and woke up in the middle of the night. Around three-thirty, he moved to another room, presumably the bedroom."

"Those things can tell what room he's in?"

"Not exactly. There's a receiver in the apartment that reports how far away the wearer is from the receiver every five minutes. Since the receiver is near the front of the apartment and the bedroom is in the back, we can make some logical assumptions about where he is based on the distance."

"I thought they used GPS or something."

"They do, sort of. When the wearer is outside, the unit records its GPS location. Next time it gets close enough to the receiver, the GPS data is transmitted automatically. We have the ability to query an individual monitor if we need to, but they don't transmit their location data in real time unless we remotely turn it on. Most of the people wearing them don't know that. They just think Big Brother is always looking over their shoulder."

"Huh," Allen said. "Guess I never needed to know the technical details."

"Regardless, Charles Reese wasn't in, or even near, Shelby Winston's apartment the night she was killed."

CHAPTER EIGHT

DEPUTY RENEE WATTS had been sitting in her car since midnight. Four hours ago, she had been excited to be on her first stakeout. Now she was trying to figure out how she would stay awake for the next four. Just a year out of the police academy, she was still considered a rookie by her fellow deputies, which gave her the privilege of drawing the midnight to eight shift of babysitting duty. She wasn't even sure exactly what she was supposed to be doing. Beyond keeping an eye out for Charles Reese, of course.

She had relieved Deputy Stan Trout just before midnight. He had been watching Reese since yesterday afternoon. According to what Stan had passed on, Reese had gone to supper at a diner out by the highway. He had stuck around reading the paper and drinking coffee until about eight o'clock, then gone home, not violating his nine o'clock parole curfew. The lights in his apartment went out around eleven thirty. Since then, everything had been quiet.

Reese's apartment was on the third floor, facing the street. The front door was the only way out of the building without setting off the fire alarm, which meant there was no way he could leave the building without her seeing him. And unless he was smarter than most ex-cons, he wouldn't know she was there.

She was in her personal car, a 2006 Honda Civic, about as generic as you could get. She had parked across the street from the building, but not right in front. They hadn't taught stakeout procedures in the academy, but it seemed like common sense to not sit right in front of the place you were watching.

Technically, doing covert surveillance wasn't in her job description. The sheriff had been very clear that this wasn't a required assignment and none of the deputies was under any obligation to volunteer. In spite of that, they had all signed up for the extra duty. She knew Crawford had done it because he had been working the case with the sheriff since the beginning. For Renee, it was all about the overtime pay. She suspected the same was true of the other deputies. Nobody got into law enforcement for the pay, especially in a small sheriff's office like Woodford County, so anytime they could make an extra nickel, they tended to jump on it.

The instructions from the sheriff had been pretty basic. Try not to be noticed, keep a log of everything that seems relevant, follow Reese if he leaves the apartment, but don't stop him. And stay until you're relieved by your replacement. The sheriff had been very emphatic about that.

Except for Shelby Winston, Renee hadn't been around for the murders this guy had supposedly committed. Whoever had killed all those women was one messed-up dude. The evidence that she knew about didn't point to Charles Reese, though. From what she had heard, it didn't point to anybody. They hadn't gotten anything from the crime scene that didn't belong there.

Renee's money was on the boyfriend. Norris didn't think so, and neither did Crawford. They kept telling her that she hadn't seen the body. The boyfriend's alibi had checked out, and they were both convinced that there was no way he could have done that to her in the time he had. Renee tried to point out that other than the broken door latch, there was no sign of anyone else ever being in the apartment. The boyfriend probably broke the latch himself to make it look like someone had broken in. Or maybe Shelby had locked him out because he'd come home drunk and he'd broken into his own apartment. Then he'd attacked her for locking him out.

Gus had just shaken his head and kept saying that she hadn't been there, she hadn't seen it.

Well, the report had been pretty vague on some of the particulars about the condition of the body. The real details, along with photographs of the body, would be in the M.E.'s report, but she hadn't seen that yet.

Renee finished off her second Mountain Dew and tossed the empty bottle on the passenger floorboard, along with several others and a few fast-food bags. It wasn't doing much to keep her awake, but it did make her have to pee. After four hours and two twenty-ounce bottles, she was beginning to get uncomfortable. What had been a small tickling an hour ago now felt like a bowling ball in her belly. She had thought about trying to use one of the empty pop bottles, but decided that would probably end up with pee all over the place. And she didn't want to go outside. Someone might see her, which would be embarrassing at best. Being a cop and all, it might get her fired.

She shifted positions and loosened her belt, hoping to relieve some of the pressure on her bladder. Nobody had told her about this part of the job. Probably another *haze the rookie* thing. Or maybe it was just that a department full of men didn't think ahead about it, since they could just pee on a tree or something when a bathroom wasn't handy. Whatever the reason, she knew she wasn't going to last another four hours.

Renee tried to take her mind off of her bladder. It was a trick she used to overcome the boredom as well as the swelling pain in her abdomen. Growing up, she had spent countless hours in tree stands hunting deer. One of the first things her dad had taught her about deer hunting was you can't kill a deer if you're sitting on the couch. Which was his way of saying you had to put in your time in the woods. Most days you wouldn't shoot at all. You'd sit in your stand for four or five hours, go in to warm up and grab lunch, then spend another four hours in the stand until it was too dark to see. The hardest thing to learn about hunting wasn't how to shoot—it was how to sit in a tree all day without falling asleep. She was finding that a stakeout was a lot like deer hunting.

Hunting wasn't the only thing she had learned from her dad. He had taught her to drive a tractor and perform basic engine maintenance and repair. She had learned how to ride a four-wheeler when she was five and a dirt bike by the time she was eight. Her dad had called her his "Little Firecracker," a nickname that had stuck with her all through high school, probably as much for her flaming red hair as for her wild personality. She sometimes wondered if maybe he'd brought her up as a tomboy because he had wanted a son instead of a daughter. Or maybe that was just all he knew. It didn't really matter. They had been best friends and had done everything together when she was growing up. If he had wanted a son, he had never said anything to her about it. Even in her T-shirt and jeans, ripped and muddy from playing in the woods, she had been Daddy's Princess.

Since Renee had left home to go to college and the police academy, she didn't see him as often as she would like, although they talked on the phone two or three times a week. She smiled thinking about what he would have to say about her current predicament. He had taught her how to take care of her business outside, but her dad had also taught her modesty, so she wasn't looking forward to pulling her pants down in someone's front yard.

She groaned at the growing pain. Front yard or not, she was going to have to go. Giving in to nature, she opened the door and stepped out of the car, looking for options. Just standing made her feel better for a minute, but then the urge came back stronger than before.

The tree next to her car would have to do.

She ran around to the passenger side of the car and looked around, hoping that at four o'clock in the morning on a quiet suburban street, there wasn't much chance that anyone would see her. Even so, she positioned herself between her car and the tree to minimize her exposure. She unzipped her jeans, took one last look around, then pulled down her pants and panties together and squatted in one move.

Relief immediately flooded through her as she watered the grass, as her dad had called it when she was five. In the quiet morning, the sound of her pee hitting the grass was almost deafening. It seemed loud enough to wake the whole neighborhood. And it kept coming. She was sure someone was going to drive down the street, lighting her up in their headlights, or that some early riser would come out of his house to get the morning paper. That the morning paper hadn't been delivered yet didn't cross her mind. The thought of being caught outside with her pants around her ankles was oddly both exciting and terrifying.

Just as she thought she was going to get away without being caught, she heard the sound of a big diesel engine turn onto the road.

*

Charlie actually laughed out loud as the truck turned onto the street and sent the whore pig scurrying around the tree. There she was, sitting on the ground, with her pants pulled down, trying to hide in the shadows as the truck rumbled toward her. He thought about calling 9-1-1 to complain about the woman peeing on the street. Since he lived in the Ashford city limits, the Ashford Police Department would get the call instead of the sheriff's department. It might be fun to watch the city doughnut eaters harass the county pig. As entertaining at that would be, though, he decided it wasn't worth letting them know he had spotted their spies.

Besides, seeing her there in the grass with her ass hanging out excited him. In fact, it gave him an idea. She might make an interesting project. And that excited him even more than seeing her sitting on the street half naked. He knew he would have to be extra careful because the cop fuckers would want revenge after he was done playing with her. He was sure he could outsmart those morons any day of the week. The concern would be that even if they had nothing on him, they would still suspect him, so he would have to be extra careful not to leave any evidence behind.

Butterflies of excitement filled his stomach at the prospect of taking out one of James' deputies. That would be even better than yesterday.

Sheriff James had questioned him for an hour. First he had tried to pretend that it was all about a mistake, that maybe Charlie hadn't expected her to come home and had panicked. Like that would ever happen. No dirty-ass cunt whore would ever surprise him and cause him to panic. He wondered what the smug-ass sheriff would have thought if Charlie had told him the truth about the slut whore. Actually, he probably wouldn't have understood. He would have made some bullshit speech about how she was just an innocent girl, tired from a long day at work.

Charlie knew better. She was a disease, just like all the other ones.

Charlie had dreams where he could cleanse the filth at will. Sometimes he wondered why the state didn't issue permits for hunting dirty slut whores like they did for other nuisance animals. Of course, if they did, he would have competition and finding a trophy whore would be harder, so it was probably better they didn't. Not having a permit wasn't going to stop him anyway. It wasn't like he cared whether or not he was doing a public service. He did it for fun.

He supposed the sheriff and that cunt whore from the State's Attorney's office would think that he had some mental condition that made him kill. They might even find a shrink to come up with a name for it. It would all be bullshit. Charlie knew he wasn't one of those fucked up in the head serial killers they did TV shows about. His dad had taken him to a shrink after his mother disappeared—the principal at his school had threatened to call family services if he didn't. The doctor had said Charlie was perfectly normal. Besides, he just played with dirty slut whores because it was convenient. He would play with anybody, though he had never killed a man. He didn't think it would be as fun. Even the skanks usually had smooth skin that felt good to rub. And the blood showed up so nice on their pale, hairless bodies. On a man, with hairy arms and chest, it wouldn't be as satisfying. That and, of course, the dirty whores deserved it.

Still, cutting Sheriff Fucktard's balls off and feeding them to him while he was still alive would be enjoyable.

He would have to think about that. Maybe he would give them to Mittens to play with.

"What would you think about that?" he asked the cat. Mittens just looked up at him and blinked. He scratched her behind the ears.

"Would you like to play with Fucktard's balls? Maybe chase them around the room a bit before you eat them? Like little mice that can't run away." He laughed. Mittens yawned.

The fucking asshole certainly deserved it. After he had realized that Charlie wasn't biting on the whole mistake approach, the sheriff had tried to convince him that even if it hadn't been an accident, confessing would make it easier on him. If not for Charlie's superior self-control, he would have laughed in the sheriff's face at that. The fucker hadn't said a word about any of his other projects. Obviously, he was trying to make Charlie think that they didn't know about the others. Like he was some kind of imbecile or something.

Unless they were even dumber than he thought and didn't realize all those dead whores were connected. Wouldn't that be a fucking trip.

Charlie had just sat there, looking at him until he shut his pie hole.

After questioning him, the sheriff had to let him go. Charlie could tell the asshole had been pissed even though he had tried to hide it. He had even walked Charlie to the front door of the station and said, "Have a nice day, Mr. Reese." That had almost made the whole thing worth it. He had even offered to have one of his deputies drive him home. If he had offered to drive Charlie himself, he might have accepted, if only to gloat a few more minutes. But Sheriff Shitforbrains hadn't offered that. Probably didn't have the balls.

Charlie had even gotten out in time to make it to work without being too late. He had told the boss-man that he had gotten tied up with his parole officer and left it at that. After another dull day on the loading docks, he had decided that he needed to go out hunting in spite of the cops he knew would be watching him. He was still scouting, so they could watch him all night for days. They wouldn't even be able to get him for pissing on the sidewalk. Unlike Whore Pig.

Charlie turned away from the window. There was unlikely to be anything new he could learn tonight. Although he could function with only four or five hours of sleep, he couldn't pull all-nighters anymore. Not like when he was younger. Or maybe being locked up for four years had made him soft.

Lying on his bed, he thought about what it would be like to play with Whore Pig. He felt a small pang of regret that he wouldn't get to start tracking her until the cops stopped watching him. He decided, in the meantime, he would keep shopping. Maybe he would find a better project.

But he didn't think he would.

*

Renee sat on the ground holding her breath waiting for the truck to pass her, sure the driver would see her, maybe even stopping to see if she was okay. Or worse. Maybe he would see her sitting there with her pants down and think she was an easy target and try to rape her.

Where had she left her gun? *Dammit!* It was in the car. Why hadn't she grabbed it when she'd gotten out of the car?

She tried to calm herself. It was just an early morning delivery truck. Maybe delivering doughnuts to convenience stores before the morning rush hour. The street was dark; she was behind a tree. He wouldn't see her as long as she sat still.

Sitting still seemed impossibly hard. She felt like she had ants in her pants. Except her pants were around her ankles.

Finally, the big diesel rumbled by the tree she was hiding behind. She glimpsed the driver sitting in the cab, sipping his coffee from a styrofoam cup. He didn't turn his head or make any indication that he had seen her. She breathed a sigh of relief and watched it pass Charlie Reese's apartment.

She stopped. Maybe it was her eyes playing tricks on her in all the excitement, but she thought she had seen the curtains move. Was he watching her? Maybe it was the air conditioning blowing the curtains. The report she had read said he had a cat. Maybe it was the cat walking past the window.

Renee's heart jumped into her mouth as the truck's brake lights flared up. It came to a stop at the end of the block. Stop sign. The brake lights went out and the truck started to move again. She didn't move to pull her pants up until the truck's taillights disappeared, just to be sure. She didn't want the driver to see her in his rearview mirror. Once it was gone, she looked back to Charlie's apartment and watched for a few more seconds. She saw no more movement. It must have been her imagination.

"Uff da! It's a good thing my pants are down," she whispered to herself, "or I'd have pissed myself."

She looked around again to make sure no one was watching, then stood up, pulling her jeans up as quickly as she could, and hurried around to the other side of the car. She slipped into the driver's seat and closed her eyes. The sound of her heart pounding in her chest and her own ragged breathing filled her ears.

Finally catching her breath, she checked her watch and made a note about the curtain movement on her log sheet. It was probably not worth mentioning. She just wanted to be thorough, not really knowing what was important and what wasn't. She left out the part about seeing it while her pants had been around her ankles.

Renee lit a cigarette, taking three tries to light it. Her hands were shaking so bad the lighter kept going out. She took a long drag and held it before exhaling.

"Next time I'm bringing a pickle jar."

*

Allen stood in the station's kitchen, staring at the coffee maker as it gurgled and chugged out the black sludge that fueled the sheriff's office. After tossing and turning for hours, he had gotten out of bed, showered, and come into the office early. He wasn't quite sure what being there would accomplish, just that it was better than staring at his bedroom ceiling.

He knew Charles Reese was their guy. He just couldn't prove it. He couldn't even get the smug bastard on a simple parole violation.

Somehow Reese must have figured out how to remove the ankle monitor. The techs couldn't find any evidence of tampering, so their conclusion was that it hadn't been removed. All they found was a cat hair, which didn't seem that unusual since Reese owned a cat.

Allen still hadn't figured that one out. Why in the hell would he own a cat? Reese was a cold bastard. He didn't have any of the charisma that Allen had read most serial killers have. When they finally nailed him, there wouldn't be anyone claiming that "he's such a nice man, always so friendly, I can't imagine that he did all those things they say he did."

Watts had interviewed several of his coworkers. They had all said the same thing: Charlie was an asshole. He kept to himself and barely talked to anybody. He wouldn't even say "Good morning" to his coworkers. The only thing good any of them had to say about him was that he worked hard. He certainly didn't seem like he had any kind of empathy in him for an animal. Besides, Allen had always thought that serial killers liked to kill small animals, not keep them as pets.

The coffee finished brewing and Allen poured a cup, hoping it would perk him up after not sleeping all night, though unless it magically made him figure out how to nail Charles Reese, it would probably just give him heartburn. He walked back to his office and sat down behind his desk to review the case files for the hundredth time. Most of them he could recite verbatim by now, but he kept reading anyway, hoping there was something, some small piece, that he had missed in the previous reads.

Allen wasn't even convincing himself with that lie anymore. He just didn't know what else to do until he got something new.

He had Reese under surveillance for now, although only at night. With just five deputies in the department, Allen couldn't set up around-the-clock surveillance and still manage to take care of the normal county policing business. He was relying on Reese's parole officer to report any absences from work.

Allen was more concerned about the evening coverage anyway. All but one of Reese's kills had been late at night or early morning. With the amount of time Reese spent with his victims, Allen suspected that even that one had started in the early morning. He probably liked to stalk his victims at night too.

But Charlie Reese was smart. He wouldn't do anything obvious now that he knew the police were interested in him. Allen just hoped that he didn't figure out they were following him. At least that way they might catch him in a parole violation or some other minor thing that would get him off the street for a while. Hopefully sooner than later.

Unfortunately, they couldn't keep up the surveillance for very long. The budget wouldn't allow it, for one thing, and as much as his deputies liked the overtime pay, they had lives outside the department. So did he, for that matter. Ginnie wasn't very happy with all the extra hours he had been spending on this case since Shelby Winston had been killed. Allen had tried to convince her that now that they knew who did it, the case would begin to move faster. While that was true, she knew as well as he did that *faster* didn't mean he could spend less time on it. Trying to convince her otherwise had been a mistake. That fight, as much as the case itself, had resulted in his sleepless night. He loved his wife and kids. He just didn't understand why she didn't see how important it was to get Reese off the street.

Ginnie knew all about the case, of course. Allen didn't keep secrets from her; he had just left out some of the gorier details. So it wasn't like she didn't know how serious this was. But for some reason, she just didn't understand why it was even more important now than before. The simple fact that he had confronted Reese could change his pattern. He might not wait a year until he killed again. Certainly Allen wasn't going to wait a year to nail him.

In any case, now that they knew who Charles Reese was, Allen was determined not to let even one more girl be butchered by that monster. He was going to dig into Reese's life, find every little dark corner where a piece of the puzzle might be hiding. Of chief interest was what Reese did with the hearts. There was always the possibly that he ate them, a la Stanley Dean Baker, but Allen didn't think so. He suspected that Reese kept them as trophies. He just needed to figure out where.

Obviously not in his apartment. They'd been through that with the proverbial fine-toothed comb. Reese didn't own any property and as far as Allen could tell, he didn't have any living relatives in South Dakota. He planned on getting some help from Kim Barrett's office to look for out-of-state relatives, although Allen figured that was a long shot. In any case, he couldn't do much of anything until morning. Or rather later in the morning.

Allen sighed and rubbed his eyes. He picked up Stan's report, then set it back down. It was basically worthless. The short version was that Reese had eaten supper, then gone home and gone to bed. Stan reported the apartment lights went out around eleven thirty and Deputy Watts had relieved him just before midnight. Watts wouldn't be back from her shift for another three hours, but he doubted her report would show much different. If anything interesting had happened, he would already know about it. He had given his deputies permission to text or call at any time if something happened that would help with the case.

He would read her report anyway. Cases were usually solved on the small details, sometimes from seemingly unrelated investigations. For now, all Allen could do was reread the case files for eight murders.

Allen pulled up Shelby Winston's files, both from her murder and from the break-in three years ago.

Details. That was what would matter.

Opening the first folder, he sat back in his chair and began to read.

CHAPTER NINE

"HEY, WATTS! GRAB a beer?"

"Not tonight, Austin," Renee answered. She and Deputy Austin Phelps had just finished their shift.

"What do you mean *not tonight*? You got a better offer?" Grabbing a beer after shift wasn't exactly tradition, but it was common enough. The single deputies almost always participated.

"Actually, I do," she answered, flashing him a sly smile. "She's a five-foot-two brunette and she's much prettier than you!"

"Hey!" Phelps said, grasping his hands in front of his chest in mock distress. "I didn't know you swung that way. Can I come too?"

"In your dreams, Phelps. In your dreams."

"No, seriously, you're going out with a chick tonight?"

"Relax, Cowboy. It's just an old friend from high school. She moved to Florida to go to school at Florida State or University of Florida or something. I always get those two confused."

Austin laughed. "FSU is the Seminoles and UFL is the Gators."

"Fuck you, Phelps." Renee laughed too.

"Anybody I know?" Austin had grown up in Woodford County just like Renee. They had both gone to Ashford High School, but Austin graduated several years before Renee.

"Shirley Drake. She lived over by Arlington. You might have known her brother, Bradley. He's getting married this weekend."

"Yeah, I knew Brad. We weren't friends or nothing, but I knew who he was."

"Well, that's why Shirley's in town. We're going to The Silver Bell for supper."

"Oooh, fancy. She must be special," Austin teased. The Silver Bell was the closest thing to fine dining in Ashford, South Dakota.

"Shirley picked it. I guess she's not used to good country cooking now that she lives in the big city."

"Why the hell would anybody move to Florida?"

"I don't know. She wants to be a vet and thinks they have a good vet school down there. Besides, she always hated it here. She's planning on staying down there when she finishes grad school."

"Whatever. Too damn hot in Florida."

"No shit. I couldn't stand being sweaty all the time. That would suck rotten canal water." Renee picked up her bag. "Gotta run. Don't want to be late for my date!"

"Alrighty then. Next time?"

"You betcha!" Renee headed out to the parking lot.

Stepping out into the cool fall air made Renee shiver a little. She smiled. The fall was her favorite time of the year. It was early October and already there had been a few mornings with frost on the ground. Winter was going to come early this year.

Renee had grown up on a farm in Woodford County and, other than the two years she spent at the University of South Dakota studying Criminal Justice, had lived her whole life here. By sheer luck, a spot had opened in the sheriff's office around the time she was finishing up her associate's degree. The sheriff had offered it to her before she had even graduated.

She had known Allen James most of her life. He and her dad, Kelly, had been friends since before she was born. He told her that hiring her had nothing to do with their friendship, but Renee was never quite sure.

While she had been at the police academy, he had hired her to do office work to start learning how the department ran even before she got her star. He even helped her with some of her course work, especially the procedures classes. He had offered to help her with the firearms training, but after he saw her shoot, he'd realized that she was probably a better shot than he was. Raised on a farm, she had been shooting rifles since she was six, shotguns since she was eight, and handguns since she was twelve. She could field strip her service pistol, a Springfield Armory 1911 Model 9mm, with her eyes closed.

Growing up on *Law & Order* and *CSI*, she had decided that she wanted to be a cop before high school. At ten and eleven, her friends thought that was a great idea, wanting to be firemen and cowboys—or cowgirls—themselves. But as they got older and hormones started turning them into women and men, all her friends started making fun of her career choice. When the girls started talking about becoming models, or singers, or maybe doctors or vets, Renee was in the back fields with the boys shooting paper targets and clay pigeons. While they were reading *Teen Beat* and *Seventeen*, she had been reading *Crime Magazine* and *Guns & Ammo*.

Not that she had been all tomboy. She had spent plenty of time at the mall and at the movies with her friends and even wore dresses to school dances. But she had always been more comfortable in a flannel shirt and well-worn blue jeans. The biggest problem had been finding a boy able to handle being with an aggressive girl. Teenage boys were easily scared off by that.

So were grown men, apparently.

Since high school, she hadn't had a single relationship that lasted more than a few dates. She liked to be wined and dined by a man. She just didn't take shit from anyone, which had scared off every man she had ever dated. Carrying a gun for a living probably didn't help with that. The only guy she had dated who wasn't scared off had been a complete asshole. The only good thing about that relationship was that she had been the one to end it for a change.

But today, she wasn't thinking about that. She was thinking about a long hot shower and then a girls' night out with her old best friend. It would be Renee's first girls' night in a while. She was looking forward to catching up with Shirley, but even happier that the overtime surveillance assignments had stopped. The cop shows she had watched as a kid never really showed how mind-numbingly boring that was. At least in a deer stand, you could relax and enjoy nature. After a while, even the extra money wasn't worth it. So when the sheriff had gotten everyone together to tell them that the budget couldn't justify the overtime to watch Charles Reese anymore, no one had been particularly upset.

Renee climbed into her Civic. She missed her old pickup truck. It had been her dad's before he'd given it to her when she got her driver's license. It had survived college and the police academy, but when she graduated the academy, she had decided that it was time to put the old girl down. She couldn't afford much on a small county deputy's salary, but the Civic was reliable and even handled okay in the snow, unlike the old Chevy pickup.

She pulled out of the parking lot, one of the local country radio stations blaring on the radio. She had to turn tight to avoid hitting a dingy white panel van parked across the street from the parking lot exit.

With all the parking available you had to park right there?

Keith Urban came on the radio. She started singing and forgot all about the white van.

*

Charlie watched her pull out of the parking lot and turn left, the same direction he had parked the van half an hour earlier. He was oddly excited to begin his hunt at the cop station.

He had tried yesterday, but had parked facing the wrong way. He had a fifty-fifty shot of picking the right direction and had picked wrong. All that buildup driving to the station, then parking and waiting for her to leave. He had watched her walk to her car without a care in the world, completely oblivious to the hunter across the street. Then she pulled out and drove the other way. All he could do was watch her in his rearview mirror. But he was patient, so he didn't get mad. He had known that he might need a couple of tries to get on her tail with no one noticing.

So the second try was the charm.

As it was, he had waited a week after the cops had stopped following him around just to make sure they weren't trying to throw him off. So one more day hadn't mattered at all. Today he was facing the right direction. When she had passed him, he started up the van and pulled out, keeping a safe distance so she wouldn't notice. It turned out they didn't go far. Ashford wasn't a very big town anyway and her apartment was only ten minutes away in the rush hour traffic.

He watched Whore Pig pull into the driveway of a small apartment building and drive around back. He parked the van on the street a few doors down and waited to see if she would come around to the front of the building or go in through some back door. After five minutes, he hadn't seen her so he assumed that was the case and that she was tucked into her apartment by now. He got out of the van, carrying a small box under one arm wrapped and taped up like a shipping container.

The apartment was a two-story building with a balcony on the upper floor on each side. The lower floor apartments had patios with tall privacy fences to prevent seeing into the apartments through their big sliding glass doors unless you went around to the side. Someone walking by or coming up to the building on the main sidewalk wouldn't be able to see in. Which was perfectly okay for Charlie.

Charlie walked up the sidewalk to the building, whistling like a delivery man that was too happy with his job. He stopped at the door and found the mailboxes built into the wall. Four mailboxes, four apartments. He didn't bother trying the door. It was probably locked anyway.

While waiting for the surveillance to end, Charlie had done some research on the internet and found out Whore Pig's name was Renee Watts. Now he pretended to check the label on the package, then the names on the mailboxes. He found her name on the mailbox labeled Apt. 2. He guessed that the lower numbers were for the first-floor apartments with Apartment 1 being on the left and Apartment 2 on the right. He would find out tonight.

Charlie quickly scribbled the name and address of one of the other apartment occupants on the address label of the package and put it on the ground under the mailboxes. As he walked back down the walkway, he resisted the urge to turn to look at what must be his target's apartment.

Back in his van, he relaxed and smiled to himself. Mrs. Campbell would sure be surprised by the box of extra-large Trojans someone had anonymously sent her.

Charlie climbed into the back of the van and sat down on the bench seat behind the driver's seat. He made a note of the time in a small notebook, then set up a tripod between the driver and passenger seat. He attached his video camera to the tripod and aimed it at the apartment building. He set it to capture a single frame every five seconds, then hit record. Finally, he opened a bag of chips and a bottle of water and sat back to wait.

He assumed Whore Pig was slutting herself up to go out on a Friday night, probably to flirt it up with the local yokels or maybe drive down to Sioux Falls to spread her legs for some city slicker.

Regardless of where she did or didn't go, Charlie would be there. And at the end of her slutfest, he would follow her home and get the first of his research videos. He didn't have a key to her apartment yet, so it would just be from the outside, but it was the first night. Patience was the most important thing in the hunt. It was what separated him from those who got a date with the state. Well, that and the fact that he was smarter than those fucktards. His brief stay in the graybar hotel had made that perfectly clear. There wasn't a single person in there besides himself that was smarter than sack of turnips, as his dad used to say. That included the hacks.

Charlie Reese was patient and smart. He had learned from the mistake that got him busted last time and he wasn't going to make it again. He sat back munching on his chips and waited.

*

Renee took her time getting ready. Shirley's flight hadn't gotten into Sioux Falls until late afternoon, so they weren't meeting until eight thirty. Even after a long hot shower, she had time to watch a movie before getting dressed, which only took her twenty minutes. She wore jeans, but since they were eating at a nicer restaurant instead of a roadhouse bar, she chose a nice blouse in favor of a T-shirt. She owned a dress or two and a couple of skirts. She just didn't wear them except to weddings and funerals. Makeup consisted of mascara and lip gloss. Growing up, she had never gotten into the whole makeup thing. One of the perks of her job was she didn't need to figure it out now. As for tonight, even though

Shirley wore dresses and makeup, she had never cared that Renee didn't. That was one of the reasons Renee liked her so much.

Like a lot of girls, and guys for that matter, Shirley had talked about getting out of Woodford County since she had been old enough to understand the concept. Unlike most of them, she had actually followed through. The day Shirley left had been the second saddest day in Renee's life, after the death of her mother. She had felt like she was losing a sister.

Shirley had only been back a few times since she'd left. Mainly just Christmas break and a week at the beginning of every summer. Renee kept promising to visit her in Florida, and she hoped to be able to keep that promise one day.

Renee had checked her watch at least ten times during the movie, knowing she was being silly. The movie was two hours long and eight o'clock wouldn't come before it was over. By the time eight did roll around, Renee was almost giddy to see her old friend.

She pulled out of the driveway of her apartment building a little after eight o'clock. The ten-minute drive would get her to the restaurant well before eight thirty, but she couldn't sit in her apartment anymore.

She looked both ways before turning right onto the narrow street. A white van parked a couple of doors down on the left caught her eye. She didn't remember ever seeing a van there before. It was probably a plumber or an electrician, but she had an uneasy feeling. There was something familiar about it. She turned right and looked at it in her rearview mirror. Just a van, like any other.

Shifting her focus back to the road in front of her, singing along with the radio and dancing in her seat.

*

Charlie felt the familiar tingle in his gut as the blue Civic pulled out of the apartment driveway. He turned off the video camera, pulled down the tripod, and stowed them on the floor, before climbing into the driver's seat. Luck was with him: the Civic turned away from him. He wouldn't have to turn around to follow Whore Pig to whatever debauchery she was planning for the evening.

The Civic turned onto Route 14 toward downtown Ashford. Downtown consisted of three blocks of US Route 14, spreading one or two blocks to either side of the main road. Then it was back to apartments, houses, and, a mile down the road in either direction, fields. The town square, located between the eastbound and westbound lanes, ran for the entire three blocks. It wasn't much more than a fountain, which only ran six months of the year, and park benches along a path through grass and flower gardens. Green space, the city council called it.

During Christmas—meaning from mid-November through the first week in January—the town square was decorated with colored lights and a Nativity scene with a lily-white Mary, Joseph, and Jesus, which always struck Charlie as odd. Jesus was from the Middle East, so he should look like one of those Arabs, not some pasty white fuck from England or Sweden. Or South Dakota. Having not spent much time in church as a kid, and none as an adult, Charlie figured he must have missed out on that explanation. And after Achmed Abdul-Jabar and his band of merry men had flown airplanes into the Twin Towers in New York back in 2001, he decided that having a Jesus that looked like he was from South Dakota was better anyway.

This time of year, the town square just had a few couples walking along, holding hands or eating ice cream one last time before the cold moved in for good. The streetlights gave the water in the fountain a strange amber glow. To Charlie, it looked like a fountain of piss. Driving by, he watched a man toss a coin into the water. Wishing to get up the skirt of the slut standing next to him, no doubt.

That's the easy part, Brother, Charlie thought as he passed. *It's doing it so they can't scream for help that takes talent.*

He smiled and shifted his attention back to the Civic that was pulling into a parking spot half a block in front of him. He drove past without slowing and watched in his rearview mirror as Whore Pig climbed out of the car. For a moment, it appeared she was watching the van, but then she turned and walked into The Silver Bell.

Charlie turned into a side street and parked the van. If she had recognized it, he would have to ditch it and get another vehicle. Panel vans worked well for his hunts because he could set up his camera and relax in the back without being seen by passersby. The downside was they didn't blend in. At least not in the land of pickup trucks and four-wheel drives. The risk of Whore Pig recognizing it was too great. Tomorrow, he would have to make a trip to Big Frank's Used Cars. For tonight, he was stuck with it. He would just have to be more careful.

He got out of the van and walked back to Main Street, the name for Route 14 inside the Ashford city limits. He walked slowly toward The Silver Bell, pretending to look at the sky and the fountain. He walked past the front window of the restaurant and glanced in, trying to appear bored and uninterested.

Whore Pig was sitting at a table with another woman. A brief chill of excitement ran down his back. Maybe he could play with two at once. He had often fantasized about it. The thrill was brief, however. Trying to catch two at once would be too risky. And he wasn't ready tonight anyway.

Charlie turned away and continued walking before anyone would notice him watching. There was an ice cream parlor next door. He walked in and ordered the biggest ice cream sundae they had and took it across the street into the square. He found a bench facing the restaurant and sat down to watch.

Sometimes everything seemed to go his way. He couldn't ask for a better setup. At least for this stage of the game. He blended into the background, just another anonymous stranger sitting on a bench, enjoying his ice cream.

When he had finished his sundae, he pulled out an e-book reader from his jacket pocket. The e-book reader was a stalker's best friend. He could sit anywhere, pretending to read without worrying about whether or not there was enough light to read by. He had gotten this one from a woman who had left it on the table at a diner while she'd gone to the restroom. He had simply walked by her table and pocketed it. He didn't know much about how to use it, but he had figured out how to turn it on and open a book. Unfortunately he was stuck with what was on it, which was a series of crappy romance novels. Not that he really needed to pay attention to what he was reading, anyway. It was just a prop.

For the next hour, Charlie sat and watched the restaurant, pretending to read, waiting for his target.

A shiver ran down his spine. Must be a chill from the cool fall air and the ice cream.

A growing sensation of being watched settled over him. He tried to ignore the feeling. He glanced around, first looking for cops then, not seeing any, looking for anyone that appeared to be not doing what they looked like they were doing. The irony of that wasn't lost on him. There were only a few people on the street, and none of them were paying attention to him. No one was sitting like he was, pretending to be oblivious to everyone around him. And yet the feeling continued to grow, closing in around him, transforming into the familiar dream-like sensation, the sense that he was watching himself through someone else's eyes. He rubbed his eyes with his fists, trying to break free.

"Go away," he said under his breath.

*

"It's been fun, but I have to go," Renee said, looking at her watch. "I have to work in the morning."

"Yeah, I have to get up early too," Shirley said. "Kendra decided that they needed to have a morning wedding. Something about starting their new life together at the start of a new day or some other mystical nonsense."

"Ugh. That sounds torturous. Are you sure he's happy?"

Shirley laughed. "Yeah, they're like peas in a pod. Brad's gone all hippy since high school."

"Are they serving beer at the reception?"

"Oh, the reception isn't until five o'clock."

"What are you supposed to do until then?"

"I'm just going to hang out with Mom and Dad. Too bad you have to work. What are you doing tomorrow night? Since Josh couldn't make it, you could be my plus one."

"I don't know. I don't really know Brad or any of his friends."

"Come on. It'll be fun. Weddings are a great place to pick up guys that aren't total creeps."

Renee grinned. "I have been in a bit of a dry spell."

"Great! I'll tell Brad you're coming. He'll be glad to see you. You know he had a crush on you when we were seniors, don't you?"

"Brad? He never said anything."

"Yeah, well, he was embarrassed because he's so much older."

They both laughed.

"Okay, but I really have to go now," Renee said, standing.

"Yeah, I know. Me too. I forgot how much fun we have."

"You're the one that moved away. You could always move back."

"Or you could move to Florida. They have cops there too, you know."

"I don't think so, sister."

"Well, we still have tomorrow night," Shirley said. "I'm going to stop by the ladies' room. See you tomorrow?"

"Yep, see you then." They hugged, then Shirley turned to the restrooms and Renee headed for the door, digging her keys out of her jeans pocket.

Outside, Renee noticed a man sitting across the street on one of the benches in the town square. He was hard to miss. He appeared to be muttering to himself and waving his arms in the air like he was being attacked by gnats or flies. He had his hat pulled down and collar turned against the cold, hiding his face in shadow. The cop in her almost made her walk across the street to see if the man was all right. The weight of her gun in the small of her back reassured her. She watched for a few more seconds and decided he was just a harmless homeless guy battling whatever demons had put him on the street in the first place, so she turned and got into her car.

Pulling out of her parking space, she looked in the mirror and saw the man stand and start to walk across the street behind her. Satisfied the homeless guy was okay, she turned up the radio and headed toward home.

*

The woman came out of the restaurant and began walking toward her car. She paused and looked at him for a moment. He thought she was going to walk over to him. Instead, she turned back toward her car.

He knew she was in danger. He tried to yell, to warn her, but the only sound that escaped his mouth was his own labored breathing. He stood up and began to walk toward her. His pace quickened as she reached her car. She opened the door and climbed in without looking back. She didn't know the danger that was coming for her. He had to reach her and warn her.

She started her car and pulled away from the curb before he could get to her. He thought he saw her look back at him in her rearview mirror as she drove off. He watched her taillights move away and then fade into darkness.

CHAPTER TEN

ALLEN READ THE email from Ken Simmons twice before picking up the phone and dialing a number he had memorized weeks ago. The automated system answered on the first ring.

"Thank you for calling Decker Electronic Monitoring Services. If you know your party's extension, you may dial it at any time. For Sales, please press 1. For Technical Support, press—"

Allen dialed in the extension for Woodford County's dedicated support rep.

"Decker Services, this is Sabrina. May I help you?"

"Hi, Sabrina. This is Sheriff James."

"Hello, Sheriff. Looking for logs on your favorite parolee?"

Allen winced. Clearly he was calling too often.

"Yeah, I need to know where he was from seven o'clock last night until now."

"Just a minute while I pull up his records." Allen heard her clicking away on her keyboard. "The logs show he arrived home at 3:42 p.m. yesterday and never left."

"Are you sure? No tamper alarms?"

"No. Nothing. The last poll from the system was fifteen minutes ago and he was still at home then."

"Okay, thanks."

"No problem, Sheriff."

Allen hung up the phone and stared at it. If Ken's account was accurate, Charles Reese hadn't been home last night. The monitoring company's logs may have shown he had been at home, but they were wrong. They had to be. The bastard was on the hunt and Allen was going to stop him before he killed anyone else.

He picked up the phone again and dialed the State's Attorney's Office.

"Thank you for calling the Woodford County State's Attorney's office. Our office hours are Monday through Friday, eight a.m. until five p.m."

"Shit," Allen said to himself, hanging up the phone. He had forgotten it was Saturday. He opened his Rolodex and flipped through the cards until he found Kim Barrett's contact information, then dialed her cell phone number.

"Kim Barrett," Kim answered after a couple of rings.

"Hey, Kim. It's Allen James."

"Good morning, Sheriff. What can I do for you today?"

"Sorry to bother you on the weekend, but I have a favor to ask you."

"Is it about Charles Reese?"

"Yeah. I know he's beating his monitoring somehow. He was downtown last night but the monitoring company shows he was home all night."

"How do you know he was downtown?"

"I have a..." Allen paused, trying to decide how best to put it. He couldn't very well tell her he had a Psychic Friend. "I have a CI that said he saw him last night. He said it looked like Reese was following some woman. Listen, I'll be straight with you, Kim. I think he's found a new target and I really don't want to wait until he kills her too to bring him in."

"Is your CI willing to testify?" Kim sounded skeptical. Allen knew he had nothing.

"Not if he can help it. Help me out, Kim. There's got to be something we can do."

"Allen, you know as well as I do that unless you have concrete evidence, you can't send him back to prison. And if you keep harassing him, he'll have grounds to sue your department for wrongful prosecution. Hell, Allen, you don't even know if this is your guy. You're just making a guess because he broke into Shelby Winston's apartment a few years ago and then she was killed after he got paroled. That doesn't even count as circumstantial evidence. There's absolutely nothing tying him to her murder. It really could just be a coincidence."

"Come on, Kim. You don't really believe that do you? This guy is playing us and you know it."

"What I know is that you have nothing on him and if you keep it up, you're going to find yourself on the wrong side of the table. Look, I don't know if Reese is your guy or not. He's certainly creepy enough, but that doesn't make him guilty. Until you have some actual evidence, there's nothing I can do."

Allen sighed. "I get that, but there has to be something we can do. If nothing else, we need to make sure he's not tampering with his ankle monitor."

"You checked that when you brought him in for questioning back in September. Our techs said it hadn't been tampered with."

"Yeah, but they may have missed something. I want to send it back to Decker and have them go over it. Just to see what they can find. We can send a tech out to swap his monitor. Not even a deputy. Tell him that we received a battery fault warning or some bullshit like that."

"Okay, fine, but be careful, Allen. You're obsessed with this guy. Try to keep an open mind and remember that he might not be your killer."

"Okay, I know. I appreciate the concern."

"I'm serious, Allen. Don't fuck yourself on this."

Allen smiled. Kim didn't cuss often. When she did, it meant she was serious.

"I'll be careful. Thanks, Kim."

"Bye, Allen. Call me when you get the results back from Decker."

"I will."

Allen hung up the phone and called the county IT lab. He got their voicemail, then remembered again that it was Saturday. The IT guys didn't work weekends unless there was an emergency and unfortunately, this didn't count, so he opted for an email instead. Once he sent that off, he replied to Ken's email to see if he could provide a better description of the woman Reese had been following last night.

Ken had seen the name of the restaurant, so maybe he could talk to the staff to see if they could tell him who had been in last night matching the description.

Another small-town advantage—everyone knows everyone.

*

Charles Reese was pissed. And people make mistakes when they're pissed. So he was pissed about being pissed.

It wasn't just that Whore Pig had seen him last night, though he didn't think she had recognized him, so he should be able to manage that. It was that feeling that someone had been in his head again. The cops could stop him on the street and search his car or come in and search his apartment and he wasn't worried because he knew they wouldn't find anything. They had no idea where to look, so he could maintain his privacy. But if someone could get inside his mind, to see what he was doing—or worse, know what he was thinking—his privacy was no longer private. The fuckknocker that was digging into his brain was violating his privacy. And that was something Charlie wouldn't tolerate.

He walked to the bathroom to splash cold water on his face. He had to calm down. Anger wasn't helping the situation.

He stared at himself in the mirror and took a deep breath, resisting the urge to smash the reflection.

The pounding in his chest subsided.

The problem was he didn't know who the fucker was. God help him when Charlie found him. Actually, even God wouldn't be able to help him. Charlie knew ways to make the asshole suffer real good. He was going to figure out who this motherfucking cocksucker was and make him pay. He was going to wish he had never been born. He would unleash the unholy wrath of Hellfuck on him.

He took another deep breath, trying to maintain control.

He may not understand how the fucker was doing it, but he knew how to stop it. At least, once he knew who it was. He couldn't do shit until then. After all, secrecy was how Charlie had survived all these years. He had never talked to anyone about his hobby so there was no one to expose him. Except this fucker trying to mind-fuck him. Someone spying on his innermost thoughts could be a real problem.

That was the one thing that Charlie was truly afraid of. This ass-hole had to go. Oh, how he was going to make this fucktoad suffer. Charlie had never had the need for revenge before. At least, not like this. Now that he did, he was thinking that he might enjoy it as much as his hobby.

It all came back to figuring out who it was. He had a feeling it was Sheriff Shitforbrains. That would be ironic. He hadn't been able to pin anything on Charlie, even with getting into his head. Probably some cop rule about having real evidence or something. Which meant that Charlie would have to be careful. If he accidentally revealed his hiding place, Shitforbrains might be able to get him. Maybe.

He had to consider the possibility that it was someone else though. If it wasn't the sheriff, whoever it was must be feeding information to him. Surely that fucktard hadn't put so much effort into questioning him and following him just because he had been caught breaking into some worthless whore's apartment. Bring him in for questioning, sure. But Shitforbrains seemed obsessed with him, so if he wasn't digging into Charlie's mind himself, the fucker who was had to be telling him all about it.

Regardless of who it was, Charlie would need to figure out how to protect himself until he found the fucktard. He had already figured out that it happened mostly in the evenings when he was getting ready to go to sleep, though there had been the time a few weeks ago when it happened in the morning. Then last night when he was wide awake.

But it always seemed to happen when he was calm and relaxed.

Was that it? Was he somehow vulnerable when he was relaxed? He didn't know the answer to that, but it was something to consider.

Another thing he had noticed—every time it happened, the feeling was stronger than the time before. And that led to the thought that if the connection was some kind of bond or tunnel between them, and that bond was getting stronger, why couldn't Charlie turn the tables and look back through the connection himself? Maybe read the shitfuck's thoughts and see through his eyes. That only seemed fair. What's good for the mind fucker is good for the mind fuckee, right?

Charlie tried to remember all the times he had felt that strange dreamlike, crowded sensation in his brain. What had it been like? Had he known all along and just not put the pieces together?

He thought not. Remembering how it had been back in the State Hilton, he had just had a queasy feeling, like he had been on a boat. It had always come in the evenings when he had been in his bunk thinking about his past projects. Right before falling asleep. He especially remembered thinking about Sandy, his first project. He had been sloppy on that one, at the bottom of the learning curve. He hadn't shaved his hair off and hadn't thrown away his clothes and tools when he was done. He had been smart enough to wear gloves, otherwise his stay with the State would have been a lot longer. That one had definitely been his hardest, but even with the mistakes, Sandy was his favorite. It had been the most exciting. He remembered dreaming about that one and waking with the queasy feeling that he now knew to be Fucknuts spying on him.

Which got Charlie to thinking about what he might have revealed in his dreams. Had he dreamed about his trophy room? Presumably not, because if Sheriff Shitforbrains knew about that, Charlie would be in jail already. He had obviously dreamed about the Big Day with his projects, and possibly about scouting and tracking them. Maybe it wasn't the sheriff. Maybe it was someone else who hadn't passed everything on to the sheriff. Or maybe not everything went through.

It didn't matter. Charlie was going to put a stop to it. He was going to reach through the mind tunnel and grab the fucker by the balls. He would find out who it was. And then he would play a new game.

Charlie smiled. Oh yes, it would be epic.

*

Allen received Ken's description of the woman in his vision—or whatever it was called—in less than half an hour. The description was vague, but Allen recognized it immediately. Petite with long, curly, red hair, drove a blue Honda Civic.

Renee Watts.

He felt a little sick.

"Hey, Boss." Gus Norris stepped into his office while Allen was reading Ken's email.

"Morning, Gus. What's up?"

"Watts was supposed to relieve me at eight o'clock but she's not here yet."

Shit. Allen glanced at the clock: 8:23. He realized hadn't seen her yet either. Not that he had been looking for her until just now. He didn't always see his deputies check in at the beginning of their shifts, but on a weekend when the office staff wasn't working, he generally noticed someone walking into the building.

"Have you called her?"

"Yeah, three times. I keep getting her voicemail."

Shit. Ken's dream hadn't told him what happened after Renee drove off. Had Charlie followed her home from the restaurant?

"Can you stay on duty for a bit while I try to track her down?" Allen tried to hide his concern.

"Sure, Boss, but my kid's got a football game this afternoon and I'd like to be there for it."

"Okay, thanks Gus. I'll make sure you're off in time to make the game."

"Great, thanks!"

Gus turned to leave, then turned back. "You think she's okay?"

"Sure, she probably just overslept. I heard her say something about going out with an old friend last night. Probably had a few too many and slept through her alarm."

"This is Watts we're talking about, right?"

"Go on, I'll let you know when she gets in."

Gus left and Allen pulled out his cell phone. If Ken was right, she hadn't stayed out late drinking. He pulled up Watts' contact information on his phone and hit Voice Call. It went straight to voicemail without even ringing.

Shit.

Based on his pattern, Allen wouldn't expect Charlie Reese to kill again for another year. But what if he had been spooked when Allen had brought him in for questioning? Or maybe he had spotted the surveillance Allen had put on him and he decided to go after one of his deputies as revenge? In hindsight, maybe it had been a bad idea to let Renee go on the surveillance assignments. He knew what her response to that would have been, but had he put her in danger by exposing her to Charlie Reese? Or maybe Reese had seen her at the station the day he had been brought in for questioning.

To Allen, his deputies were his family and the idea of having one of them hacked up by a monster like Charles Reese was too much to think about. Especially Renee Watts. She was the youngest of his deputies and even though he wasn't supposed to think of her differently just because she was a woman, he couldn't help but feel a little more protective of her. She was like a daughter to him. The other deputies looked at her like a little sister. Sure, they gave her a hard time like they would any rookie, but when it came down to it, they looked out for her more than they would have a guy.

If Reese had gone after her, he might not make it to trial. Allen knew he would have to try to bring him in alive, but he wasn't sure he would be able to stop one of his other deputies from playing judge, jury, and executioner. That would have been true regardless of whether or not Watts was a woman. It would just be worse for Reese because of the way they all felt about her.

Allen's thoughts were interrupted by voices out in the main room. He got up to investigate and almost ran into Gus in the hallway.

"Hey, Boss. Look who decided to show up!"

Renee Watts walked up next to him, looking a little sheepish.

"Where the hell have you been?" Allen barked, more with relief than anger.

"Sorry, Sheriff. I got a flat tire and my cell phone was dead."

Allen looked at her for a minute, then shook his head.

"Okay, Gus, you can take off. Thanks for staying. Watts: in my office. Now."

Renee followed him back into his office and sat in one of the chairs on the visitor's side of the desk. Allen sat in his own chair and leaned forward.

"You know what the policy is for tardiness, right?"

Renee stared down at the floor and nodded.

"Goddammit, Watts, I thought you were dead!"

She looked up in surprise.

"What? Why would I be dead? It was just a flat tire. I'm not even thirty minutes late."

"Forty-five. You're supposed to be here fifteen minutes before your shift starts."

"Okay, forty-five, but why would you think I was dead just because I was late?"

Allen sighed.

"Were you at The Silver Bell last night?"

"Yeah. I had supper with an old friend from high school. How'd you know that?"

Allen paused. He was being overdramatic.

"You were followed."

"Followed? By who?"

"Charles Reese."

"Charlie Reese?" Renee's eyebrows raised as much as her jaw dropped. "Why would he be following me?"

"My guess is that you're his next target."

"Holy fuck."

"Yeah. Holy fuck. Did you see anything last night? Anyone that looked like they might be following you?"

Renee thought about it for a minute. "Well, there was a guy sitting in the park across from The Bell when I came out. He looked like he was a vagrant. He was acting a little strange, but most of them do. I saw him cross the street behind me when I got in my car, but he didn't chase me or anything."

"So he didn't follow you home from the restaurant?"

"I don't think so," she said. She paused, thinking. "But there was a white van at my apartment last night that I hadn't seen before. I didn't really think much of it at the time. The only reason I noticed it at all was that there was a white van that looked just like it parked across the street from the station last night when I left. Do you think that was him?"

"Maybe. What I do know is that we need to get you some protection."

"I think I can handle a creep like Charlie Reese."

"I have no doubt that you can, but I would feel better having someone else watching your back until we can get proof he's violating his parole and get him back behind bars."

"Wait a minute. How did you know he was following me?"

Allen looked away. What was he going to tell her? That some part-time psychic from West Virginia had a vision? Oh, but he's not just some whack job—he writes crime novels. That wasn't going to make her feel any better.

It certainly didn't make Allen feel better.

"We got an anonymous tip. Someone saw him downtown last night. They said he looked like he was following a woman who fit your description. So you can see why I was concerned when you didn't show up on time."

"Shit. I'm sorry, Sheriff. I really did have a flat tire. And I forgot to plug my phone in last night."

Allen decided there was no reason to continue to admonish her. Shit happens and she was usually very reliable. Being told that a lunatic suspected of killing at least eight other women was hunting you was probably punishment enough.

"Well, don't let it happen again. In the meantime, clock in and get to work. I'll come up with something before your shift is over."

"Okay. Thanks. And I really am sorry."

"All right, go on. Get out of here. I have work to do." Renee got up to leave. "And make some more coffee, Rook," he added.

*

Renee left the sheriff's office feeling like she was walking through a dream. Only this dream was a nightmare. She wasn't sure how to take the news that she was being followed by a serial killer. It wasn't the kind of thing they teach you to deal with at the police academy, or anywhere else for that matter.

She had looked right at Charles Reese last night without recognizing him and that bothered her even more. She was a cop. She was supposed to be observant and pick up on the little things. What kind of cop didn't even recognize a suspected serial killer that she had been assigned to stake out just a few weeks ago?

For the first time since deciding to become a cop, she had real doubts about her career choice.

While at the police academy, she had dealt with her share of the "good old boys" bullshit, not just from the instructors, but from some of the candidates too. She had been accused of being a lesbian and had been the brunt of countless sexual innuendos and jokes from some of her fellow cadets. Some of the instructors had tried to get her to quit saying that being a cop was no job for a little girl and that she was too weak to protect herself, which would put her fellow officers in danger trying to cover her ass. And yet through all of that, she had never questioned her decision to become a cop. She used it to fuel her determination to succeed. The day she'd graduated from the academy had been the proudest day of her life. It had held extra sweetness because several of her harassers had washed out before graduation.

Working at the sheriff's office, Renee had taken a lot of razzing, but it was all "being a rookie" type of nonsense, like making coffee and washing the cruisers. Having worked in the office while at the academy, by the time she had graduated, the other deputies saw her as just one of the guys. Most of the time when they were standing around talking about guy stuff, they forgot she was a woman—sometimes to their collective embarrassment—which was fine with her. It made her feel like she was part of a close-knit family rather than the target of some macho bullshit like she had experienced at the academy. Nothing she had experienced on the job had shaken her confidence in her ability.

Until now.

And the sheriff wanted to put her under a protection detail? That would be the ultimate humiliation. Her eyes burned with tears of frustration. She rubbed her eyes, refusing to let anyone see her cry, even though there was no one in the office but her. She grabbed a radio off the charger and hurried to the door.

What she really wanted to do was crawl into a hole and die.

*

"Jesus," Ken said to himself, reading the email from Sheriff James.

Ken and Sara were eating lunch on the deck, enjoying what would surely be one of the last warm days of the year before fall descended on the mountains. Most of the summer haze was gone, leaving a bright, blue sky with what some painters called happy clouds meandering above them. The rich red, orange, and brown leaves beginning to show in the trees marked the coming of fall, but the light, warm breeze held no hint of the cold winter winds to follow. They had been discussing whether or not they would see an early winter when Ken's cell phone dinged with the arrival of Allen's email.

"What is it?" Sara asked.

"The dream I had last night. I told Allen about it and they figured out who the girl in it is." Ken's mouth was dry causing him to have trouble talking.

"I thought you weren't going to talk to him about it anymore? You promised!"

"I had to tell him. It turns out the girl Charlie was following was one of Allen's deputies. He seems to be pretty concerned about it. She saw him last night but didn't realize who it was she was seeing."

Sara stared back at Ken, the blood draining from her face.

"So you were actually seeing what was happening? It wasn't just thoughts or impressions? You actually saw him?"

"Not exactly. It was more like I *was* him. But I didn't have any control over what I—he—was doing."

"Ken?" Sara was visibly shaken. "What does it mean?"

"I don't know," Ken replied. He felt like Sara looked. He suspected that he didn't look much different either.

"Did...did he know that... You know... That you were there?"

"I don't know. I think maybe." Ken thought back to the time he had seen Charlie in the bathroom mirror. Clearly Charlie had known that something wasn't right then. And last night, hadn't he heard Charlie say something like *get out* or *go away*? So it was possible that Charlie knew, or at least suspected that there was someone in his head. Not that Ken really understood what that meant. How he could be inside another person's mind didn't make any sense to him.

A few days ago, Ken had done some research on the subject. Or at least tried to. He hadn't been able to find anything specific, other than information on movies and TV shows where a psychic could get into someone's mind and see through the target's eyes. He had learned a lot about remote viewing, where a person could see events and places far away. He had even read that the US Government had researched it. *Project Stargate* was a secret Army project to investigate the use of psychic phenomena for military applications, including remote viewing, to look for Soviet military secrets. There had even been a book and a movie made about the project. Ken's reading seemed to indicate that most people saw it as a joke. The government eventually shut down the program because they felt they hadn't gotten any useful information out of it.

While the research had been interesting, Ken hadn't been able to find anything that helped him understand his situation. What he had really hoped to find was a way to stop it from happening. Most of what he found was from people describing their personal events or trying to figure out how to do it. He hadn't seen anything from anyone trying to turn it off. Even articles he had found where people described their experiences didn't really match what was happening to Ken. Mostly they were short episodes lasting a second or two. He hadn't found anything talking about episodes that lasted minutes. And he hadn't seen anyone discussing the experience from the other person's perspective and whether or not the other person was aware of what was happening.

"Ken, what if he finds out who you are? What then? You promised you wouldn't do…whatever it is any more."

"I'm not doing it on purpose. Last night I was sleeping. The only reason I even sent Allen the email was because it looked like Charlie was following somebody. I thought it was just a dream. I didn't think it was a real vision or anything. I sure as hell don't want to do it. Whatever *it* is."

"Well now that they know it's him for sure, they're going to arrest him, aren't they?"

"They don't have any evidence. All they really have is a bunch of stories from a guy who makes up stories for a living. They need actual proof that he's done something wrong. Even last night, he was just sitting on a bench across the street from the restaurant that the deputy happened to be eating at. The only reason they even know that he was there and what his intentions are is because of my dream."

Sara turned away and stared over the tops of the trees in the valley below the house. Ken sensed what she was thinking. Sara had always believed in psychics and ghosts and angels, but this was different. This wasn't just a sideshow psychic reading your palm or dealing out tarot cards to tell your future in some vague narrative that could be shoehorned into almost anyone's life. Whether you called it remote viewing or clairvoyance or something else entirely, it wasn't your everyday spiritual shit.

Maybe a better question was, why Charles Reese? He had never met the guy, so why him? Why not Sheriff James? Or one of Charlie's victims. Certainly that made more sense than being in the head of a serial killer, right? Ken didn't normally write from the antagonist's point of view, so if you looked at it strictly from a writing perspective, getting into Charlie's head made no sense. Thinking about it now, he supposed the book should have been written from Tammy Knight's perspective. With a healthy dose of Detective Alan St. James. Cory Rivers should have been a complete mystery until the very end.

Ken couldn't remember ever making a conscious decision to write from Cory's perspective. He had started the book with Detective St. James arriving at the scene of Sandy's murder. It was his first homicide case as a detective. Ken had explored Alan's emotions as he worked through the room culminating in his discovery that her heart was missing. Later, he had written the actual murder from Cory's perspective and added it before his original opening. But he didn't remember when he had made that switch.

When reviewing the first draft, he had decided to put more focus on Cory and less on Detective St. James, which changed the whole feel of the book. Instead of a story about a detective chasing a serial killer, it had turned into one about a serial killer outwitting a detective. He had even started to empathize with Cory, though he would never admit that out loud. At the time, it never occurred to him to wonder why he was empathizing with someone as evil as Cory. He had just assumed it had to do with telling the story through Cory's eyes. Now that he knew that Cory's story had come from a real life monster, that thought made him queasy.

He knew Sara wasn't concerned with who the main character was in *Terror in Suburbia*, or why he had channeled Charles Reese instead of Allen James.

The look he had seen in her eyes was raw fear. She was afraid of Charlie. Afraid he might find them. Afraid of what he would do if he did.

Sara shivered as she turned back to Ken.

"I'm scared."

Ken got up, walked around the table, and put his arms around her.

"There's nothing to be afraid of. He's all the way in South Dakota and has no way of knowing about me. Or us."

But as he looked out over the trees himself, Ken wasn't so sure that he was telling Sara the truth.

CHAPTER ELEVEN

CHARLIE HAD HIM pegged as a cop the minute he walked in. He wasn't in uniform and didn't carry a gun, but Charlie could tell. The kid was dressed in khaki pants, a white polo shirt, and some kind of office shoes. Charlie couldn't read the logo on his shirt from across the warehouse—not that he needed to. He knew it would be the Sheriff's Office logo. The little shit could have been there for anybody. The truck depot hired a lot of ex-cons, probably some kind of kickback from the county, but Charlie knew he was there for him.

The warehouse foreman intercepted the piglet before he could get too far into the warehouse. After a brief exchange, the foreman pointed at Charlie. The kid nodded and started off toward him. No point in running. The little fucker wasn't here to arrest him anyway. They'd never send a kid to bring in an ex-con by himself. Besides, he didn't even look like a real cop. More like a gofer.

Charlie leaned against a post and cleaned his fingernails while he waited for the brat to make it across the warehouse floor. The kid glanced side to side at the other ex-cons as he walked. They just glared at him while they stacked their boxes on pallets and loaded them onto trucks. Charlie suppressed a grin, preferring to meet him with a scowl.

"M-Mr. Reese?" the pimply faced punk asked when he reached Charlie, his high-pitched voice cracking like a nervous teenager's.

"Yeah," Charlie said, still working his fingernails.

"My name's J-Jack Fitzgerald. I'm from the Woodford County Sheriff's Office. I'm here to swap out your ankle monitor."

Charlie kept his head down, hiding his surprise. There was only one reason they would want to swap out his ankle monitor. Whore Pig had recognized him following her. The monitor would show he had been at home and they wanted to know why.

"What for?" Charlie asked, managing to maintain a neutral tone.

"Your m-monitor sent a battery fault s-signal last night. That means that the battery is failing. Eventually, it'll stop holding a charge. That happens to rechargeable batteries all the time. It's part of their normal lifecycle. They can only take so many cycles before they don't have enough capacity anymore. We swap out ankle monitors before that happens. Nothing to worry about."

The kid was lying to him. Charlie knew what a battery fault meant. That wasn't what was going on here.

"Isn't the battery indicator supposed to flash if there's a problem with the battery?" he asked.

"It's supposed to," Geek Pig replied. He looked over Charlie's shoulder when he answered. "S-sometimes they don't. It's a firmware bug. It's been a problem for years. The manufacturer knows about it, but they say they can't reproduce it in the lab, so it's never been fixed."

Yeah, right. Don't ever commit a crime, asshole. You can't lie worth a shit.

"So you want to change it here?"

"We can do it here. I have a new one already programmed up. It'll just take a minute." The kid was still avoiding eye contact.

"Whatever. Make it quick. My boss is getting pissed."

The kid looked around, but Charlie's boss was nowhere in sight.

"Okay, I just n-need you to pull up your pant leg."

Charlie grunted at the kid and pulled up his left pant leg to reveal the ankle monitor. He looked down at the kid on his knees in front of him. If he grabbed the back of the kid's head and brought his knee up, he could turn college boy's pretty face into a bloody pulp. Without plastic surgery, his nose would be permanently fucked up. He would think of Charlie every time he looked in the mirror.

As satisfying as that would be, it wasn't worth the price.

He scowled again as the kid swapped out the monitor. He didn't think they would find any evidence of tampering. He had been too careful. His concern was the extra attention he was getting right after the clusterfuck of Friday night. His lifestyle depended on anonymity. All this scrutiny would make it impossible to play his game.

"Okay, we're all done." Geek Pig stood up and brushed off the knees of his pants, even though there was no dirt.

"Whatever. I gotta get back to work." Charlie turned and walked over to the pallet he had been loading and tried to ignore the little cocksucker. He was going to have to be more careful. Something bad was about to happen and he needed to figure out how to deal with it before it fucked him.

*

Instead of going to lunch, Allen drove into downtown Ashford to the County Administration building. The Sheriff's Office should have been in the admin building. The not-so-secret story behind the separation was that when the admin building had been built in the 1950s, the sheriff and the Ashford police chief had been mortal enemies, ironically for reasons no one could remember. The sheriff had refused to work inside the city limits. Instead, he kept the Sheriff's Office at the old administration building outside of town. By the time a new sheriff was elected in the early '60s, there had been no room at the new building, so the Sheriff's Office stayed where it was. Only the computer crimes division office was in the admin building.

Larger counties had separate computer crimes and IT support departments. Woodford County couldn't justify that, so the computer crimes division filled both roles. Having their office in the county admin building simplified that arrangement. They actually did more IT support than criminal investigation anyway. The division itself consisted of just Jack Fitzgerald and Kari Dunn.

Even as small as they were, Allen thought they were a pretty competent team. They only had to pull in help from the state occasionally, and usually that was due to lack of equipment, not lack of brain power. He felt fortunate to have them, even if they did both look like they were still in high school.

Allen walked in to the IT lab where Jack Fitzgerald was sitting at a work bench, eating lunch.

"Jack," Allen said.

Jack jumped at the sheriff's voice and coughed, choking on his sandwich.

"Sorry, didn't mean to scare you."

"It's okay," Jack said between coughs. "I should know better than to eat with my back to the door."

"I just stopped in to see how it went with Charles Reese."

"Fine, no trouble at all. He's pretty creepy though."

"More than you know," Allen said. He hadn't told Jack he suspected that Charlie was a serial killer. He figured it was hard enough on the kid to face the guy on his own. Allen had decided to send Jack by himself to reduce the possibly of raising Charlie's suspicions. He didn't want him alone with Charlie though, so he had him do it at the truck depot where at least there were other people around.

"Why's that?"

"Gut feeling, I guess," Allen lied. "In the interview the other day he just seemed like he thought was better than everybody around him. Anyway, what'd you find?"

"Nothing, Sheriff. Same as before. The diagnostic showed no evidence of tampering. Do you still want me to send it off to Decker?"

"Yeah. Overnight, A.M. delivery. I'm sure he's managed to take it off and I want to know how."

"Okay, I'll take care of it right after lunch."

"Great, thanks, Jack." Allen turned to walk out.

"Hey, Sheriff?"

"Yeah?" Allen stopped and turned back.

"One other thing. There was a lot of cat hair on it again."

"Well, we know he has a cat."

"Yeah, but this seems to be more than you would expect from just casual contact."

"Maybe the damn thing likes to rub on it. Cats like to rub on people's legs, don't they?" Allen didn't care for cats. He had always been a dog person.

"I suppose. It just seems odd."

"Okay, make a note of it, then, and include it in your work order to Decker."

"Will do. Thanks, Sheriff!"

Allen turned and walked out before Jack could come up with anything else. Damn IT kids were always trying to be detectives. Allen decided to stop by Kim Barrett's office. Maybe she had a change of heart about getting an arrest warrant for Charlie.

*

Charlie didn't like to take unnecessary risks. It was one of the reasons he had stayed out of the eyes of the law as long as he had. He planned his hunts to the last detail. The only thing he didn't plan was the specifics of the cutting. Like any artist, he couldn't plan that part. He had to wait to see how the canvas spoke to him. But everything leading up to that was meticulously detailed days, if not weeks in advance. He even had contingency plans in case things didn't go right. He was being even more careful with his contingency plans since the fuckup that had landed him in the big house for three years.

So when Charlie was presented with a new situation, he would take his time and analyze it before jumping in. Acting without thinking was what got lesser men caught. Charlie was not a lesser man. He studied new situations to determine the risks and rewards. That was the case now.

Discovering that someone had been reading your mind, exploring your innermost secrets, would be hard enough for an average person to handle. When those secrets could result in a needle in the arm… Well, Charlie had reason to be upset. Not that he was afraid of dying. He knew he would one day. He just wanted it to be on his terms, not at the whims of twelve random nitwits.

The encounter with the piglet that had changed out his ankle monitor confirmed that last Friday's disaster would have bigger consequences. The situation was worse than being spotted by his target and being mind-probed by some nosy fuckturd. Charlie needed to lay low for a few days, to evaluate and reconsider. There was no point in exposing himself to Whore Pig again until he was ready. He was in no hurry. If she had recognized him at the town square then she might be on the lookout for him. The cops may be stalking him again too, although he doubted that. He was sure he'd be able to spot a cop watching him from a mile away. Regardless of whether or not they were watching him, he needed to be careful.

Charlie was used to being in complete control over his life. Even when he had been in prison, he had maintained mental discipline and kept control over everything that happened to him, except for the not being able to leave the prison part. When something came along that was outside of his control, he would evaluate, then either take control of it or remove himself from the situation thus restoring control to his life. Having two events surprise him within minutes of each other had shaken him. When the third came along a couple days later, Charlie had decided that he needed to regroup.

Instead of tracking Whore Pig, he had spent the last several evenings watching television. He particularly enjoyed *Forensic Files, Most Evil*, and other real-life crime dramas. Partly, he liked to see if there were any new forensics techniques he needed to be aware of, but mostly he enjoyed seeing the mistakes amateurs made that got them caught. Most of the time, the shows were just a simple distraction.

What he did most, however, was think. He had the start of a pretty good plan for what to do once he caught the fucker that was poking around in his mind. What he lacked was a plan on how to figure out who it was. He had never much thought about telepathy, or any other psycho-shit for that matter. He had known plenty of grifters, especially when he was in prison, and knew the basics of how gypsy fortune tellers would hustle money from shit-for-brains morons that believed in that bullshit. He had just never considered that any of it might be real.

Trying to come up with a plan to deal with something he didn't understand was frustrating him. He thought maybe the next time it happened, if he concentrated hard enough and focused on the other person, then maybe he could make it flow the other way. It wasn't much of a plan, but it was all he had.

Not willing to risk being caught by the cops and not having a solid plan for dealing with the asshole in his head, Charlie spent the evenings on the couch staring at the TV, thinking, and watching Mittens play with mice, eventually just lying in bed waiting for sleep to come. During the day, the problem consumed most of his time at work. Not that moving boxes around required more than a couple of brain cells. Still, he was beginning to wonder if maybe he was overthinking it. Even so, he spent most of his waking hours considering his options.

By the time he felt the strange sensation again, almost a week after the clusterfuck downtown, he had pretty much decided what he had to do.

*

Virginia "Ginnie" James tried to relax on the couch in the James' family room, playing *Candy Crush* on her phone. Some singing talent reality show was mumbling on the television in the background. She told people she liked to watch it. Really, she just turned it on for background noise, not paying much attention to who was voted off and who moved on. This time of night was consumed with games on her phone. Especially lately.

Being a cop's wife wasn't easy during the best of times. The fear that her husband would be hurt, or God forbid killed, by some mindless drug addict or desperate criminal weighed on her mind every time he left for work. Even after more than fifteen years, Ginnie still worried. Although she didn't talk to Allen about it anymore, the fear was always in the back of her mind.

She understood why so many cops were divorced. That was what had happened to Allen's best friend, Phil Crawford. Twice. Although the first one, Grace, had only been his fiancé. She had just up and left after a fight one night. Phil never saw her again. Actually, nobody did. Ginnie would never do that, but if she didn't love Allen so much, she would have left a long time ago.

Then Allen had decided to run for sheriff. She clearly remembered the day he came home from work with the announcement that Bill Wade was retiring. She had jokingly told him to not even think about running. But after a few days, he had come to her and said he wanted to do it. They had argued about it, but in the end she had agreed so long as he promised not to let it consume his life. At the time, their kids had been five and three and she didn't want to be a single parent because her husband worked eighty hours a week.

To his credit, he tried very hard to keep that promise. He tried not to stay at the office past suppertime and on the weekends, he did as much as he could from home. He had taken time off for family vacations and had been able to make most of Greg's, and later Amber's, sporting events. Everything seemed to be going well until earlier this year.

When Allen became obsessed with catching a serial killer.

He had suspected that there was a serial killer running around the area for a long time, but with so much time between the murders, he didn't really have a lot to go on. The last murder had been five years prior. He had almost forgotten about it—except that he kept the open case files on his desk and reviewed them every couple of months. Then Phil had brought him that damned book.

Phil had been around for all of the murders and knew how Allen felt about them. Ginnie didn't think Phil was obsessed with the case like Allen, though she had never talked to his ex-wife about it. The way Allen talked, Phil seemed to want the whole thing to just go away. On the other hand, when Phil had given Allen the book, Allen became even more obsessed with catching the guy. He had spent weeks going through the book and comparing it to case files, highlighting passages, and bookmarking sections.

Ginnie had tried reading it. She had to put it down before she even finished the first chapter. Way too much gore for her taste. She wondered about what kind of person could come up with that kind of stuff. When she'd found out K. Elliot Simmons was married, she wondered how his wife could sleep next to a man with all of that in his head. Allen had told her that the murder scenes in the book were just like the real thing. She supposed that seeing all those poor girls mutilated was messing with his head, which was all the more reason he needed to step back from the case.

When the young woman had been butchered back in September, Allen had taken it personally, even flying out to West Virginia to discuss it with Ken Simmons, although Ginnie had no clue how that would help. She had hoped that he'd come back realizing the book had nothing to do with the real murders and he was just imagining a connection. Instead, he had come back even more convinced that the book was real and would help him catch the killer. Now Allen was spending almost every waking minute on the case. She had tried to tell him he wasn't helping himself, that he needed to take a break from time to time. She felt he was too close to the case, couldn't see the forest for the trees or something. He had dismissed her concerns, telling her that he wasn't going to be able to rest until he put the guy behind bars permanently. He was convinced he knew who it was. He just needed proof.

For the last couple of months, Allen had worked every day, twelve or more hours a day during the week and almost as much on the weekends. He allowed himself to sleep "late" on Sundays, getting up at seven thirty instead of his usual five o'clock. Even on days he didn't go to the office, he worked from home in his study. During the week, Allen left for work before anyone else in the house was awake and most days didn't get home until the kids were in bed. They only saw him a few hours on the weekends. Ginnie saw him for an hour or so most nights, though some nights she wouldn't see him at all unless he woke her climbing into bed.

The toll it was taking on Allen was obvious. Unfortunately, Allen wasn't aware of the toll it was taking on *her*. In the morning, she would have to get the kids up and ready for school on her own. She would get herself ready for work, then make them breakfast, pack their lunches, and make sure they were out the door in time to catch the bus. At least this year, Amber was old enough to walk herself to the bus stop.

Ginnie worked at Fletcher's, the only pure bakery in town. She had quit waitressing shortly before Gregory was born, but when Amber started first grade, Ginnie had decided to go back to work. She had tried waitressing again, but quickly realized the good money in waitressing was during supper and she only wanted to work while the kids were in school. Eventually, Clyde Fletcher had offered her a job working at his bakery. He even gave her the summers off, replacing her with high school kids who were on break. It was the perfect job, except that now that Allen was gone all the time she had no help at home.

Ginnie had stopped even making supper for Allen. He was never home for it anyway. She cooked enough for her and the kids, but left Allen to fend for himself. And she didn't feel one gosh darn bit guilty about it, either. If he was going to be a jerk and leave everything up to her, he could fix his own damn supper. She had hoped he'd get the message: *Hey, Bub! You have a family here, you know.* But he didn't seem to be getting it. In fact, he had just started eating supper at the office.

After cleaning up from supper, Ginnie would spend a couple of hours sitting in front of the TV, playing her games and reading Facebook posts. Tonight was no different, except she felt the end of her rope slipping from her fingers. As the talent show ended and *Dateline* started, the silent rage she had been holding down began to rise.

Allen Nathaniel James was going to get an earful tonight, just wait and see. She didn't care how tired he was when he got home—she was going to jerk a knot in his tail.

*

Charlie was watching an exposé on Robert Hansen when the first signs came.

He had heard of Robert Hansen before, of course, but the show about his life revealed more into his character and, more importantly, his craft. Hansen would kidnap strippers and fly them out to the remote wilderness in his private plane. There, he would send them into the woods, naked, where he would hunt them until he killed them. Charlie thought that was way too risky. The chance of one of the bitches getting away was too high. In fact, that was what ultimately led to Hansen's downfall. One of his toys escaped while he was loading his plane. Not smart. Even though he had some friends lie for him and give him an alibi, the Butcher Baker was doomed to be caught.

Charlie felt a slight pressure in his chest and throat. Maybe just indigestion from the Mexican fast food he had eaten for supper, maybe something more. He sat up to focus.

The narrator began talking about Hansen's bakery, where he would sell doughnuts to the cops who were investigating the disappearances of his victims. He would listen to them talk about the missing strippers while he worked behind the counter.

That made Charlie smile. Stupid cops.

The pressure spread to the back of his head, feeling like the onset of a migraine. Now Charlie was sure: Fuckface was trying to get into his head again. Only this time, Charlie wasn't frustrated or mad. This time he was ready.

His smile grew as the feeling got stronger.

Now the television narrator was talking about a movie that had been made about Hansen and his game. Charlie wondered if anyone would ever make a movie about him.

He closed his eyes and tried to relax and let the claustrophobic feeling grow. He wanted to make sure the connection was good and strong before he tried anything.

*

Ken's eyes slowly cleared and the dream came into focus. He was sitting on a couch in a small living room. A television flickered in the corner. A cat was at the other end of the couch. It looked up at him and yawned, then went back to licking its paws. He could see his legs and his feet, but they weren't his. His hands were clasped across his waist and they weren't his, either.

He wasn't himself. He was Cory Rivers.

He began to notice Cory's thoughts, sense them rather than hear them. He was looking for something. No, not something. Someone. Finding this someone was important. His life depended on it.

Cory knew Ken was there. That was who he was looking for. He had to find Ken.

He had to kill Ken.

*

Charlie sensed the intruder now, felt him looking around the room. He sensed the fear and confusion. Charlie took a deep breath and focused. At first, it seemed like he was grasping at air. He would get close, then it would slip away. But Charlie didn't give up. Oh no, Charlie would never give up. The intruder's thoughts felt like whispers in his mind. Charlie concentrated on those thoughts, listening, searching.

Images swam before his mind's eye, mountains and trees, a house in a clearing on a hill, a woman sleeping in her bed, peaceful and oblivious to the chaos swirling around her. The intruder's thoughts grew louder. He could almost hear the words rising from a cacophony of voices. Then names.

Cory Rivers, Ken, Sara. Simmons.

*

Ken jerked awake, his head pounding. All he could see was a fuzzy flickering light. He rubbed his eyes with hands that felt like balloons. Slowly, his vision cleared. The flickering light was coming from the television. Reaching for the remote, he noticed he wasn't in his bed. He was on the couch. Confusion washed over him. He was sure he had gone to sleep in bed.

Something touched his feet, making him jump. It was just the cat licking his toes. He relaxed.

"But we don't have a cat," he said.

He jumped again at the sound of his voice. It wasn't his. He looked around and realized he wasn't in his house. He wasn't even in his own body. He was in Charlie Reese's body, but this wasn't a dream or a vision like he had experienced before. He wasn't just hearing Charlie's thoughts or seeing through his eyes.

This time he really was Charlie.

The pounding in his head was making it hard to concentrate.

A thought began to form at the back of Ken's mind, rising to his consciousness the way a bubble of air rises from the bottom of the ocean. If he was in Charlie's body, where was Charlie?

Could Charlie be in *his* body? In his bed? Next to his wife?

"Sara!" he shouted.

The cat looked up at him, tilting its head and giving a soft meow. He stared at the cat and the cat stared back.

Satisfied there was no danger, the cat put its head back down and closed its eyes.

Ken tried to think. His mind was fuzzy. He felt drunk. He couldn't focus. He knew he had to get home. Charlie Reese, the evil monster who had been torturing and killing women for years, was lying in bed next to Sara.

"Charlie! Get the fuck out of my body!"

Ken heard a low laugh in his head that made his skin crawl.

"You get the fuck out of mine, Ken Simmons. That's right. I know who you are now."

Ken's mind raced. How could his mind be in Charlie's body and Charlie's mind be in his? It didn't make any sense.

"But what I want to know is how the fuck you know who I am?"

What did that mean? Ken didn't know Charlie. Not really. He knew Cory.

But Cory was Charlie.

"Who the fuck is Cory?"

Cory Rivers. Charlie Reese. They were the same, really, even if the book was a little different from real life.

"A book? You wrote a fucking book about me?"

Charlie didn't know about the book. Why would he?

"How? How did you get into my fucking head?"

"I don't know. I'm sorry, I didn't mean to. I thought I was making it up, I swear."

"And you told Sherriff Shitforbrains about me? All this trouble over some little pissant like you?"

"Please, leave me alone. I won't say anything more to anybody, I promise."

"I don't think so, asshole. I'm going to find you. I'm going to find you and cut your fucking balls off and shove them down your fucking throat. Then I'm going to make you watch while I play with your fucking whore."

"Leave her alone, you sick fuck!"

Charlie's laugh filled Ken's head, echoing in his mind, drowning out all his thoughts.

"Oh, I'm going to enjoy doing her. Her skin is so soft. Hmmmm… Her hair smells nice. I could kill her right now. Wouldn't that be fun? I could kill her and the cops would pin it on you."

"No! Leave her alone!" Ken shouted again.

"My hands are around her neck, Kenny. All I have to do is squeeze. Should I do it now? Whaddya think, Kenny? Should I do her now?"

"No," Ken whispered. "She didn't do anything to you."

"But you did, you fucking cocksucker! And her death will be on you."

"Please," Ken pleaded. "Don't hurt her."

That laugh again.

"Pinning her death on you would be fun, but I have bigger plans. I won't kill her until you can watch. I'll tie you to a chair and cut off your eyelids so you have to watch. Then I'll start on your whore and show the little cunt what she's worth. You'll see it all, Kenny. You'll get to watch me cut her. I've been learning how to cut off strips of skin without the bitch bleeding out. We can play for hours. Days even. Then when I get bored with her, you can watch while I cut her open and take out her fucking heart. I'm real good at that. It'll still be beating in my hand. Would you like that, Kenny? Your cunt's heart beat for the last time in my hand?"

Ken felt sick. Charlie laughed.

"Don't worry, I'll take my time. I'll go real slow. It'll be loads of fun, don't you think, Kenny?"

Ken tried to answer, to tell Charlie to go to Hell and leave Sara alone. The thought of that monster touching her, of hurting her while he sat helpless on Charlie's couch was too much. He couldn't move, couldn't think. He put his face in his hands, sobbing in frustration as much as fear.

As he sat, his hands and feet went numb. The sound from the television dimmed. As the numbness crept up his arms and legs, his vision began to fade. Charlie's presence was like a cold slime covering his body. Numbness consumed his mind. Consciousness faded. He was drifting away, fading into nothing.

Sleep was coming.

Maybe it had all been a dream.

Tomorrow…

CHAPTER TWELVE

AROUND TEN O'CLOCK, Allen pulled out of the parking lot and headed for home. He had spent another day of banging his head against the wall trying to find a way to bust Charles Reese and had nothing to show for it but a massive headache. He was looking forward to getting home and getting to bed, hoping sleep would help. Tomorrow would be a new day.

He drove in near silence, the only sound the rumble of the truck's big diesel engine. He didn't even turn on the radio. He used to use the fifteen-minute drive home from the station to de-stress. Used to be he would leave the job at the office and not bring it home. The drive had been some kind of magical buffer that kept home and work from blending together. That was the way it used to be, back when he'd been just a deputy. Now that he was sheriff, he didn't have the luxury of leaving the job at the office. Now he spent the drive thinking about work rather than forgetting about it.

Since he'd first been elected sheriff eight years ago, the barrier between work and home had slowly eroded until there was no more *work* and *home*. There was just work at his office in the Sheriff's Office building and work in his office at his house. When Allen had first talked to Bill Wade about running for sheriff, Bill had told him not to do it. He had told Allen that it would consume his whole life. Allen hadn't understood what he meant at the time, but he did now. Maybe he should go to see Bill and get some advice before it was too late.

He made a mental note to add that to his ever expanding list of things to do. He couldn't go see Bill this late at night anyway. He probably wouldn't get a chance until Reese was behind bars again, which he hoped would be soon. All he needed was some proof that Reese had been tampering with his ankle monitor. Then he could at least bring him in on a parole violation while they built a case for the murders.

First thing on tomorrow's agenda was a call to Decker to find out what the deal was with the analysis of the monitor. They had had it for almost three full days. What was taking them so long?

Allen watched the road ahead as it passed under the beams of his headlights. Cornfields flanked either side of the road, hidden in the dark, moonless night. He knew the fields were empty, with mostly just beets and pumpkins left to harvest this time of year, yet all his headlights showed him was the asphalt of a long, straight road running through rural South Dakota. He couldn't prove there were empty cornfields on either side of him any more than he could prove Charles Franklin Reese had murdered eight women.

He hadn't even been able to convince Frank Harrington, the Ashford Police Chief, that there was a serial killer loose in the county, although he hadn't talked to him about it since Jordan Rosenbaum had been killed five years ago. Maybe he should set up a meeting with Frank and show him the new cases he'd found. Frank was stubborn, but he wasn't a fool. With eight cases with virtually identical MOs sitting in front of him, even Frank Harrington would have to admit there was a connection. Then maybe he would lend some help. He probably should have gone to Frank after Shelby Winston's murder. Old habits die hard.

Allen knew hanging his hopes on a parole violation wasn't good enough. But it would be good enough to protect Renee Watts. With luck, he would have Reese behind bars by lunch tomorrow. Then he would go home early and take the whole weekend off. He felt like he hadn't seen his family in weeks. Especially the kids. He was going to make it up to them as best he could this weekend. Maybe even take the family out to Lake Thompson on Saturday and rent a boat.

And he should probably take Ginnie out to supper on Friday night. They had had a few arguments about the amount of time he was spending on Charlie Reese. He knew it wasn't fair to put her through it, but he wouldn't be able to live with himself if Reese killed another girl. At least he could make it up to her once he put Reese was behind bars.

The trouble was, he wasn't sure he would be able to do that. He had a sneaking suspicion the reason the analysis of the ankle monitor was taking so long was because they couldn't find anything. He had insisted that Reese had to be doing something to make the system think he was home when he wasn't. He wanted them to look for even the tiniest evidence that it had been tampered with.

Even though Watts hadn't been able to confirm it had been Reese in the town square last week, Allen was sure of Ken's vision. So Reese either had some kind of gadget that would transmit fake data to the base station in his apartment and block the real data from the monitor, or he had figured out a way to taking the monitor off without detection. The techs had assured him that removal wasn't possible without triggering an alarm. And even if he had managed to get it off, the monitor sensed body heat; if it was off for more than a thirty seconds or so, it would have sent an alarm for that.

Regardless of what the evidence was showing, Allen was sure Reese was the right suspect. Everything in his gut told him that Charlie Reese was evil and would kill someone as easily as eat a hot dog.

More to the point, Allen was getting an increasingly strong feeling that something really bad was going to happen and happen soon. Reese possibly stalking one of his deputies was adding to his sense of urgency. And with Watts adamantly refusing to have another deputy follow her around, Allen had alarms bells going off in his head. He wondered why he hadn't reinstated the surveillance on Reese when he'd found out he was after her. That had been a mistake. He would have to rectify that first thing in the morning, in spite of the budget issues. With one of their own on the line, his deputies would probably do it for free if they had to.

*

Renee was sitting in the living room of her small apartment watching *The Tonight Show* and eating strawberry ice cream. Jimmy Fallon was having one of his famous lip sync battles. She had just discovered

Jimmy, having been a Letterman fan until he retired, and she found herself giggling until her sides hurt. Finally, a commercial break rescued her from asphyxiation.

Renee normally worked second or third shift so she didn't usually get to see the late night talk shows. Tonight was an exception. This week, she was scheduled for both Friday and Saturday night, so she'd gotten Thursday night off. Used to working nights, she could hardly ever go to sleep before two o'clock.

In a small community like Ashford, the only thing to do on a Thursday night was sit in a bar and get hit on by warehouse workers and farmhands who had come straight from work, not bothering to shower first. She was turned on as much as the next girl by a strong, sweaty man working a tractor or swinging a hammer; she just didn't want to sit next to him all night in a stuffy bar. Besides, this time of year, Thursday nights were football nights, and tonight the boys would be more interested in Matt Hasselbeck than Renee Watts.

She used the commercial break to take her ice cream bowl back to the kitchen. She was thinking about getting another scoop when she thought she heard a soft thump coming from down the hallway. She stopped and listened, wishing her gun wasn't in her bedroom. She held her breath, straining her ears. Nothing. It was probably the kid upstairs. Her upstairs neighbor was a single mother with a five-year-old son, who sounded like a herd of elephants running across her ceiling. Renee suspected that the kid didn't have a strict bedtime because she would hear him at all hours of the night. Normally it didn't bother her, but ever since she had found out that Charles Reese might be stalking her, she had become paranoid and noticed every sound the kid made.

Not hearing anything more, she took her bowl into the kitchen and decided on popcorn and a movie instead of more ice cream. Popcorn was her favorite snack, even though the microwave variety wasn't as good as the crunchy butter salt at the movie theater.

The sound of the microwave and popping corn masked any possible noise from the toddler upstairs.

Or of an intruder.

She leaned out to the hallway and looked toward her bedroom.

"You're going to drive yourself crazy if you keep jumping at every little bump in the night," Renee said aloud, and went back into the kitchen to wait for the microwave to finish like a normal person.

When it was done, Renee poured the popcorn into a bowl and took it into the living room. Just to be sure, she walked to the patio door and pulled the curtain aside to look outside. The tall fence around the patio blocked her view of the street and the front walkway. All she could see was the concrete slab outside the glass door with a small charcoal grill and two plastic chairs. No one out there. She checked the lock and the security bar, then went to the front door to double check the locks there.

On her way back to the couch, she paused at the hallway and listened.

No noise.

"Dammit," she muttered and walked down the hallway to her bedroom. Flicking on the light, she looked around the room. Everything was in place. The window was closed. The closet doors were open, dirty laundry spilling out into the room. Her uniform was lying on the dresser along with empty coke cans and a half-eaten breakfast sandwich. The sheets and blankets on her bed were bunched up on one side. Her service pistol was on the nightstand next to her bed, right where she had left it.

She walked across the room and picked it up. She looked at it in her hands, trying to decide if she was being cautious or paranoid.

"You're being ridiculous, Watts. There's nobody here. You're letting that asshole get into your head." She laughed at herself, but took the gun to the living room with her.

Satisfied the apartment was secure, she went back to the couch. She had an odd urge to be working instead of sitting home alone. When she had rented the apartment a year ago, the first floor had seemed like a good idea. The patios on the first-floor apartments seemed bigger and more practical than the balconies on the second floor. She hadn't worried about security. Ashford was a safe community and besides, she was a cop. Everyone knew it. You'd have to be crazy to break into a cop's apartment.

Crazy like Charlie Reese.

She picked up her gun again, then shook her head. She was just being skittish. She tucked it under the pillow, then folded her legs up and pulled the bottom of her nightgown down over her feet. Almost as an afterthought, she grabbed the comforter off the back of the couch. Still feeling a little paranoid, she turned the volume down on the television, listening for noises.

After a few minutes, she relaxed and forgot all about bumps in the night. She looked for a pay-per-view movie to watch, settling on a chick-flick about a city girl who falls in love with a bull rider. Normally an action flick fan, Renee thought a good tearjerker was just the ticket to take her mind off Charlie Reese.

*

Allen knew Ginnie was upset as soon as he walked in the door. She was sitting on the couch, watching TV and playing with her cell phone like she always was these days. Supper had been cleaned up and the dishes washed because he rarely made it home in time to eat with the family. The kids were in bed because they had school in the morning. Everything looked normal, but he could feel it—the air was too thick.

Allen hung his jacket on a hook next to the door and walked through the kitchen to the living room with trepidation.

"Sit down," Ginnie said without looking up from her game. "We need to talk."

Allen's heart sank. He had known this was coming. He had just hoped that he would have been able to fix it before she said anything. No such luck. He sat down in the recliner across from the couch and waited. His gut told him it would be best to let her vent before he tried to defend himself.

Ginnie put down her phone and turned off the television, then turned to look at him. Her eyes were red from crying, but he couldn't tell if the look on her face was anger or sadness. Maybe it was both. He felt a pang of guilt.

"I'm done," she said finally. "I can't do this by myself anymore. You're never home. I'm raising our kids by myself. They hardly ever see you. *I* hardly ever see you unless you wake me up in the middle of the night with your snoring. Something needs to change."

Ginnie paused, waiting for a reaction or for effect he wasn't sure. He was about to reply when she went on.

"When you decided to run for sheriff, you promised me that it wouldn't consume your life. *Our lives.* I understand that from time to time things come up that you have to deal with, and I accepted that a long time ago. But now you're almost never home and even when you are home, you're not really here. You're working in your office or talking to somebody on your phone. I'm not going to accept that anymore."

"Gin, you know I would rather be home than working," Allen pleaded. "But this guy Reese is a monster. I have to get him off the street before he hurts someone else. How would you feel if it had been your daughter he had killed?"

Wrong answer.

"Dammit, Allen! You aren't the only cop in the state! If there really is one guy doing all these killings, why isn't anyone else worried about it? Even Kim Barrett thinks you're wrong about Charles Reese and she's harder on men that attack women than you are! Face it, *Sheriff,* you might be wrong about this guy. And even if you're right, what good is it doing you to work all damn day every day of the week? It isn't getting you any closer to catching him. Heck, Allen, your best lead is a guy who writes fiction novels for a living."

Ginnie hated bad language and never used it herself. Hearing her use *damn* twice in one day was shocking enough. Twice in one minute told Allen to tread carefully.

"Okay, I get it. I'm sorry. I know this has been hard on you too, but I know Charlie Reese is a serial killer. I just have to prove it. Kim doesn't believe it because she thinks there's no way Reese could get his ankle monitor off without setting off alarms. But she's just being naïve. I'm hoping to have an answer to that tomorrow. If it comes back that he's been tampering with it, we can arrest him on a parole violation. At least that'll get him off the street, then we can relax and take our time building a case against him for the murders. I wouldn't be able to forgive myself if he hurt someone else before I could arrest him and I didn't do absolutely everything I could."

"Including throw away your family?" Ginnie fumed.

"That's not fair. I'm trying to protect my family, along with all the other families in the county."

"What's not fair is having to raise two kids by myself! What's not fair is doing your laundry and never even seeing you. What's not fair is you making everyone else a priority instead of your family!"

The tears were flowing now. He knew there was no way he was going to convince her that he had to do what he was doing for the good of the county, including her and the kids. All he could do now was damage control.

"Okay, what should I do then? I can't just ignore it. Charles Reese isn't going to stop what he's doing just because I'm not at work. Look, I really want to be home. I don't like spending all my time working. I miss my family. I just don't know what else I can do here. Help me figure out what I can do and I promise I'll do it."

"I want you home. What are you doing at the office fifteen hours a day? For Pete's sake, Allen, you're burning yourself out. You could have the clue you need to solve this thing sitting right on your desk, but you're too tired to see it."

Allen stopped because he suddenly understood she was right. He really wasn't making any progress on Charles Reese. During normal business hours, he was busy with his normal duties. Before and after he would just sit and research cases from other parts of the state, looking for similar murders, hoping that if he found one, it would have some piece of the puzzle that would help him prove Reese was guilty. But in the weeks since Shelby's murder, he had come up with nothing. He had gotten nothing back from his inquiry with the FBI, so he had sent out requests directly to every county sheriff's office in the state and then to the state police in neighboring states. Those inquiries hadn't turned up anything other than the cases he already knew about. His own research had resulted in the same.

Maybe he was wasting his time at the expense of his family. Maybe he really just needed to step back and take a breath. Look at it with fresh eyes. The idea that the break in the case was staring at him the whole time—and he was too wrapped up to see it—scared him. He would put surveillance on Reese again. Maybe even beg Frank Harrington to lend a few officers so his guys didn't get burned out.

"You're right," he said finally. "I'm working this thing too hard. Taking a break might be the best thing for the case. Tomorrow's Friday. If I'm lucky, I'll have what I need to scoop him up and I won't have to worry about it. If not, I'll put surveillance on him and take the weekend off. We can go out to the lake on Saturday and get away for a bit. Then Sunday, I'll spend the day at home and I won't do anything beyond check my email unless an emergency comes up. After that I'll see if I can come up with a longer-term plan. Okay?"

Ginnie smiled for the first time since he'd walked in the door. "I knew you'd see it my way if I kicked you in the butt hard enough."

Allen smiled back. "I'm sorry. I really am. Come on. We're both tired. Let's go to bed."

The both got up and met in the middle of the room. Allen put his arms around Ginnie and held her tight, her head resting on his chest.

You really screwed the pooch on this one, asshole, he thought. *It's a good thing she's an understanding woman or you'd be sleeping in the car tonight.*

He kissed the top of her head. "I love you," he whispered to her.

She squeezed him tighter in response. They stood like that for a few minutes before turning out the lights and heading for bed. As they walked down the hall, Allen thought about Renee Watts. On a whim, he decided to text the deputy on duty to tell him to sit on Reese's apartment unless something else came up.

As he crawled into bed, Allen hoped he wasn't too late.

*

The movie had gotten bad reviews, but Renee liked it anyway. She thought the girl was an idiot, but the guy was hot. Turning off the TV, she wondered why all the hot cowboys fell for the city girls.

If I ever met a hot cowboy, I'd make sure he'd never look at a city girl again.

She grinned to herself as she turned out the lights and headed to the bathroom to brush her teeth. It was probably because more city girls watched movies than country girls. All the movies about country girls had them falling for city guys. Maybe Hollywood thought that the city was better than the country and everyone in the country wanted to move to the city. Or maybe she was just reading too much into it.

It was almost three o'clock in the morning before Renee finally went to bed, making sure not to forget her gun. She put it back in its place on the nightstand before going to the bathroom to pee and brush her teeth.

"Just because you're paranoid doesn't mean they aren't out to get you." She stuck her tongue out at her reflection and giggled.

Feeling better, she went back to her bedroom, turned out the light, and slipped into bed. She shivered as the cool sheets touched her bare legs. Soon, she would need to start turning on the electric blanket before bed. Tonight, however, the coolness felt good. She adjusted the pillows and snuggled under the blankets, then completed her bedtime ritual by reaching over to the nightstand to make sure her gun was in easy reach.

It wasn't there.

She stretched her arm across the nightstand groping in the dark. Not finding it, she turned on the light.

"Looking for this?"

Renee stifled a scream. At the end of her bed stood Charlie Reese.

She struggled to control the panic and fear. He had her gun. He was pointing it right at her.

"Make a sound, whore, and I'll shoot you right there. You understand me?"

She nodded, trying not to let her panic show. Panic wouldn't help her. Her mind raced to come up with a way out. The safety was off. If she tried to run, he could kill her before her feet hit the floor. Her cell phone was on the other nightstand, but she couldn't get to that without him seeing her. She needed a distraction. Her eyes darted around the room looking for something—anything—that could help her. She found nothing.

"If you shoot me the neighbors will hear it," she said, trying to sound calm. "Everybody knows you've been following me. They'll catch you before breakfast. I wouldn't expect you to make it to jail, though."

The threat sounded weak in her ears. Apparently Charlie didn't take it seriously either.

"Shut up, Whore Pig! Your cop buddies couldn't catch a cold. They may think they know something, but they ain't got shit on me."

Charlie sneered at her as he walked to the side of the bed. She tried to slow her breathing. She was only going to get one shot at this, so she needed to stay calm and wait for the right moment. She kept her eyes on the gun. It never wavered. Charlie had it pointed at her chest, which limited her options.

"We have more on you than you think," Renee lied. "We have your DNA from Shelby Winston's apartment. We're just waiting for the analysis to come back from the lab."

Charlie laughed. "You're so full of shit. If you had my DNA from that bitch's apartment, you would have arrested me weeks ago. It doesn't take a month to do a DNA match. You must think I'm a fucking idiot."

"No, it takes a week or so," she said, trying to think of a plausible excuse. "It just took us a while to get the sample."

"Bullshit." He stopped next to the head of the bed, looking down at her.

Renee's gaze shifted between the gun and his face. He was holding it in his right hand. He had made the mistake of holding it out in front of him. If she timed it right, she could swing her arm into his, knocking the muzzle of the gun away from her. She would have to swing her legs off the bed at the same time and try to kick him in the balls.

"Don't even think about it, bitch."

She hesitated for a second, then took a deep breath, readying herself for the strike. Gathering all of her strength, she exploded off the bed, swinging her left arm into his right, knocking it away from her. She tried to use the momentum to swing herself off the bed, her left foot aiming for his crotch. She missed, kicking him in the hip instead and sending a wave of pain up her leg. She ignored it, trying to get her balance before he could react.

Her head exploded in stars. She fell back onto the bed, the blow to her ear from his fist disorienting her. Before she recovered, he grabbed her wrists and pulled her toward the headboard. She struggled to break free, managing to get her right arm loose. She tried to roll away from him, twisting her other arm out of his iron grasp. He yanked her back toward him and his fist came down on her mouth and chin like an anvil. Dazed from the blow, she collapsed. With a final tug, Charlie pulled her hands to the headboard and used a pair of handcuffs—probably her handcuffs—to keep them there.

Her head was still spinning, the tangy taste of blood filling her mouth. Now completely helpless, she started shivering with fear. Her cotton nightgown was already soaked in sweat and clinging to her body. She opened her mouth to scream for help. Before any sound came out, Charlie shoved a ball of cloth in her mouth, gagging her and making her cough. He pulled out a roll of duct tape from his jacket pocket and ripped off a long strip. He slammed the tape across her mouth, securing the gag. The smell of plastic filled her nose as she tried to catch her breath, air wheezing through her nostrils.

Charlie stood up, his scowl changing to a grin that made her shake even harder. Hunger filled his eyes.

"That's better," he said. He grabbed the sheets and blankets that had gotten wrapped around her during the struggle and pulled them off the bed, leaving her lying in her damp nightgown, hands pulled up over her head. The cool air on her sweaty skin sent a chill through her body, causing another round of shivers. Tears welled in her eyes, but she refused to give him the satisfaction of seeing her cry. Her lungs burned.

He licked his lips as his eyes wandered over her body. She looked away, the duct tape pulling at her skin as she turned her head.

"I should fuck you with your own gun, Whore Pig. You'd like that, wouldn't you?" He dropped the gun on the bed between her feet as he laughed. "Too bad I have to be somewhere else. We could've had a lot of fun." Charlie pulled a Bowie knife out of a sheath on his belt. He looked at it, turning it over slowly, lovingly. "Too bad," he said again.

Renee watched, helpless, hoping he would let her live, knowing he wouldn't. She thought about her dad, wishing he were here to protect her like he had when she was a little girl. She remembered a time when she had been eight years old—she had fallen off her bicycle and skinned her knee in the gravel driveway. She'd run into the house crying. Her mom had been baking an apple pie with fresh apples from their orchard. She'd screamed for her daddy, but he wasn't there. He was in the fields. Her mommy had held her close trying to calm her down, but she'd wanted her daddy. Only Daddy could fix it.

The knife rose up in the air and came down. Renee squeezed her eyes closed as the blade entered her stomach. To her surprise, she felt no pain. Maybe he hadn't stabbed her after all. Then she felt the tugging as he ripped the blade through her flesh and up to her chest. She felt warm fluid spill across her belly and down her sides. The scent of blood and bile drifted up to her nose and she realized she was smelling her own insides.

Renee noticed that everything was quiet. The sloshy sucking sounds of Charlie's knife dicing her insides faded away. The feeling faded from her fingers and toes.

She was sleepy. So sleepy.

CHAPTER THIRTEEN

ARA SAT IN silence at the kitchen table with her coffee. Ken had told her about his dream. She couldn't think of a useful response. *I told you so* sat at the front of her mind, but it seemed pointless to voice that thought. All she knew for sure was that she was scared. It was a fear she had felt only once before.

The night Ken had been shot.

She couldn't remember most of the details of that night. They had been in Pittsburgh visiting her parents. Her father had made reservations at Ruth's Chris Steak House, where they were going to celebrate her mother's sixtieth birthday.

As they had walked down Third Avenue, a man had stepped up to them and said something, but she couldn't remember what. She remembered thinking the man had come up to Ken for an autograph. When he had pulled his hand out of his pocket, she'd expected to see a paperback or notebook and a pen. That he had a gun hadn't registered with her until she had seen the muzzle flash. She had felt, rather than heard, the explosion of the gun firing. The pain in her ears, then the disorientation, bits and pieces of seeing Ken on the ground, blood, screaming. At some point paramedics arrived. The next clear memory was her father driving her to the hospital.

That ride to the hospital, not knowing if Ken was dead or alive, had taken a lifetime. That had been the worst fear of her life. She expected to get to the hospital and find out that he had died in the ambulance or that he was in a coma with permanent brain damage, a drooling vegetable if he did wake up. She had known in her heart that the best she could hope for was that he would have enough of a brain left to remember her, and yet even hoping for that much had seemed like foolish fantasy. The only man she had ever loved besides her own father was gone. She had lost the most important part of herself. The twisting knot in her stomach, the uncontrollable shaking and sweating, the cold that penetrated her bones, the yawning feeling of standing on the edge of a towering cliff in the dark.

That was the fear she was feeling now. Ken was sitting right in front of her, but she had the same feeling of not knowing if he would live or die. She couldn't tell if he understood that his life was in danger. He sat with his untouched coffee cup between his hands looking at her with what? Guilt? Concern? She couldn't tell. She was having trouble thinking clearly.

She knew none of this made any logical sense. How could Ken see inside the mind of a man living half a continent away? And then, how could that man turn around and see inside Ken's mind? A rational person would say it was a dream, nothing more. But Sara believed there was a lot more to the world than what you could see with your eyes and touch with your hands. The human soul wasn't just a bunch of neurons firing off in the brain. To Sara, it was just a plain fact that the soul transcended the physical body and as such existed outside of it.

Even so, if not for the preternatural fear in her gut, she would have a hard time accepting the possibility of a person possessing another person's body like Ken had described. Reading minds was one thing, but swapping bodies? That was science fiction. Or maybe a Disney movie.

Yet her heart told her it was true.

"Are you okay?" Ken asked.

Sara didn't answer right away. Was she okay? She didn't know.

"What are we going to do?" she asked instead of answering him.

Now it was Ken's turn to pause. She didn't think he had any more idea what to do than she did.

"I think maybe we need to take a trip. Maybe that trip to Jamaica we were talking about a couple of years ago."

"For how long? A week? A month? What happens when we come home and find him waiting for us?"

Ken didn't answer, so they sat in silence a few more minutes.

"I'm going to email Allen and see what he thinks. The guy's on parole. You don't really think he would risk going back to jail for violating his parole just to come after me?"

She didn't answer out loud, but in her mind she did. *Yes.*

*

Allen sat at his desk, waiting for a call back from Decker Electronic Monitoring Services. They were on the West coast, so he wouldn't hear back from them until after ten o'clock. After the confrontation with his wife, he really hoped they had something he could use.

He checked his cell phone for missed calls. He had left a message for Chief Harrington as well. The chief better not take until ten o'clock to call back. In the meantime, Allen had assigned Phil Crawford, who was on first shift today, to take over surveillance of Reese's apartment until he could work out a plan with the Chief.

Maybe he would get lucky and it wouldn't even come to that. If he got something from Decker, he'd have Reese in lockup before lunch.

To pass the time, Allen was reading the case files for Margaret Hale, Rachel Pierce, and Alexis Morrison. Again. He figured he didn't have anything else to do, and these were from outside Woodford County, so he wasn't as intimately familiar with them as he was the others. He wasn't expecting to find anything new, but it was better than picking up smoking again. Maybe.

Alexis Morrison was first on the list for no reason other than her case file was on top. He skipped the summary and moved straight to the witness statements. There were no actual witnesses, of course, but the sheriff's deputy had gotten statements from neighbors and other household members. Her parents had been out of the house for the weekend and discovered her body on Sunday afternoon when they got home. The only other member of the household, their niece Drina, claimed to have been home but hadn't heard anything. She had been sleeping down the hall.

There was a side note from the deputy saying the girl claimed to know who the murderer was because she'd dreamed about it. The deputy hadn't recorded anything more about it. Allen picked up the phone and called the Deuel County Sheriff's Office.

"Deuel County Sheriff's Office, Nina speaking. How may I help you?"

"Yeah, Nina. This is Sheriff James from Woodford County. I need to talk to one of your deputies, a Marsha Holt?"

"I'm sorry, Sheriff, but she's not on duty right now. Can I ask what this is in regard to?"

"I'm reviewing a case she worked on a few years ago. We have a similar case up here and I wanted to ask her a couple of questions to see if we can maybe help each other out."

"Well, like I said, she's not on duty this morning, but if you give me the case number and your phone number I'll get a message to her."

"That'd be good." Allen gave her the numbers. "Please have her call me back as soon as possible. It's pretty important."

"I'll pass it on, Sheriff. You have a good day now!"

"Thanks, you too."

He hung up the phone, no further along than before.

"Jesus, I can't catch a break this morning," he muttered to himself.

He was about to check in with Phil when his computer dinged. A new email. Allen pulled it up hoping it was the report from Decker. It wasn't. It was from Ken Simmons and what it said made his blood run cold.

He picked up his cell phone and called Phil.

"Hey, Boss," Phil answered.

Allen skipped the pleasantries. "Any sign of Reese yet?"

"No. He hasn't left for work yet."

"Okay. Keep a close eye out. I have reason to believe he might try to head out of state."

"New information?"

"New something. I got an email from Ken Simmons." Ginnie and Phil were the only people he had talked to about Ken's visions.

"Did he see Reese packing for a trip or something?"

"Worse. Reese saw him and knows who he is now. According to Ken, Reese is planning on heading to West Virginia for payback."

"Jesus. Do you believe him?"

"I believe that he believes it. And since everything else he's seen has been accurate, I think we need to take the threat seriously."

"Okay. I'll call you if I see him leave. I'm assuming he's not planning on going to work today. If he was, he would have left by now."

"Yeah, I agree. He's got other plans for today. Hopefully Decker will give us what we need to bring him and we can all relax a bit."

"What if they don't?"

Allen had been trying not to think about that. "Let's just hope they do. Anyway, one thing at a time."

"Okay, Boss. I'll keep my eyes peeled."

"Thanks, Phil."

Allen hung up. He really didn't know what he was going to do if Decker came back with nothing. Maybe he'd have Watts pick him out of a lineup or something. He doubted that would be enough for an indictment since even the worst lawyer could get that thrown out, but it would get Reese off the street for a few days.

He turned back to his computer. He needed to tell Ken something. He was probably shitting his pants right now. The least he could do was reassure Ken that they wouldn't let Reese get out of the state. If he tried that, they wouldn't have to worry about an ID from Watts. And as long as he kept the surveillance up, Reese couldn't get to either of them.

Six months ago, Allen would have filed Ken's email under "K" for "Krackpot." Hell, two months ago he would have dismissed it as nothing but a bad dream of an overactive imagination. Now he was surprising himself by accepting Ken's message at face value. Shaking his head, he hit send on the reply.

Not for the first time in the last month, Allen craved a cigarette.

*

"Allen says they have Charles Reese under surveillance," Ken said to Sara after reading Allen's reply.

"Why don't they just arrest him?"

She knew why. Even now, all they had was her husband's visions. Her question was more about frustration.

"If he tries to leave the state, they'll know and they'll arrest him then."

"Unless he manages to get away from them before they catch him."

"They're professionals. He won't get away. Besides, even if he did, I'm sure Allen would let us know."

"And then what?"

"We leave. Just like we talked about."

Leave. Go to Jamaica. Then what? They could spend the rest of their lives running from him. If this Charlie guy was half as bad as Cory Rivers from Ken's book, she didn't want to ever meet him. She thought again about how she wished that Ken had never written that book. It was the creepiest thing he had ever written. At first, she hadn't even recognized the writing as his. He had insisted that it was just a result of having gone through his own trauma—a cleansing of his own demons or something. She didn't know whether to feel better or worse to find out that the story had actually come from Charlie Reese.

Then there were the dreams. She hadn't told Ken, but she had been having nightmares about Cory Rivers, too. In her dreams, he was chasing her through the woods, slashing at her with his knife, laughing at her and calling her "Kenny's little cunt." Last night, she had dreamt that he caught her. She had tried to run, but she had been moving in slow motion, like running in a swimming pool. He had just reached out and grabbed her hair and pulled her back into his arms. She had felt his hot breath on her neck as he ripped off her nightgown. Then he had tied her to a bed and stood over her, snarling.

As she'd lain there, naked and tied to a bed in the middle of the woods, he changed. His teeth had become fangs, like a wolf or a bear, and his fingers had turned into claws. What had really terrified her, though, were his eyes. Red, glowing coals set in deep, dark pits. When he looked at her, his eyes seemed to burn into her skin like hot pokers.

She shivered at the memory.

"I think we should pack some clothes and put the suitcases in the car," Ken was saying. "Just in case. That way if we have to get out of here quick we can just go."

"That's why I married you," Sara said, smiling to hide what she was really feeling.

"Because I know how to run away?" He smiled at her, but it was a thin, weak smile that mirrored her own fears.

"No," she said, wrapping her arms around his waist. "Because you're smart." She rested her head on his chest. "Everything's going to be okay, right?" she whispered.

"Yep. Everything will be just fine." His voice didn't sound any more confident than his smile.

They stood in the middle of the kitchen, holding each other for a long time. Finally Ken broke the embrace.

"Come on, we need to pack," he said, and started off for the stairs.

Reluctantly, Sara followed him.

*

Allen was still waiting for Decker to call back at ten o'clock. Chief Harrington had called him back around nine. He had told Allen he would discuss the request with the city finance manager to see if they could swing the overtime. He promised to get back with Allen before the end of the day. So with that half of the equation still up in the air, Allen was juggling his own numbers to see how much he could manage on his own. He was coming to the conclusion that he would have to bring in the County Engineer, the Park District, and the dog catcher to get enough people to cover the surveillance.

The phone rang, interrupting his thoughts. He picked it up with the first ring still echoing off the walls.

"Sheriff James."

"Good morning, Sheriff. This is Neal Ramirez with Decker Electronic Monitoring Services returning your call."

"Hi, Neal. I called regarding an ankle bracelet we overnighted to you on Monday. I need to know the status of the analysis."

"No problem, Sheriff. I can help you with that. Can you give me your Decker Account Number and access code?"

Allen recited them by memory.

"Okay, great. Can I put you on hold while I pull up the information?"

"Sure," Allen said. What was he going to say? No? He tried not to grit his teeth in frustration and failed. The ridiculously cheery hold music just irritated him more. He was sure someone had spent millions of dollars on a study to determine what kind of music should be played while customers were on hold to keep them calm. Whoever had done that study was a fucking moron.

"You still there, Sheriff?"

"Yeah, I'm here." *Where else would I be?* he thought, but didn't add.

"Great. I have the information here. It looks like that unit is still in the process of being analyzed. It says there was a rush put on it and they started looking at it Tuesday afternoon. That's strange. It normally doesn't take more than a day or two to run all the diagnostics and do a physical inspection of the device. Maybe there was a problem. It happens from time to time."

"So when will you know something?" Allen could feel his frustration boiling.

"As I said, Sheriff, it normally only takes a couple of days so I would expect someone to get back with you in the next day or two. If you haven't heard back by Monday afternoon, you can try calling back."

"I'm sorry, Neal, but that isn't going to cut it. I need to talk to someone who actually knows something. Can you transfer me to the guy who's actually doing the analysis?"

"Oh, I really wish I could, but I can't do that. I don't have access to that information and the operations facility is on a different phone system from us. I'm sorry. Is there anything else I can do for you?"

"Apparently not." Allen clenched his teeth to keep himself from unloading on the guy. He knew yelling at the kid wouldn't get him anywhere. He was just some poor schmuck sitting in a call center with a bunch of other drones.

"Okay. Thank you for calling Decker Electronic Monitoring Services. Have a nice day!"

Allen slammed the phone down, unable to hold back his frustration anymore. *By Monday Renee, Ken, and Sara could all be dead and Charles Reese could be in Timbuktu.*

Fuming, he picked up the phone again and called Kim Barrett.

"Good morning, Sheriff. Are you calling me to get a warrant put together for Charles Reese?"

In spite of her concerns about violating Reese's civil liberties, Allen knew she wanted the scumbag off the streets as much as he did.

"Not yet. Decker hasn't gotten back to me with the analysis yet and their support drones can't tell me what the holdup is. I was wondering if you could call the account rep and light a fire under their ass."

"Sure, Allen. I'm on my way to a deposition. Can it wait until this afternoon?"

"I would really appreciate if you could get to it sooner. I have a bad feeling that something's about to blow up. The sooner I can get him behind bars the better."

Kim sighed on the other end of the line. "Okay. I'll see what I can find out."

"If you could just get the account rep to have one of the lab techs that's working on the analysis call me direct, I can handle it from there. They just won't put me through to them."

"Okay. I have to go if I'm going to get this done and still make my deposition."

"Thanks, Kim. I owe you."

"You're damn right you do. A steak supper would be a good start."

Allen smiled as he hung up. If he could get Reese behind bars today, he'd buy her a steak supper every week for the rest of the year.

He sat back and was contemplating an early lunch when his cell phone rang. It was a South Dakota area code, but he didn't recognize the number.

"Sheriff James speaking."

"Hello, Sheriff. This is Deputy Holt from the Deuel County Sheriff's Office returning your call."

He had completely forgotten about her.

"Deputy Holt! Thanks for getting back to me. I just had a couple of questions for you regarding a homicide you worked a few years ago." He pulled open the file for Alexis Morrison's case.

"Well I'm at home right now and all of my notes are on file at the station, but I'll see what I can remember. What case?"

"Alexis Morrison, August 2011."

There was a long pause before Deputy Holt continued.

"I remember that one. It was bad. It was the most fucked-up thing—I'm sorry, the worst crime scene I've ever seen. We never got very far in that one. No witnesses, no real physical evidence. Just that woman torn to pieces. It was like something out of *Saw*."

"Yeah, I know. We've had a few like it in Woodford County. We know of one in Moody County and another in Lake County. I'm pretty sure it's the same guy."

"Wow. I didn't know there were others. A serial killer? Here?" Allen could almost feel a shiver running down her spine through the phone.

"Yeah. That's why I'm hoping you can help me out. I noticed in your report you mentioned a niece that was living with the Morrisons at the time. She was home at the time of the murder?"

"Yeah. She was an odd one. She claimed that she was sleeping, but I don't know how anyone could sleep through what was going on just down the hall."

"This guy is good. We had a victim here where her parents were sleeping down the hall when she was killed. I don't understand it either, but somehow he does it."

"Still seems odd to me. Anyway, we suspected her for a while, but there was nothing tying her to it, except that she was in the house at the time. We never found a murder weapon and there were some bloody boot prints in Alexis' room that were too big for anyone living in the house."

"That's about all we've seen too. This guy's pretty careful about leaving evidence."

"Apparently. Anyway, so the niece, I don't recall her name—"

"Drina is what you wrote in your report."

"Right, Drina. Like I said before, she claimed to have slept through the whole thing, but that she had a dream about the guy. Maybe if she had been a kid, I would have suspected that she had actually seen him and her mind turned it into a dream. Some kind of childhood defense mechanism or something."

"That's what the report says, but you didn't elaborate on it."

"No, because it seemed irrelevant. I know I took notes about what she said, but since it wasn't really evidence, all I put in the report was that she said that she had dreamed about the guy. I could get the details out of my notes the next time I'm at the station if you like."

"That would be great. I have a suspect and it would be interesting to see if her dream matched. Not that we can use it for evidence, but there's some other... Let's just say that if her dream killer matches our guy, I wouldn't be surprised."

"If you say so, Sheriff. One other thing, since you are taking dreams as witness testimony. I remember she said she was going to cast a spell or a curse or something on the guy. I probably have the exact wording in my notes. I remember she looked like some kind of gypsy and talked with a foreign accent. Russian or something."

"A gypsy girl dreams about the killer and then puts a curse on him," Allen said, almost to himself.

"Like I said. Since you're talking *X-Files* stuff anyway."

"Yeah, I know. Maybe I'm just grasping at straws. I'm pretty sure I have the right guy, I just don't have any evidence to bring him in. Anyway, thanks for calling me back. If you could just email me your notes when you get a chance, I would appreciate it."

"No problem, Sheriff. Wish I had more for you."

Allen put his cell phone down, trying to decide if the new information helped.

CHAPTER FOURTEEN

ALLEN HAD JUST gotten back from lunch when his phone rang. "Sheriff James," he answered, hoping Decker was finally getting back to him.

"Hi, Sheriff. This is Brian Grigsby at Decker Electronic Monitoring Services calling you back regarding the ankle monitor you sent us."

"What did you find?" Allen was in no mood for small talk.

"Well, first off, I apologize for how long it took to get back to you, but there were some strange findings. At first, it looked like there hadn't been any tampering. We ran a full diagnostic check on it and didn't find any problems. We checked the data on the monitor and there wasn't any corruption and it matched the logs that were uploaded from the base unit. There weren't any obvious physical signs of tampering, although it had obviously gone through a lot of wear and tear. Does the person who wore it have a physical labor job?"

"He works in a warehouse loading trucks. Why?"

"Most ex-cons end up working in some kind of physical labor so we're used to seeing these with dings and scratches. I don't know how much physical damage loading trucks would cause, but this one was really beat up. But like I said, in spite of that, there didn't seem to be any sign of tampering. At least not at first."

"So you did find something?"

"Maybe. We found what looks like a dog hair or maybe a cat hair in the latching mechanism and it seems unlikely that it would get there except when the unit was put on. Does he have a dog or cat or some other pet?"

"Yeah, he has a cat, but the last time it was put on, we did it at the station. We took it off to inspect it while we questioned him about a case we're working on. Then we reinstalled it before we released him. And there aren't any cats here."

"No one changed it out after that?"

"No."

"Then I would say he somehow managed to get it off and back on without the system detecting it."

"How is that possible? Doesn't it throw an alert immediately when it's removed? Even when we change them out, there's a record of it in the logs."

"That's the way it's supposed to work and I've never seen it not work that way. But even if he did get it off, the lack of body heat would cause it to flag. So unless he took it off and put it right back on, we would still have a record of it and we don't. That's what took us so long. We're trying to figure out how it could possibly be removed without at least one of the two alerts going off. We can't figure any way of doing it. In all of our tests, both alerts went off just like they're supposed to. So our official report has to say we can't find evidence of tampering."

"But you just said there was a cat hair in a place where it could only get there when the monitor was put on."

"Yeah, but without evidence that it was removed or installed by someone other than your technicians, we can't say when that hair got there. Maybe it fell off his clothes when you were putting it on him the last time.

"So that's it? That's all you have?"

"I'm afraid so. Sorry I couldn't give you what you were looking for."

Allen hung up the phone and leaned back in his chair. He closed his eyes and rubbed his temples to try to relieve his stress headache. He had no idea how Reese had managed to get his ankle monitor off without setting off alarms, but he had obviously done it. He had been downtown a week ago past his curfew and his monitor said he had been at home.

"Fuck it," he said to himself. He was going to have to rely on Watts identifying him even though she hadn't recognized him at the time. At least that it was something. He picked up the phone and called Deputy Trout, who was supposed to be watching Reese's apartment right now. He had relieved Crawford at lunchtime. Reese still hadn't left his apartment today. Allen called Trout on his cell phone just in case Reese had a police scanner and was listening in.

"Hey, Sheriff. What's up?"

"Are you still at Reese's apartment?"

"Yeah. No sign of him. His car is still parked in front, but there's no sign of him or the van Watts saw the other night, so if that was his, he could be out in that right now."

"Shit. Hold tight. I'm coming out there with Phil. I'm going to get an arrest warrant."

Allen hung up and called Kim Barrett.

"Allen! People are going to start talking about us if you keep calling."

"Let them talk. Listen, can you whip up an arrest warrant for Charles Reese and email it to me?"

"Sure. Did Decker find something?"

"Nothing they're willing to stand by, but it's enough to confirm my Deputy's report of seeing him downtown." Well, not really, but it was close enough.

"Allen, we have to have real evidence, not just your gut feeling."

"They told me there was a cat hair inside the mechanism. It could only get there when you latch it. The last time we put that one on him was at the station and it wasn't there when our guys looked at it. That means it got there later."

"It would help if your CI would do a lineup."

"Unfortunately, I can't make that happen. Come on, Kim. It's a stupid parole violation. I'm not asking you to give me a warrant for the murders yet."

There was a pause while Kim thought about it. "Okay, Allen, I'll get it for you. But you better be sure about this. It sounds pretty flimsy. I'll have it to you as soon as I can."

"Perfect. I'm heading to his apartment right now."

Allen hung up, then called Phil Crawford to tell him to meet him and Trout at Reese's apartment. He grabbed his jacket and ran out the door.

*

Deputy Stan Trout had only been watching the apartment for a little more than an hour. In that time, he had seen several people come and go, but none the right size and build to be Charles Reese in disguise. He had been studying the picture of Reese he had on his clipboard while watching the apartment, so he was pretty sure that he would recognize him if he came out. So far he had seen no one even close.

Even so, the call from Sheriff James had put him on edge and he found himself checking his mirrors far more frequently than he had before. He wasn't the rookie anymore—that honor belonging to Watts now—but he didn't want the bust to go fubar because of him. He relaxed a few minutes later when a sheriff's cruiser pulled up behind him. He got out of his car and walked back to meet Deputy Crawford.

"Anything?" Crawford asked.

"Nope."

"Sounds like the boss has had enough. I guess we're going to bring him in for parole violation for when Watts saw him downtown last week."

"Sure hope he knows what he's doing. She told me that she couldn't be sure if it had been Reese or not." Stan and Renee were pretty close since they were the two newest deputies in the department.

"She'll be fine. Just because she didn't recognize him at the time doesn't mean she can't pick him out of a lineup."

"Yeah, but she's seen pictures of him. Even Daffy Duck would be able to get that lineup thrown out."

"That's the prosecutor's problem," Phil replied.

"I'm sure Kim Barrett'll have something else to say about that."

"Probably. Sometimes I wonder if she remembers which side of her bread is buttered."

Stan snickered.

"Show time," Phil said, looking down the street past Stan. He turned around and saw the sheriff's car coming from the other direction. Phil got out of his cruiser and the pair hurried across the street and down the block to where the sheriff parked. He was waiting for them in front of Reese's apartment building, checking his phone.

"Everything okay, Boss?" Phil asked.

"Yep. Just got the warrant from the SA."

"Did you tell her what you told me? Sounds like a pretty weak case."

"I told her what she needed to hear. It's not like we rushed it. It took me almost a month to get the damned warrant."

The sheriff looked around behind the deputies. "Is Gerry here yet?" Gerald Danowicz was Charlie's parole officer.

"I haven't seen him," Stan said.

"All right, let's go. I'm not waiting for him. I want to go home early today."

"Guess it's good to be the king." Phil grinned at the Sheriff.

Stan always felt a little awkward when Phil would razz the sheriff. He knew some of the other deputies felt the same. The relationship between Phil and the sheriff was different than for the others, having been friends long before Allen had become sheriff. The sheriff dished it right back at Phil, so he guessed it was okay. He just couldn't imagine saying some of the things Phil said.

The sheriff closed his cruiser door and looked at them.

"I want your guns out when we go in. He may have been passive last time, but I'm guessing this time he's going to know the gig is up. Desperate people do desperate things and I don't want anyone getting hurt. Got it?"

"Got it, Boss," Phil said.

"Yes, sir," Stan replied.

Sheriff James looked at them one more time, then turned toward the apartment. Stan could tell the sheriff was on edge. He just couldn't figure out if he was scared or excited. Maybe a little of both. The boss had supposedly been after this guy for almost ten years. Stan looked at Phil who looked back at him, then they followed a few steps behind the sheriff.

His heart raced as they stepped through the door to the apartment building. The sheriff glanced back at them again before mounting the stairs to the third floor.

Charles Reese lived in Apartment 3D, which was the first apartment on the right as they got to the top of the stairs. The sheriff unsnapped the thumb break on his holster and looked back at Phil and Stan. Taking the cue, Stan and Phil drew their weapons. They both nodded to the sheriff. He nodded back and turned his attention to the door.

"Mr. Reese! Sheriff's Office!" the sheriff shouted, knocking.

They waited, but no one answered.

The sheriff turned to Phil. "Head outside, make sure he isn't climbing out a window or something."

"Got it," Phil replied and bolted down the stairs and out the door.

The sheriff banged on the door louder.

"Sheriff's Office! Open the door, Mr. Reese!"

The door to the apartment across the hall opened and Stan swung around, bringing his gun up. In his sights was an older man in sweatpants and a white T-shirt. When he saw the gun pointed at him, his hands shot up in the air.

"Don't shoot!" he squeaked. "I'm the apartment manager!"

"Do you have the key to this apartment?" the sheriff asked, lowering his weapon. Stan hadn't even seen him swing it up. He lowered his own weapon, keeping it in front of him with both hands ready to bring it back up at the first sign of trouble.

"Of course! I have keys to all the apartments in the building. They're in a lockbox in my closet." He made no effort to move or put his hands down.

"I'm sorry if we scared you, Mister…?"

"Fowler. Doug Fowler."

"Mr. Fowler. You can put your hands down. You're not in any trouble. Can you get the key for Mr. Reese's apartment for us? I'd rather not have to break the door down."

"Of course! Of course! They're in the closet behind this door," he said, lowering his arms, but keeping his hands up. "I need to close the door to get to the closet."

"Okay, that's fine, Mr. Fowler."

Stan watched while the sheriff talked, trying to calm the old man. Another skill Stan needed to improve on. He moved to one side so he could keep an eye on Reese's door while Sheriff James walked across the hall to wait for Mr. Fowler to come back with the key.

"Here it is," he said, opening the door again. "Apartment 3D. Is Mr. Reese in trouble? He's a perfect tenant. Very quiet, never calls with a problem in the middle of the night. He's been here since he was paroled last spring."

"Well, he violated his parole by being downtown after his curfew," the sheriff answered. He smiled and said, "Rules are rules, after all."

"Oh, dear. What happens now? I'll need to lease the place out to someone else. When will his stuff be moved out?"

Stan sensed the sheriff's frustration.

"Sir, that's for another day. Today, we just need to take Mr. Reese into custody. He's responsible for the rent until his lease is up. If he can't or won't pay it while he's in prison, then you will have to follow normal eviction procedures. Right now, I just need the key."

"Oh, I'm sorry. Here you go." The apartment manager handed the key to the sheriff.

"Thank you, sir. Now if you could just go back into your apartment, we'll return the key when we're finished."

"Oh, right, right! You don't need me standing around getting in your way. I'm right across the hall, Apartment 3A. Just knock on the door when you're done. I'll be here. I don't have anywhere to be this afternoon."

"Okay, thank you, sir. Now just move inside for your own protection."

"Okay. Just let me know if you need anything else. I'll be right here." The old man smiled.

"Okay, fine. Thank you again. Now please close the door." The sheriff was beginning to lose his cool, but the apartment manager finally closed the door. Stan suspected he was watching them through the peephole.

Sheriff James turned and looked at Stan with a scowl. Stan had to suppress a laugh.

The sheriff moved to Charles Reese's door and knocked one more time.

"Mr. Reese, we're coming in," he said as he turned the key in the lock.

He moved to the side and looked at Stan. Stan raised his weapon, finger on the trigger, and pointed it at where Reese's center of mass would be if he was standing behind the door.

The sheriff reached over and turned the doorknob. Still looking at Stan, he mouthed, "One, two, three."

On three, he pushed the door open while simultaneously pulling back from the opening. Stan looked down the empty hallway and nodded to the sheriff. He nodded back, then swung around into the entry and started down the hall, checking doorways as he went. Stan followed the sheriff down the hall.

In less than two minutes, they had cleared the apartment and determined that Reese wasn't there.

"Dammit," Sheriff James said to no one in particular. He keyed the mic on his radio and called Phil. "Crawford, you got anything out there?"

"Negative, all clear," came the staticky response.

"Dammit!" the sheriff said again, and then into the mic, "Okay, come on up and help us search the apartment." He turned to Stan. "Trout, are you sure you didn't see him leave this morning?"

"Positive. I even had my binoculars in the car to get a better look at every person who came out of the building this morning. There wasn't anyone who even looked close."

"Fuck!" the sheriff said, slamming a doorframe with the side of his fist. He turned to Phil as he walked in. "What about you? You sure you didn't see him leave?"

"No way that bastard snuck past me, Boss. There were only five people that came out of the building this morning and two of them were women."

"Where the fuck did he go?" the sheriff yelled.

"I don't know," Phil said. "Maybe Phelps saw something?" Deputy Phelps had been watching the apartment when Phil took over this morning.

"Call him. Then call Norris. He was watching the place before Phelps." Sheriff James pounded the side of his fist on the doorframe again. "Who is this guy? Fucking Houdini? Jesus Christ, somebody must have seen something!"

"On it," Phil said, obviously glad to have a reason to step out of the room. He glanced at Stan and grimaced as he left.

Stan had never seen the sheriff this upset about something and wasn't sure how to react. He had seen him pissed before, of course. He would give whoever messed up a verbal lashing, then give one to the rest of the deputies as a reminder that they were a team. If one person messed up, it was on all of them. One time, he had even seen the sheriff yell and throw a radio across the garage. Stan had left his radio on top of his cruiser and driven off. It had fallen off and broken, so when the sheriff had thrown it, he was just finishing the job. It was the second radio Stan had broken in two months. That was the only time the sheriff had yelled at him, and Stan knew he deserved it. He hadn't even balked at having to pay to replace the second radio.

Seeing the sheriff like this actually worried Stan. He looked like he was ready to rip somebody a new asshole, literally. Stan stepped back a few steps into the living room to give him some space, wishing he had a job to do to get him out of the apartment.

He was about to ask if the sheriff wanted him to start canvassing the neighbors when he heard something. It was a soft squeaking noise. He had noticed a terrarium full of white mice when he had come in, but the sound was coming from behind the couch. His first thought was that maybe one of the little bastards had gotten out. Then he heard the sound again and realized it was a cat. He walked over to the couch and peered behind it.

"Hey, Sheriff! You're gonna wanna see this."

"What is it?" the sheriff said, walking over. He knelt on the couch next to Stan and looked over the top. "You gotta be fucking kidding me."

Sitting behind the couch was a white cat with black paws. Wrapped around its midsection was an ankle monitor, its status light glowing bright green.

CHAPTER FIFTEEN

ALLEN SLAMMED THE phone down. Still no answer from Watts. Damn cell phones. Watts wasn't his only deputy without a landline. She just seemed to have more trouble keeping her cell phone charged than the rest. He hoped that was all it was. He had sent Norris to check on her after his first call went to her voicemail. He wanted to go himself, but he needed to get the manhunt started. Norris was a good man. He'd find her and get her to check in.

He had left Crawford and Trout at Reese's apartment to see if they could find any clue to where he might be headed, although Allen was pretty sure he knew the answer to that question already. He knew it wasn't the fault of any of his deputies that Reese had managed to get out without being detected. If anything, it was his fault for not keeping up the surveillance, though he knew that was being overly critical of himself. There had been no way to keep a deputy parked outside Reese's apartment or work twenty-four hours a day indefinitely.

Knowing that didn't make him feel any better.

Allen had been on the phone since he had gotten back to the office. Phil had relayed the reports from Phelps and Norris, though they didn't help much. Norris had arrived at Reese's apartment shortly after eleven o'clock last night and had stayed there until Phelps relieved him around twelve fifteen. In that time, he hadn't seen anyone go in or out of the building. Phelps had stayed until about eight o'clock, when Crawford had relieved him. All he had seen was the newspaper delivery guy and a young woman leaving around six forty-five. Apparently, the rest of the apartment residents didn't have to be at work early. All the reports really told him was that Reese had been on the run since before eleven o'clock last night.

He had issued a BOLO for Reese, but without knowing what he was driving, catching him quickly was unlikely. Hell, they didn't even know for sure when he had left. Allen had tried to get the South Dakota Highway Patrol to put up some roadblocks to see if they could catch Reese trying to sneak out of the state. He had asked them to set up checkpoints on the interstates and major highways, but they only agreed to do it on US-14. They said that shutting down interstate traffic to look for a fugitive wasn't practical and they wouldn't do it unless the Attorney General told them to.

Allen knew there wasn't any point in arguing with the guy. The State Boys stuck by their rules and no backwater county sheriff would get them to change their mind. Kim Barrett could probably convince the Attorney General's office to do it, but by the time the request made it through all the red tape, Reese would be long gone. Even the checkpoint on US-14 was pretty much useless by now, assuming Allen's guess that Reese had been on the run since before eleven o'clock last night was correct. If he was headed to West Virginia, he would probably be at least to Indianapolis by now.

His call to the FBI had been a little more fruitful. He had told them that Reese might be headed to West Virginia to look for Ken Simmons. He hadn't wanted to tell them that Ken had a psychic connection with Reese, so he made up something about Reese being upset that Ken had written about murders that Reese was suspected of perpetrating. It was weak, but it was better than the truth. At least for an official report to the feds.

The guy he'd talked to in the Sioux Falls RA said he would pass the information on to the Pittsburgh Field Office and they would hand it over to the right Resident Agency in West Virginia, but that he should probably contact the local law enforcement agency directly. It would take time for the information to filter through the system.

Before Allen got a chance to call West Virginia, his cell phone rang. Kim Barrett. Shit. With all the chaos, he had forgotten to call her.

"Hey, Kim."

"What the hell happened this afternoon?"

"It's a mess. Reese is gone."

"How in the hell did that happen? He's wearing a goddamn ankle monitor!"

"Yeah, about that. I think we need to find a new vendor for ankle monitors. We found his monitor on his fucking cat."

"What? How did he get it off without setting off an alarm?"

"That's what I've been trying to figure out for the last four weeks! I knew he was doing it, but you wouldn't back me up on it, now he's gone, I can't find Deputy Watts, and he's probably on his way to West Virginia to go after Ken Simmons and his wife."

"Hey, don't blame me. You're the one who didn't have anything on the guy. And what does West Virginia have to do with it? Who is Ken Simmons?"

Allen decided the same white lie he told the FBI was good enough for Kim. At this point, the rest didn't matter anyway. "Ken Simmons is a writer. He wrote a book about a serial killer that's very similar to Charles Reese. Apparently, Reese isn't happy about that. He contacted Simmons last night. He threatened him and his wife. I found out about it this morning, but I've had Reese's apartment under surveillance since last night."

"Jesus, Allen. Why didn't you tell me all of this sooner?"

"Tell you what? That some guy in West Virginia wrote a book and the main character in the book is a lot like Charlie Reese? You would have thrown me out on my ass, and don't give me any bullshit that you wouldn't."

There was a long pause before Kim answered him. "Okay, maybe or maybe not. I guess it doesn't really matter now. The important thing is catching him. What do you need from me?"

Allen told her about his conversations with the Highway Patrol and FBI.

"I need to call the Pocahontas County Sheriff in West Virginia to see if he can put some men on the Simmons' house. If you can get some backup at the state level, maybe we can catch him before he gets there."

"Okay, I'll see what I can do. When this is over, you and I need to have a long talk. This shouldn't have happened. If we're lucky, only one of us will lose our job in November."

Allen hung up. Politics. He had always hated that part of the job. Maybe being voted out of office wouldn't be such a bad thing. He could use a vacation after all of this.

But first things first.

He dialed Gus Norris' cell phone. His hope that Watts had just forgot to charge her cell phone again was dwindling.

*

Ken's hands were trembling so much he dropped his cell phone. It bounced on the carpet and landed underneath his desk, but he didn't notice. He was staring out the big picture window at the early fall sky, but he wasn't seeing any of it. He felt a chill as the blood drained from his face. His hands were numb. His heart seemed to be trying to break out of his chest and the lump in his throat made breathing difficult.

Ever since the last "dream" about Charlie Reese, Ken had been bracing himself for the news that Charlie was coming. Now that he had gotten it, it didn't seem real. It was just another part of the nightmare. Allen had promised that he would keep an eye on Charlie, that Charlie wouldn't be able to make it out of Woodford County, that he and Sara had nothing to worry about.

The email he had just read from Allen proved that to be a lie.

Ken looked up at Sara as she walked into his office.

"Hey, Ken, what do you want to do for—" She stopped as soon as she saw him. "Kenny? Are you okay? You look sick."

Ken only nodded his head. He found he wasn't able to speak yet. He held up a finger while he tried to swallow the lump still stuck in his throat.

"Drink," he finally managed to croak out.

"You want a drink? Water? I think we have some tea."

"Whiskey."

"Oh shit. What's wrong? Did you have another vision?"

Ken shook his head. He went to the bar and grabbed two glasses and filled them with ice from the mini-fridge. He picked up a bottle of Crown Royal, slid it out of its purple sack, and filled one glass almost to the top and the other halfway. He handed the half-full glass to Sara and took the full one for himself. He led her over to the couch and sat down.

"Okay, you have your drink. Now tell me what's going on."

Ken took a long swallow of his drink and looked out the window. He couldn't look at her.

"Charlie Reese is missing," he finally managed.

Sara's jaw dropped and her eyes widened. "What do you mean missing?"

"Allen went to arrest him this afternoon and he wasn't in his apartment. They know he was at work yesterday and they've been watching his place since last night so they think he left sometime before that."

"Is he coming here?" The pitch of her voice had gone up a step or two.

"They don't know, but I think based on my last encounter with him, that would be a safe assumption."

"Ken! What are we going to do?"

"I think we do just like we talked about this morning. We're already packed. Let's just grab a few last-minute items and go."

"Go where? If he's able to track us here, won't he be able to track us anywhere we go?"

"Probably, but that's why I suggested Jamaica. He might figure out where we went, but there's no way he'll be able to get on a plane to follow us there." Unless he had a good source for fake passports, Ken didn't add.

"Well, if we're going to Jamaica, I need to pack a few more things," Sara said.

"Me too. Let's finish our drinks, then I'll make the reservations while you finish packing. And don't let me forget to get our passports out of the safe."

Sara looked at him and tried to smile, but instead burst into tears. He pulled her close and held her in his arms. His own emotions tumbled and swirled around. He had never been to Jamaica, and this wasn't the ideal reason, but he was determined to keep Sara safe and this was the best he could come up with.

He squeezed her tighter. He wasn't going to let that animal get near her. He promised.

*

Allen had just gotten off the phone with the Pocahontas County Sheriff when Gus Norris finally returned his call. His conversation with his counterpart in West Virginia had been cordial, but Allen wasn't sure the sheriff was taking his concerns seriously. He did promise to send a patrol to the Simmons' house to do a welfare check, which might be enough if Ken followed through with his plan to head out of town.

"Hey, Gus," Allen said, answering his cell phone. "Did you find her?"

"Hey, Boss," Gus replied. There was a long pause. Allen was about to check to see if the call had been dropped when Gus continued. "I found her. He got her, Boss. The son of a bitch must have broken into her apartment last night. The bedroom window was jimmied."

Allen couldn't answer right away. When he did, his voice was quiet and hoarse. "Are you sure it's her?" What a useless fucking question that was.

"Yeah, I'm sure. Jesus, Boss. He butchered her! Just like the Winston girl. The son of a bitch tore her to pieces!"

Allen didn't know what to say. Neither of them spoke. Finally, Allen found his voice again. He tried to put aside his emotions and focus on the mechanics of what needed to happen.

"Okay, Gus. Here's what we need to do. You need to call the ME. Then call Phil. Have him lead. I've already got a BOLO out on Reese. I'm going to update it with the latest information, then I'll be over. I know you're not officially on duty, but wait there until I get there."

"Okay, Boss."

Allen hung up and hung his head, rubbing his eyes with one hand.

Renee was as much his daughter as Amber. She would always be that grinning, freckle-faced kid with pigtails wanting to ride next to him in the front seat of his cruiser. He'd helped Kelly raise her. She always wanted "Uncle Al" to take her swimming in the creek or hunting squirrels with a .22. He had been there for her first fish, her first deer, and her first date. He had imagined fighting with her dad over who would get the first dance with her at her wedding. He would be grampa to her kids as much as Kelly.

And what the hell was he going to tell Kelly? That some monster mutilated his daughter because Allen hadn't been able to get him off the streets? Kelly was going to be devastated. After he'd lost his wife to breast cancer, Renee had been his whole world. Allen had promised Kelly that he would keep her safe.

What kind of sheriff can't even protect his own deputies? It wasn't like they didn't know who the guy was. They'd been watching him, for Christ sake.

"Fuck!" he yelled, picking up his coffee cup and throwing it across the room. The ceramic mug shattered against the wall. Shards of glass exploded everywhere.

One thing was for sure. Charles Reese wasn't going to get away with this one. Allen swore he would chase that piece of shit to the ends of the Earth if he had to. In this case, the ends of the Earth meant West Virginia. Allen was positive Reese's next stop was a house in the mountains just outside of Murphy Creek. And he was going to make sure it was Reese's *last* stop.

Allen stared out the window at the gray sky, his jaw clenched as tight as his fists.

"You're dead, motherfucker," he whispered.

He needed to call Ginnie and let her know. She'd been right. The damn cat had been in front of him the whole time and he hadn't been able to see it. Even the kid in IT had been more concerned about it than he had.

His eyes burned with grief and anger. He may as well have killed Watts himself. His own incompetence had killed her. All he could do now was hope it didn't kill Ken and his wife too.

Ginnie wouldn't be happy about the sudden trip to West Virginia. He hoped she would understand. She had known the Watts family almost as long as Allen. She hadn't been as close to Renee, but surely she would be just as upset. She would know why he had to go.

Allen picked up his phone to call home, then put it down. Better to go home and talk to her in person.

*

Sara had finished packing their last minute items: toiletries, bathing suits and beach towels, and sandals. In a smaller bag, she'd packed two sets of clothes for each of them. She was a somewhat experienced traveler and knew packing a couple of days' worth of clothes in a carry-on bag was a good idea when traveling by plane, especially when flying internationally.

She had also made a list of things they would need to pick up on the way to the airport. Sunblock wasn't something they used much in the mountains. And she didn't know how easy it would be to get things like Tums and Tylenol in another country.

She was just finishing up when Ken came in.

"I'm almost ready," she told him as he walked through the door.

"Take your time. The latest flight leaving today is at eight o'clock." With the four-hour drive to Pittsburgh, they wouldn't be able to make that flight. "I have us booked for a six a.m. flight tomorrow morning. This time tomorrow, we'll be sitting on a beach in the Caribbean enjoying complimentary cocktails."

Ken put his arms around her. She was glad for the comfort.

"What about tonight?" she asked.

"I reserved a room at the Hyatt at the airport. We can take our time, get a good night's sleep some place where he won't be looking for us, and in the morning, we'll be right there. Everything will be okay."

Sara buried her face in Ken's chest and squeezed him. They stood together, holding each other. Ken was trembling slightly. She liked to think of herself as a brave woman. The fear and panic she was hiding from Ken was not something she was used to. Knowing that she wasn't alone in her fear made her feel better. Although she might not be able to take on a psychotic serial killer by herself in hand-to-hand combat, she wasn't some delicate flower that would wilt in the heat of the moment. She felt that Ken would need her help before this ordeal was over, so she told herself to buck up and be strong.

And even though she wasn't a mother to children, she knew she would protect her man like a mamma bear protecting her cubs.

Sara grudgingly pulled away from Ken. She looked up at him and tried to smile. He was trying to smile back. What he managed was an awkward smirk. She imagined her own attempt didn't look much better. Ken stopped trying and just bent his head to hers and kissed her.

"I love you," he whispered to her. "And I'm sorry."

"It's not your fault," she whispered back. "And I love you too. Now, don't forget the passports."

Now Ken did smile at her, and she was able to smile back. She gave him a pat on the butt and said, "Come on, Mr. Simmons. Let's get moving. We have a plane to catch."

Still smiling, Ken walked to the closet and opened the small safe they used for their important papers. The cold grip on her heart eased a little. In spite of the situation, a small seed of excitement began to take root. She started to think that maybe Ken was right. Maybe everything would be okay.

CHAPTER SIXTEEN

MITCH ARMSTRONG ARRIVED at the Simmons' house around six thirty. Rounding the last turn, Mitch drove into the clearing where the old lodge watched over the valley that surrounded it on three sides. He had never seen it in the daylight.

He had seen it once in the dark when he was a kid. Back then, Old Man Rawley still owned the place and there had been rumors among the kids about how he had set up booby-traps all around the property to keep the locals from hunting on his land. There were other rumors about him too. One of the stories they'd passed around as kids was if Old Man Rawley caught you trespassing he would kill you, then he would gut you and hang you in his barn like a deer. Mitch had never truly believed that story, but he hadn't wanted to chance it either. So other than the one time when he'd been ten and had snuck up in the middle of the night on a dare, he had stayed away. Seeing it now, he had trouble imagining the stories they had scared each other with as kids. He suspected most of the rumors were started because Elmo Rawley never went into town. He had employees run his errands for him, so only a couple of people in Murphy Creek had ever met him.

The sheriff had asked Mitch personally to come up to check on Mr. and Mrs. Simmons. He didn't really know much, just that there had been a credible tip about a threat to them. The sheriff had told him that apparently some guy from North Dakota or South Dakota or something was pissed about something Mr. Simmons had written. The sheriff out there was concerned that the whack job was going to drive all the way to West Virginia to show Mr. Simmons how he felt about it. The whole thing sounded kind of crazy to Mitch. Apparently, the sheriff wasn't taking it too seriously either because he had sent Mitch to help out with a traffic accident over on Route 92 before checking in on them.

Mitch didn't see any lights on in the house, but it wasn't quite dark yet. There were two cars in front of the house, so they must be home. He knew the Armada was Mrs. Simmons'. The Ford Taurus must belong to Mr. Simmons. That seemed odd to Mitch. Living in the mountains, he would have expected him to have a four-wheel drive like his wife. Maybe they figured one four-wheel drive vehicle was enough. The Taurus would certainly be better on gas than the Armada.

Mitch parked his cruiser next to the Taurus and looked around before getting out. He couldn't see the right side of the house from the car. On the left side was a huge deck with chairs and a table, but no people. In the front, a covered porch ran the width of the house. The entrance was a pair of large wooden doors with metal straps made to look like an old barn door. The porch light next to the doors was off, though Mitch didn't imagine they would bother turning it on unless they were expecting company. They certainly weren't expecting a visit from the Sheriff's Office.

He keyed the microphone on his radio. "Dispatch, thirty-one, ten twenty-three at One Rawley Drive."

"Roger, unit thirty-one. Show you ten twenty-three, One Rawley Drive."

He got out of his cruiser and stretched, taking in the view. The sun was just setting, intensifying the reds and oranges of the fall leaves on the trees on the hilltops, though the valley that wound around the point was already gray. The orange sunlight gave the lawn and house an eerie red glow, almost the color of blood. Mitch shivered and pulled up the zipper on his jacket. The air was cool, but it was the odd light playing on his already rattled nerves that caused the chill.

He hoped Mrs. Simmons had some coffee brewing. Probably not. Most people don't brew coffee after dinner. Since becoming a cop, Mitch drank it pretty much any time he was awake.

A barred owl hooted from a tree nearby, causing Mitch to jump a little. He laughed at himself, then looked back at the house. He still didn't see any lights. He supposed they could be watching television. A lot of people like to watch television with the lights off. Or maybe they were in a room on the other side of the house. Being the backwoods of West Virginia, Mitch knew better than to just go wandering around the property without announcing himself to the homeowner. That was a good way to get dead.

The driveway continued on to the right to a stand-alone garage. That must be the barn he had heard about as a kid. It was big enough for four or five cars. Mitch guessed they didn't use it so they didn't have to walk so far to get their cars. It was fifty or sixty yards from the house. A floodlight had been installed over the garage door and another light next to the walk-in door. Neither one were on.

Mitch stood still for a minute and listened. Other than an occasional crow, the birds had stopped singing for the day. This time of year, even the crickets had weren't chirping in the evenings. His cruiser's engine ticked as it cooled. The Taurus' engine was ticking too. Mr. Simmons must have just gotten home. Everything else was quiet.

The barred owl called out making Mitch jump again.

"Dammit," Mitch said to himself. "It's just a stupid owl. Relax."

He walked around the Taurus and the Armada and headed to the front door.

*

"Shit. I forgot my phone."

Ken and Sara had been driving for about an hour and a half and were now on the Staunton-Parkersburg Turnpike. It was still called a turnpike, even though the state stopped collecting tolls over a hundred years ago. Ken barely noticed the normally scenic drive through historic portions of West Virginia. Less than half an hour ago, the trees had been bursting with flaming color in the light of the setting sun. Now everything was turning gray in the fading twilight.

"We're not turning around to go get it," Sara said from the passenger seat.

"No, but I forgot to send Allen an email to tell him we were headed out of the country. I was thinking I would have to remember to send it when we got to the hotel, which is when I realized I didn't have my phone."

Sara pulled her phone out of her purse.

"I have some signal. I'll call him. I don't suppose you remember his phone number?"

Ken harrumphed. He had never been good at remembering phone numbers. Sara's cell phone number was the only number he remembered, and that was just because she still had the same number she'd had when they first met. He didn't even remember his own number. He relied completely on his phone's contacts feature.

"Never mind," Sara said. "I'll just call the Sheriff's Office. He'll probably be home for the evening, but maybe I can leave a message for him."

Sara got the number for the Woodford County Sheriff's Office from information. As they suspected, no one answered. She left a message on the voicemail for Allen to call her, along with her cell phone number.

They drove in silence for a while, the only sound coming from the quiet hum of the SUV's tires. Once they had gotten onto Route 28, they had started to relax. Even if Charlie Reese figured out where they were headed, they knew he couldn't follow. The problem was going to be when they had to come home. They could only stay in Jamaica for six months. He supposed that if Charlie hadn't been caught by then, they could go to Bonaire or Aruba for another six months. Either that or get some other kind of visa that allowed them to stay longer.

The real problem would be—

"What if they never catch him?" Sara asked what Ken was thinking.

"I don't know." Ken wished he could give her a better answer, reassure his wife that everything would work out and life would go back to normal.

They had to catch Charlie eventually, didn't they?

"Jamaica sounds fun and all, but I don't want to spend the rest of my life running from this psycho."

"Me either," Ken replied.

Ken turned on the headlights and lost himself in thought.

What if Charlie never was caught?

*

Mitch rang the doorbell again. Still no answer. After a minute, he tried knocking. When his fist hit the door, it swung open.

He peered into the dark hallway beyond the door. He didn't see any lights.

"Hello?" he called. "Mr. and Mrs. Simmons? It's Mitch Armstrong, Pocahontas County Sheriff's Office. Are you home?"

There was no response. He listened, straining his ears. He expected to hear a television or something, but the only sound was the ticking of a clock drifting out of the darkness. He pulled his Maglite out of his duty belt and switched it on, shining it down the hallway.

The hallway ran down the right side of the house with doors on the left and stairs leading to the second floor on the right. At the end of the hallway was another door. The glass from picture frames on the wall reflected the light from his flashlight. Just inside the door was a small table with a box holding mail. On the wall to the right of the door, a couple of jackets hung from hooks. The hardwood floor had a rug that ran most of the length of the hallway.

Runners, he remembered his mother called them.

The air was still; just the clock ticking somewhere down the hall.

"Hello?" he called again. "Is anyone home?"

Mitch was getting a bad feeling. He knew that the front door being open didn't necessarily mean anything. A lot of folks in the country didn't bother to lock their doors when they were home.

The problem was the Simmonses weren't from the country. They were from the city and city folk don't think like country folk. People from the city locked their doors out of habit, even when they were home. And if they weren't home, they would never leave the door unlocked.

Something was wrong.

He drew his weapon, checking to make sure the safety was off.

He thought about calling for backup, but decided not to. What did he have, really? A creepy feeling? He could see that one back at the station.

"All available units, rookie is scared, requesting backup."

He would hear about that the rest of his life.

"Hey, Armstrong! How's that creepy feeling coming?"

He pushed the thoughts aside and stepped into the hallway, panning his flashlight left and right.

"Relax," he said to himself. "Probably just out for a walk. Nothing to be worked up about."

He stepped over to the right side of the hallway and shined his light up the stairs. He held his breath and listened. Nothing.

"Sheriff's Office! Is there anyone up there?" he called. There was no answer. He moved back to the left side of the hall and pointed his gun and flashlight toward the other end. No one was there. Slowly, he started down the hall.

"Mr. Simmons? Mrs. Simmons? Are you home?"

Tick. Tick. Tick.

He reached the first doorway and shined the flashlight into the room. It was a sitting room with a large fireplace on one wall. It looked like it might have been the main room back when the house was Elmo Rawley's hunting lodge. He imagined the walls covered in hunting trophies: deer heads, pheasant and ducks, wild turkey, maybe even a bear skin rug in front of the fireplace. There was none of that now. It was a simple sitting room with a couch and some chairs and a bookcase on one wall.

Mitch found the light switch and flipped it on.

Nothing happened.

He flicked it a couple of times just to be sure. Still no light. Maybe it wasn't hooked up to anything. His stomach was full of butterflies and tight with tension. He stepped into the room, sweeping the flashlight left and right making sure no one was hurt and lying on the ground behind the couch or one of the tables. His uneasiness grew with each step.

Mitch's bad feeling smacked him in the back of the head. As he fell, he thought, *You really do see stars*. He had dropped his gun. He tried to reach for it. It was just beyond his grasp. His head was spinning. He managed to roll over on his back. His vision dimmed.

Just before his sight failed completely his mind registered a man standing over him with some kind of metal pipe or aluminum baseball bat. The last thought of his life was *That's the creepiest grin I've ever seen.*

*

Allen drove south on I-79, pushing the rental car as fast has he dared. He didn't care about a speeding ticket, but the delay a traffic stop would add to the drive would more than eat up any time gained by going faster. At least there wasn't much traffic at midnight. Still, the miles clicked by painfully slow.

He knew Reese had to be in West Virginia already. He hadn't heard from Ken yet and that heightened his concern. Ken was usually quick to return his messages. Now, several hours after sending the email telling Ken he was on his way, no response had him thinking the worst.

Allen's anger had subsided somewhat, but not his resolve. He had been traveling for almost six hours, between driving, flying, then driving again. It had given him a chance to process the situation, which was a good thing. If he confronted Reese without a plan, he could end up like Renee. He hoped to surprise Reese. He shouldn't expect Allen to chase him down from South Dakota.

He was trying not to think about Ginnie. She had been far more upset about his trip to West Virginia than he'd expected. When he told her about Renee Watts, she had collapsed onto the couch. As she'd started to recover, she'd realized he planned on going after Reese. That was when she really freaked out. Probably the only thing keeping her from packing up and moving out while he was gone was his promise to retire at the end of his current term in January.

Which was another thing he was trying not to think about. As much as he had enjoyed the job over the years, the whole Charles Reese case had taken everything from him. He was tired. Even if Ginnie hadn't said anything, he was pretty sure he would have come to the same conclusion. Maybe not until after he got Reese, but the result would be the same. He wasn't going to run again. He'd just have to find somebody to run in his place so that weasel Rudy Gibson didn't get it unopposed.

That wasn't her biggest issue though. Her main concern was his safety. By killing Watts, Reese had shown he didn't care who he killed anymore. Allen had promised Ginnie he would be careful. Allen wasn't concerned about that so much as he was about finding Reese. Once he found him, he should be able to deal with him. As long as he kept his cool and didn't take any unnecessary chances. Most importantly, stay professional. He couldn't let his anger control his actions.

What he really wanted to do was shoot Reese in the kneecaps so he couldn't run, then shoot him in the gut so he would die a slow, painful death. What he had to do as an officer of the law was try to arrest him and haul him back to South Dakota. Either option was better than what Kelly Watts would do to Reese if he had the chance.

Allen's jaw still hurt from that conversation. At first, Kelly had just slumped to the floor and wouldn't say anything. Then he had yelled at Allen for letting Reese get to his little girl, eventually taking a swing at him. Finally, he had collapsed into Allen's arms and cried.

"If you don't kill that sonofabitch, I will," Kelly had promised. "When I get through with him, his own mother won't recognize him."

Allen took some solace in knowing that back home, Reese would get the needle. South Dakota had executed less than twenty people in its entire history. He had no doubt that Charles Reese would join that exclusive club.

*

Ken lay in the bed staring at the ceiling of the dark hotel room. Occasionally, a small green light would flash indicating the smoke detector was working. He had spent most of the last hour trying to count the flashes. He had lost count around two hundred and fifty. He had hoped to fall asleep long before reaching one hundred.

They were safe in Pittsburgh. In a few hours, they would get up and drive to the airport's long-term parking lot, then catch the shuttle to the airport. He figured that would take about thirty minutes total, so he wanted to leave the hotel room at four thirty to make sure they had plenty of time to catch their six o'clock flight.

That meant that if he fell asleep right now, he would get three hours of sleep.

He envied Sara, who was breathing softly next to him. She never seemed to have trouble sleeping. He supposed it was a gift. She could fall asleep within minutes of lying down. Even more annoying, she could sleep almost anywhere. He remembered a time when she had fallen asleep in the lobby of a radio station while he had been down the hall giving an early morning interview. And now they were being chased by a maniac who wanted to kill them both, and she was sleeping like a baby.

Ken had just decided to go get a drink of water when it hit him. It was a crawling sensation that started on the back of his neck and moved up his scalp until his whole head felt like it was being invaded by ants. His heart quickened and his breathing shallowed. He knew what was happening but he was powerless to stop it.

Cory's voice filled his head. *"Where are you, you little fuck?"*

Ken's stomach tightened. He tried to block out the voice in his head. He didn't want to listen.

"Trying to run away? You fucking pussy. You suck my brain and make millions of dollars, but when the shoe's on the other foot, you run away like a little fucking pussy."

Ken felt more than heard Cory's laugh. A cold sweat covered his skin.

"You go ahead and run, you little bitch. That cocksucking sheriff pal of yours is coming. I'll take him out instead. Just like I did the fucking pig deputy that came to check on you and your pretty little cunt of a wife. Then when I'm done with him, I'll just go through your house to see who else you might care about and go after them next. What do you think, Fuckface? Maybe even go back to South Dakota to finish off your pal's family. Is he married, Kenny? Does he have kids?"

Ken squeezed his eyes shut and pressed his hands to his face, trying to get Cory's voice out of his head.

No, Charlie's voice.

"Ginnie Shitforbrains and two shitforbrains nuggets? I'll do them all together. I'll make her watch while I cut her snot slingers. Is that what you want me to do, fucker?"

Ken shook his head, bit his lip, pounded his fists on his temples. Nothing worked. Charlie was in control.

"You take care now, asshole. I'm going to have fun with or without you."

The crawling feeling faded away and Ken was finally able to catch his breath. The sweat dripped off his face onto the pillow, his heart pounded in his throat.

Charlie was at his house. He had killed a cop and was waiting on Allen to kill him too.

Then Ken thought about his mother, living alone since his father died a few years ago. And Sara's parents, still living outside of Pittsburgh. Charlie was going to go after them. And then Allen's wife and kids.

Unless Ken went back.

He lay in the bed shaking, his arms tight around his chest. He looked at Sara sleeping beside him. More than anything, he wanted to get on the plane tomorrow and fly away. He didn't even care where, just somewhere that Charlie couldn't get to them. He had promised he wouldn't let anything happen to her, but how could he ever look at her in the face again if he let Charlie kill her parents? She would never forgive him and he would lose her anyway.

And where would far enough be that Charlie couldn't reach his mind? Maybe even kill Sara while he controlled Ken's body?

Ken knew what he had to do. He eased himself out of bed, making sure not to disturb Sara. He dressed in the bathroom, then crept back into the main room. Ken looked at Sara one last time.

This time tomorrow, he would probably be dead.

CHAPTER SEVENTEEN

SARA OPENED HER eyes, slowly comprehending the ringing in her head wasn't a dream. At first, she thought it was the fire alarm. A moment of panic passed through her, then she recognized the sound she was the hotel phone ringing on the nightstand. She remembered Ken had asked for a four o'clock wake-up call.

"Ken, answer it already," she said without rolling over.

The phone kept ringing.

Sara tried to elbow Ken to wake him up. He was too far away, so she tried to reach behind her to grab him and shake him awake. Her hand found nothing, so she grudgingly rolled over.

He wasn't there.

The phone kept ringing.

"Dammit, Kenny," she said louder. It was just like him to get up early to go poop and leave the alarm for her to deal with. She scooted to the other side of the bed and answered the phone.

"Hello."

"Good morning. This is your wake-up call. Thank you for staying with us at the Hyatt Regency, Pittsburgh International Airport."

"Anytime," she mumbled as she hung up the phone, then louder, "It's for you, Ken."

Sara stretched, but stayed in bed. There was no point in getting up until Ken was done in the bathroom. She picked up her cell phone off the nightstand and opened up Facebook to see what nonsense her friends had posted overnight. After several minutes she called to Ken again.

"If you don't hurry up in there, we'll miss our flight."

She waited for him to give her some smart-aleck reply. There was no response. She sat up, the seeds of worry beginning to grow in her chest.

"Ken?"

Still no answer. Sara got out of bed and walked around the partition wall to the bathroom. There was no light coming from under the door.

"Ken?"

Now the worry weed growing in her was sprouting panic flowers. She turned on the light and rushed back to the main section of the hotel room, checking to see if Ken had rolled out of bed and hit his head on the nightstand.

He was nowhere to be found.

"Calm down," she said aloud. "He's probably down getting coffee. Maybe he couldn't sleep and got up early."

She checked the side of the bureau where they had left their shoes. Ken's were gone. Okay, so he had gotten up, gotten dressed, and gone for coffee. That was all. No need to go all panicky.

Sara grabbed her clothes and tried to dress as quickly as she could, fumbling the whole time—both legs into one leg hole of her underwear, shirt on inside out, socks catching on her little toe as she tried to pull them on. Then, just because Murphy wrote the damn law for a reason, she got a knot in her shoelace.

Finally dressed she raced to the desk to get the keycard for the room. What she found was a folded piece of paper with her name on it, written in Ken's handwriting. She stared at it, not able to bring herself to pick it up. She forced herself to reach out and grasp the note. Her hands shaking, she opened it.

Sara, it started. Her trembling made it difficult for her to read. *Know first that I love you. I love you more than anything in the world. Above all, I want you to be safe. So whatever you do, don't follow me.*

She wiped the tears from her eyes trying to read the rest.

I had another visit from Charlie. He's killed a cop. He knows where we're going. If I don't go back, he's planning on killing everyone I care about, including my mom and your parents. Probably Allen and his family too. I don't have a choice. I have to go. You can take the shuttle to the airport and fly to Jamaica like we planned. I'll get in touch with you when it's all over. Please, Sara. Do this for me. I couldn't bear to lose you. You are my world. The thought of things this monster would do to you... Well, you read the book. Stay safe. Love you forever. Ken.

Sara sat down on the bed, the note still in her hand. Looking at herself in the mirror she saw a woman destroyed. Her reason for living had left her alone.

When Sara had been eight years old, she'd wanted to make a cake for her daddy. She made a huge mess in the kitchen and burned the cake so bad that black smoke had poured from the oven. Her father had fallen asleep in his recliner reading the newspaper. The smoke had woken him up when it escaped the kitchen for the living room. Sara had been trying to fan away the smoke with a paper plate when he came running in. She remembered him pulling the burning cake out of the oven and throwing it out the back door. Then he had yelled at her and sent her to her room. She had been crushed.

And now she felt the same sense of betrayal and loss.

Only this time she wasn't eight.

*

As Ken made the final turn and his house came into view, his headlights lit up a black SUV with a six-pointed gold star on the door. On the other side of the truck was a man pointing a gun at him.

Ken slammed on the brakes. The man was yelling something, but he couldn't hear. He thought about putting the car in reverse and punching the gas, but decided that would result in either a bullet in the face—again—or driving off a cliff. He opted instead to put it in park and get out.

"Put your hands in the air!" the man yelled as Ken stepped out.

"Who are you?" Ken yelled back.

"Pocahontas Sheriff's Office! Now get your hands in the air or I will shoot!"

Ken complied.

"Slowly, walk around the door and turn around."

Ken did as he was told.

"Now walk backward towards me. Slowly. Now lay on the ground."

Lie *on the ground, not* lay, Ken thought stupidly, his mind racing in circles.

After he was lying on the ground, hands on his head, legs spread, he heard the deputy come around his car and stand near him, but not too close.

"You move a muscle I will shoot you right there!" the deputy screamed.

"Okay, I won't move," Ken answered. "Can you at least tell me what this is about?"

"Shut up! And don't move!" The deputy sounded as scared as Ken. Ken heard a siren in the distance. Backup, presumably.

"I live here," Ken tried again. "Will you at least tell me what's going on?"

"I said be quiet! I will shoot you if I have to! Don't make me shoot you!"

Ken sighed. The siren was getting closer. It wouldn't be too much longer before the kid's backup arrived. Then maybe he could get this straightened out.

In fact, it took ten minutes for the police cruiser to make it up the rough gravel road in the dark. By the time it pulled into the yard, Ken was cold, wet, and sore from lying on the ground. He needed to stretch, but he was afraid Twitchy McGee might blow his head off if he did.

Ken's face was turned away, so he couldn't see the new officer approach, but he heard him.

"You don't even have him cuffed yet?" the new officer asked in obvious surprise.

"Shit, Blake, you saw Armstrong! I wasn't about to get close to him without somebody else here!"

Ken wondered if they meant Mitch Armstrong. Charlie had killed a cop. He hoped it wasn't Mitch.

"You fucking pussy," the other cop—Blake—said. Ken heard him walk up.

"Sir, I'm going to put handcuffs on you for our protection. Understand you are not under arrest at this time. Do you understand?"

"Yes," Ken responded, his voice muffled because his mouth was pressed up against his shoulder. He felt the handcuffs being slapped on to his wrist. The cop pulled his arm down and behind his back, then the other arm. He cuffed Ken's other wrist, then rolled him over on his back.

"Okay, I'm going to help you up now. Don't try to run. You won't get very far."

"I live here," Ken replied. "Why would I run?"

"Are you Ken Simmons?" Blake asked him.

"Yeah. My wallet is in my back pocket."

The cop helped Ken to his feet, then pulled out Ken's wallet. Finding Ken's driver's license, he looked at the picture with his flashlight, then shined the light in Ken's face to compare. He set the wallet on the hood of the other cop's SUV.

"Mr. Simmons, you are wanted for questioning regarding the death of Deputy Mitchell Armstrong. I'm going to take you back to the station where a detective will talk to you."

"Am I under arrest now?" Ken had talked to enough cops over the years doing research to know they couldn't force him to go without arresting him.

The two deputies exchanged looks.

"Not at this time, sir, but we would really appreciate your cooperation." Blake was doing all the talking. Ken noticed the first deputy still had his gun pointed at him.

"Okay, look, first of all, can you stop pointing that gun at me? I'm handcuffed. If I ran, how far would I get running around the woods in the dark on a mountain with my hands behind my back? Second, I've had a very long night, so if I'm not under arrest, how about you just let me go inside and get a couple of hours of sleep, then I'll come out in the morning? Your detective is probably home asleep anyway, right?"

"I'm sorry, sir, but your house is a crime scene. You can't go in."

"Well I'm not doing anything until I get some sleep. I've been up all night."

"If you've been up all night you probably shouldn't be driving. If you come back with me, you can sleep a couple of hours on a cot at the station until the detective comes in."

Ken could see the deputy wasn't going to give up and since his cruiser was blocking Ken's truck, he was pretty much stuck here until the deputy felt like letting him go.

"Okay, fine, but before we go I want to know what happened at my house. You said that Mitch had been killed. Was he killed here?"

The deputies looked at each other again.

"I'm sorry sir, I can't discuss that with you," the one named Blake responded.

Ken let out a sigh of exasperation. "Fine, let's go to your station and talk to the detective."

Blake led Ken to his cruiser and helped him into the back seat. After moving Ken's truck, he pulled the cruiser around and headed back down the driveway, leaving Deputy Twitchy to continue watching the house.

*

Ken waited in the interrogation room drinking a cup of vending machine coffee. He was contemplating how things had gotten so out of control.

Two and a half years ago he had just been a writer. A successful writer, but just a writer. He had a nice home, a wife who loved him as much as he loved her, and while they hadn't managed to start the family they had talked about when they were younger, life was good. They were happy.

Now he was sitting in a police station, the prime suspect in the murder of a county sheriff's deputy—a kid he happened to know, no less—with a psychotic maniac trying to kill him and possibly his wife. And all of this after spending a year recovering from being shot in the face by a different psychotic maniac.

Ken leaned back in his chair and rubbed his eyes. He was tired from only two hours of sleep, but his exhaustion ran much deeper. He had hardly had a good night's sleep in weeks. Every time his head hit the pillow, he expected to have another encounter with Charlie. Sometimes he would lie awake waiting for it. With the news that Charlie was here, he was surprised he had slept even two hours. Ken had welcomed the coffee offered by the deputy who had brought him to the interrogation room, even if it was just from a vending machine. The cup didn't even have a very good poker hand on it—two pair with aces and eights.

Ken looked up when the door opened. A man wearing dress pants and shirt with a tie and a badge clipped to his belt walked in.

"Good morning, Mr. Simmons," he said, extending his hand. "I'm Detective Chester Parker. You can call me Chet."

"Good morning, Chet," Ken replied, taking the detective's hand.

"I apologize for the inconvenience. I heard you slept on the couch in the break room. I've slept on that couch myself. I know how uncomfortable it is."

"It's fine," Ken said. He just wanted to get this over with so he could get back to dealing with Charlie. He was out there somewhere, waiting for Ken.

"Okay, let's get started." Detective Parker set his coffee cup and folder on the table and pulled up a chair. He opened the folder so Ken could see the pictures inside. They were of a man hanging by his wrists from the rafters of a barn.

The man was naked and had been mutilated beyond recognition. On closer inspection, Ken recognized the barn was actually his garage. The man, he assumed, was Mitch Armstrong, but Ken wouldn't have been able to recognize the mangled body in the photo if it had been his own wife. He turned away from the grisly image and looked at the detective.

"Mitch?" Ken managed to say past the lump in his throat.

The detective nodded. "Did you know him, Mr. Simmons?"

Ken nodded back, but couldn't say anything.

"How well did you know him?"

Ken took a sip of coffee to wet his mouth.

"Not well. I've talked to him a few times over the years. In a small town like Murphy Creek, you tend to talk to everybody from time to time. I haven't seen him in a while, though."

"How long?"

Ken thought about it for a minute.

"I ran into him at the Fall Festival last month. My wife had talked me into riding the Ferris wheel and I ended up getting sick. I threw up on some guy and his girlfriend. They were pretty pissed about it. I think they guy was about to clock me when Mitch walked up. He managed to calm the guy and his girlfriend down. I guess he was working security or something because he was in uniform. It was the first time I had seen him in uniform since he became a cop."

"And you haven't seen him since then?"

"No," Ken answered. "What was he doing at our house?"

The detective hesitated. "He was there to check on you."

"To check on me? Why?"

"I don't have that information right now. What about your wife? Do you know if she has seen him?"

Ken could tell there was something Detective Chet wasn't telling him. He decided to let it go for the moment. "No clue. You would have to ask her."

"And where is Mrs. Simmons?"

"She's on her way to Jamaica."

The detective stiffened. It was a subtle change that most people would have missed, but Ken saw it. He had spent a lot of time interviewing people while doing research for his books and knew when someone caught a curve ball he wasn't expecting. Ken answered the question he knew was coming next.

"I was supposed to go with her, but I have some unfinished business so I changed my mind at the last minute."

"And what business would that be?"

Ken was sure that telling the detective everything would be a mistake, but the truth was better than a lie. He looked the detective in the eyes and just came out with it.

"My wife and I are being hunted by a serial killer."

The detective surprised Ken. He simply nodded and waited for Ken to continue.

"My last book was about a serial killer that was very similar to this guy. His name is Charles Reese. He thinks that I know something about him that I don't and is afraid that I'll be able to give the police the evidence they need to put him away. I don't really know anything about him, but he doesn't seem to believe that."

The detective continued to look at Ken while scribbling notes on a legal pad on the table. "Go on."

"Well, there's a sheriff in South Dakota working on the case. You can call him to verify all of this. His name is Allen James. He's the sheriff in Woodford County. I could get you his phone number, but my cell phone is at home."

"I'll do that, but for now, why don't you tell me where you were last night?"

"Yesterday, Allen told us that Charlie was missing and based on earlier events, we assumed he was coming here to follow through with his threats. So I booked us on the first flight to Jamaica and we drove to Pittsburgh last night to catch the first flight this morning. We stayed at the Airport Hyatt."

"But at five o'clock this morning, you arrived at your house."

"Charlie contacted me last night. Apparently he was at my house and knew that we were running away. He said that if I didn't come back, he would go after my mother and Sara's parents, then go after Allen and his family."

"So you felt that coming back home would protect all those people."

"What else could I do? If I ran and he killed them, it would be my fault."

"Sure, I get it. But why didn't you call the police? We could have sent someone out to check."

"You did. And you see how that worked out. You won't catch this guy."

"But you can?"

"No." Ken sighed. "He just wants me. Then maybe he'll leave everybody else alone."

"So what about your wife?" the detective asked, jotting some notes into his notebook. "Didn't she want to come back too?"

"She was sleeping when I left the hotel. I left her a note telling her to go without me and I would catch up with her in a couple of days."

"And you're sure she's on that flight?"

"I assume she is. Why wouldn't she be?"

"Mr. Simmons, we checked. We found out about your reservations out of the country last night. We called the TSA in Pittsburgh and told them to hold you and your wife for questioning. They called us when the flight took off to let us know that neither you nor your wife checked in for the flight. We know why you didn't check in, but what about your wife? Where is she, Mr. Simmons?"

An icy chill filled Ken's body. Sara should be in Atlanta by now waiting for the flight to Kingston. What was going on? Where was she?

His vision blurred and narrowed, his insides twisted in knots. His mouth moved as he tried to speak, to tell the Detective Chet that he didn't know where she was. No words would come out.

The room was spinning. He was falling…

*

"Mr. Simmons? Are you okay?"

Ken opened his eyes. He was lying on the ground. Detective Parker was kneeling over him, hands on Ken's shoulders. A deputy was kneeling on his other side, waving something under his nose that smelled like ammonia.

Ken started to cough and choke.

"That's good, Watkins," the detective said.

Ken recognized him—it was Deputy Twitchy from his house. He still looked twitchy. Watkins stopped waving the smelling salts capsule under Ken's nose, then he and Detective Parker helped Ken back up into the chair.

"Are you okay, Mr. Simmons?" the detective asked again.

Ken nodded, still woozy from fainting and the smelling salts.

Detective Parker turned to the deputy. "Randy, why don't you get Mr. Simmons a bottle of water?" Then to Ken, "You just sit here and relax for a minute. I need to make some phone calls."

The detective left and Ken was left alone to try to make sense of what the detective had told him. Charlie must have killed Mitch, then followed Ken and Sara to Pittsburgh. While Ken was driving back, Charlie had found Sara.

Ken was starting to feel lightheaded again when Deputy Twitchy—*Watkins*, Ken corrected himself—came back with a bottle of water.

"I'm sorry about last night, Mr. Simmons," the deputy said. He didn't look at Ken directly, mostly looking at the ground. He stood with his hands in his pockets and shuffled his feet. "What happened to Mitch has us all on edge. I thought maybe you might be the guy who killed him coming back for more."

Ken looked at him, but barely heard what he said. His mind was on Sara.

"Anyway, you let me know if you need anything else. More water or coffee or a candy bar or something. I'm off duty, but I'm going to hang around for a bit."

Ken nodded, but said nothing. Watkins left the room and Ken was alone again with his thoughts. The photos of Mitch strung up in Ken's garage were still sitting on the table. After a few minutes, Ken picked them up and started going through them.

Images of violent deaths didn't easily disturb Ken. He had seen plenty of crime scene photos over the years and had become desensitized to the gore. Charles Reese's murders pushed Ken's limit. Allen had shown him a couple of the photos from Shelby Winston's murder that had been too much. Mitch's murder was almost as bad. Ken wondered if Charlie had taken Mitch's heart.

When Detective Parker came back almost half an hour later, he had another folder with him. He set it on the table and sat looking at Ken with a softer expression than he had the first time. He opened up the folder and pulled out three photos.

"I talked to the Hyatt. They confirmed you checked in last night at ten o'clock." He put down the first photo. It was from a surveillance camera behind the front desk at the Hyatt. The photo showed Ken and Sara standing at the desk. The timestamp on the photo was 9:54 p.m.

"Deputy Armstrong arrived at your house around seven p.m. It seems unlikely that you could have killed him and…mutilated the body, cleaned up, and made it to Pittsburgh by ten o'clock. So pending further developments, we're satisfied you didn't kill Mitch Armstrong."

Ken nodded. The news wasn't much of a relief to him. He was more concerned about Sara. The detective put down the next photo.

"It took some time, but they found a surveillance photo of you leaving the hotel around one o'clock which would correspond with your five o'clock arrival at your house."

Detective Parker paused, then put down the last photo. It showed Sara getting into a cab. The time stamp was 4:32 a.m.

A cab. Not the airport shuttle.

"Since we know your wife was alive at four thirty, we know you didn't kill her either. But we still don't know where she is. We are trying to get hold of someone at the taxi service to figure out where she went, but no luck yet. I understand she has family in Pittsburgh?"

"Her parents live in a suburb south of the city," Ken replied. He perked up. "That's it! She must have been freaked out that I left and went to her folks' place. But I don't have my phone."

"That's okay. Do you have their names?"

"Ben and Denise Heile."

"Okay, great. What about your wife's cell phone number?"

Ken recited the number, the only phone number he ever remembered.

"Perfect. You sit tight. We'll try Sara's cell first, then we'll see if we can't get ahold of her parents and find out if she's with them."

As the detective left, Ken sat back in his chair and closed his eyes. He should have known Sara wouldn't leave without him. He should have woken her up and taken her to her parents' house himself. At least then he would know she was safe.

He tried to convince himself she had to be at Ben and Denise's house. She certainly couldn't take a cab all the way back to Murphy Creek. Sara was probably sitting in their living room waiting for him to call. Denise would be telling her not to worry, that everything would work out. Ben was probably telling her how he always knew something like this would happen. Sara was probably telling them both to stop trying to cheer her up, that she would relax when she heard from Ken.

Just maybe everything was going to be okay.

Just maybe.

CHAPTER EIGHTEEN

KEN WAS DOZING in his chair when Detective Parker came back. He was carrying two cups of coffee. He offered one to Ken as he sat down. Ken stretched before accepting it.

"Did you get ahold of Sara?" Ken asked, trying not to sound anxious.

"No, we tried several times and left voicemails, but she hasn't called us back yet. We did talk to her parents. Apparently she did go to their house this morning. She borrowed a car and told them she was going home to help you."

"Dammit!" Ken burst out. Realizing he had just yelled, he apologized. "Sorry. I'm just worried about her. She should have gone to Jamaica. Or stayed with her parents. At least that way she'd be safe."

Detective Parker didn't respond.

"What time did Ben and Denise say she left their house?" Ken asked.

"About five thirty," the detective said after a pause.

"So she should have gotten to the house by now. Do you still have a guy watching the place?"

"We do. She hasn't shown up there yet. If she does, you'll know about it as soon as I do."

"So she must be okay. Charlie didn't get her." Ken tried to sound confident. He didn't feel it.

"I'm sure she's just fine, Mr. Simmons," the detective said, leaning forward in his chair. "You just need to remember that we're trained to deal with situations just like this."

"So what happened with Mitch?"

Ken knew that was an unfair comment. Detective Chet was just trying to make him feel better. Ken wasn't in the mood for that.

The detective sat back. "Whoever killed Deputy Armstrong must have surprised him. We're looking for that person now, so that can't happen again."

"You mean Charlie Reese."

The detective hesitated again. "Honestly, Mr. Simmons we don't know that for sure. I know you and your friend Sheriff James are convinced it's this Reese character, but that just doesn't make a lot of sense. This could be someone completely unrelated. For one thing, how would he know where you live? Besides, Charles Reese isn't the first person to threaten your life, is he?"

Ken ignored the question. "You talked to Allen?"

The detective sighed. "Yes, we talked to him. He called us yesterday with the story about Mr. Reese. The sheriff isn't convinced that this Reese guy would come all the way from the Dakotas to kill you, and I'm afraid I have to agree."

"Really? Even after Mitch, you think I'm just being paranoid?"

"We looked into the guy. He's on parole for burglary. He just doesn't seem to fit the profile of a serial killer."

"Isn't that what they say about all serial killers before they catch them?" Ken glared at the detective. "So why did Mitch go to my house?"

"The sheriff sent him as a professional courtesy to Sheriff James. Look, we're just trying to keep an open mind. Deputy Armstrong may have stumbled on someone trying to break into your house. Or maybe it was personal, someone he arrested. We're exploring all the possibilities. Including your claim about Mr. Reese."

"But you don't think it's him."

Detective Parker didn't answer.

"So Sheriff James contacts you and says there's a serial killer on his way here, you send a deputy to my house to investigate, and the deputy ends up dead. Don't you think that's just a little too much of a coincidence?"

"Look, Mr. Simmons. Let's just say you're right, that this Charles

Reese came all the way from South Dakota to kill you. What do you think we should be doing that we aren't doing already?"

Ken paused. What else was there for them to do? They had searched the area around his house and had someone posted there.

"Okay, fine. Why am I still here? You know I didn't do it, so I'm not under arrest?"

"No, sir. You are free to leave any time you like. But I would appreciate if you could stick around a little longer. At least until we can locate your wife. Your house is a crime scene right now anyway."

"I don't think so. I'm going to go find my wife."

The detective opened his mouth to respond, then closed it again. He looked at Ken for a minute, then put up his hands. "Okay. Wait here for a few minutes, then I'll see you out." As he was picking up his notepad and folders, the door opened. A uniformed deputy looked in.

"Hey, Chet. You got a minute?"

Detective Parker went to the door to talk with the deputy. After a minute the deputy left. The detective turned to Ken.

"What is it?" Ken asked. "Is it Sara?"

"No. It's Frank Shaw. Apparently, he never made it home last night. We just found his body. It looks like he was tortured and killed sometime yesterday afternoon or evening."

*

Sara was almost home when the first drops of rain splashed off the windshield. She glanced up at the clouds. Her stop in Green Bank had taken her longer than she would have liked to gas up, pee, and get breakfast to go, but she felt better for it. Looking at the sky now, she was surprised at how dark the clouds had gotten since then. She was just glad she was almost home. The rain began to come down harder as she turned on to Rawley Drive.

She had called her parents from the hotel while waiting for a cab. Of course, they had been in a panic when they found out she was on her way to their house at four thirty in the morning. Not exactly sure what to tell them, she had promised to explain everything when she got there. She had used the cab ride to figure out what to say. She was afraid trying to explain the whole psychic connection thing to them would lead to a longer conversation than she had time for.

She'd ended up telling them that Charlie Reese was a psycho fan that the police thought might try to hurt Ken. It was close enough to the truth. Her dad had started in with how it was all Ken's fault for writing those appalling crime books. He was asking for trouble, it was bound to attract the crazies. This Charlie guy just proves that the first one hadn't been a fluke, yada, yada, yada. Sara had told him there wasn't time for that now, that she needed to find Ken before he did something stupid. She had managed to talk them into letting her borrow her mom's car and was on the road by five thirty.

Now, almost four and a half hours later, the adrenaline had worn off and Sara was struggling to stay awake. Even the coffee she bought in Green Bank labeled "High Octane" wasn't enough. She was driving with the air conditioning on full blast and the windows rolled down, hoping the cold air would keep her awake.

If she could just call Ken, to hear his voice, to make sure he was okay. But the dammed Radio Quiet Zone and Ken's stupid idea to not install a landline made that impossible.

Sara rolled up her windows against the rain and clenched her teeth, trying to stay awake for the last mile and a half. She leaned forward focusing on the narrow, twisting road, trying to see through the increasing downpour. Giddy with exhaustion, she thought how ironic it would be if she drove all the way back to help Ken face a killer, just to die driving off a cliff a mile from home. Fortunately, she knew this road well and had no real trouble negotiating the sharp turns, even in the near zero visibility.

She made the final turn to the house when a figure appeared in the middle of the road. He was waving his hands over his head signaling for her to stop. She pulled the car within a few feet of the man before realizing he was a cop. Confused, she tried to process why a cop would be at her house. The cop walked up to her car and she saw it was a sheriff's deputy. She rolled down her window as he approached, his uniform soaked from the rain.

"Good morning, ma'am," the deputy said.

"What's going on?" was all Sara could manage.

"Are you Mrs. Simmons?" he asked.

"Yes. What's going on? Is Kenny okay?" Surely the only reason for a cop to be at her house was because Charlie had already found Ken and now Ken was dead.

She glanced at the deputy's name badge: Armstrong.

"I'm afraid there's been some trouble," he said.

Sara's brain finally clicked, but it was too late. The deputy's hand came up, holding a stun gun. Before Sara could react, she felt the stinging burn of fifty-thousand volts of electricity surge through her body.

*

Ken looked up as the door opened and Allen James walked into the room.

"Allen? What are you doing here?"

The lines on the sheriff's face and dark circles under his eyes made him look ten years older than the last time Ken had seen him. He was wearing civilian clothes, his badge and gun attached to his belt and a visitor ID badge on a lanyard around his neck.

"Apparently keeping you out of jail." Allen sat down in the interrogator's chair. "I got in late last night. They were still processing the scene at your house when I got there and since you weren't there, I went into town and got a room for the night. I came in to the station this morning to talk to Detective Parker and found out you were being interrogated. They wouldn't let me in to see you until they had confirmed your alibi for last night."

"Sara's missing." Ken couldn't really focus on much else.

"I heard. I also heard you had planned on taking a trip to Jamaica. Right about now, that sounds like the best plan in the world. Why didn't you go?"

Ken glanced up at the video camera in the corner of the room then back to Allen.

"Charlie contacted me."

"Contacted you?" Allen asked raising his eyebrows. "As in…"

"Yeah. As in."

"Has that happened before?"

"No. Last night was the first, and hopefully the only time. He told me he had killed a cop and if I didn't come back, he'd go after everyone I cared about. Including you and your family."

Allen sat back, rubbing his chin and thinking.

"Look, they know I didn't kill Mitch..." Ken felt a pang of guilt for being glad he hadn't been there when Charlie showed up.

"Is that the deputy Reese killed?"

"Yeah, but they don't believe it was Charlie. Even after they figured out I hadn't killed Mitch, they still think he wouldn't come all this way. They even thought I was responsible for Sara's disappearance until they talked to her parents."

"I know. If I had known you were here I would have come in earlier. It might have helped. Sorry."

"Doesn't matter now. I just want to get out of here. Do you know when they're going to let me go? They said I wasn't under arrest, so they can't hold me."

"Right now I think they are assuming that Sara will show up at the house and the deputy there will send her down here to pick you up. They'll want to talk to her too, even though they probably already realize that she doesn't know anything."

"Well I'm not going to just sit here waiting for something to happen. Charlie Reese is out there and my wife is missing. I need to find her!"

"Okay, just relax. I get it, but if you get worked up like that they'll try to come up with some way to keep you here. Remember that they lost one of their own last night, so they're going to be a little touchy. I know how they feel. Reese killed Renee Watts yesterday morning."

"Jesus." Ken clenched his teeth against the panic that was trying to take over. Charles Reese may even be worse than Cory Rivers. He shuddered at the thought. "I'm sorry, Allen. Did you tell Detective Chet?"

"I told him, but like you said, they think their guy was killed by somebody local. He thinks I'm off the reservation. He even told me to go back to South Dakota and stay out of their investigation."

"You're not going to do that, are you?"

"Hell no! I may be out of my jurisdiction, but this asshole killed one of my deputies. Only she was more than that. She was family. I've known her almost her whole life. Reese is going to pay for it." Allen stopped and took a deep breath. "Come on. Let's get you out of here and see if we can't find Sara."

*

Sara struggled against the rope that bound her hands to the legs of the chair, even though she knew it was pointless. The rope was wrapped from her wrists almost to her elbows, keeping her arms tight against the rear legs. Her ankles were secured on the outside of the front legs so that only her toes touched the floor, giving her no leverage. Not that it mattered. She was still feeling weak from the stun gun.

Charlie had carried her into Ken's office and tied her to the chair. She didn't know how long she'd been here, only that her arms and legs were tingling—either from the stun gun or from being tied up in such an awkward position. Either way, the tingling was becoming painful.

Charlie came into the room, carrying a knife. The knife was huge. Sara couldn't take her eyes off it.

"What do you want?" Sara managed to say, her voice trembling in spite of her efforts to hide her fear.

Charlie smiled, but said nothing. He walked toward her, holding the knife by the blade and slapping the handle into his other hand. As he walked, his smile faded into a scowl. Cold sweat dripped down her neck. He stopped in front of her, his feet almost under the chair. Charlie moved the blade of the knife to her throat and used it to force her chin up so she was looking at his face.

"Your fuckface husband fucked up my life and now I'm going to fuck up his," he said, almost spitting out the words. He bent down so his nose was almost touching hers. She smelled his sweat and sour breath. She tried to turn her head, but he pressed the blade of the knife harder into her jaw, forcing her to stay still.

"I had the perfect project planned out," he said. "It would have been my best one yet. But Fuckface had to go stick his nose where it didn't belong, so I had to kill her early. I didn't even have enough time to play with her. But I'm going to make up for that. I'm going to play with you instead. I don't even have to worry about being quiet here. You can scream as loud as you want and no one will hear you." His mouth twisted into a grotesque grin as he stood up and pulled the knife away from her throat. "But we have to wait for the Fuckface. I promised him he could watch. He likes to watch me." Charlie laughed.

Sara relaxed a little. He wasn't going to kill her yet.

Charlie's hands flashed out and grabbed the neck of her T-shirt. With one swift pull, he ripped it down to the waist. Sara screamed in surprise and tried to pull away.

"But that doesn't mean we can't get started without him," Charlie said, his grin widening.

Her eyes began to burn with tears when the cold steel of the knife touched her bare skin as he finished cutting away her T-shirt.

"Please, don't hurt me," Sara said, knowing how desperate and pathetic it sounded even as she said it.

Charlie stood up, holding the remains of her shirt, and laughed again, a cold, hollow sound that made Sara's flesh crawl.

"Oh, I'm going to hurt you. I'm going to hurt you in ways you can't even imagine. Maybe I'll cut Fuckface a little too. Would you like that? Watching him suffer for what he's making me do to you?" He grinned as he watched her reaction. She tried not to show it, but she knew he could see everything. Her pain. Her fear. Her anger.

"It was an accident. Ken didn't mean to hurt you. He didn't even know who you were at first." She tried to sound confident, but her voice was thin and squeaky to her ears.

"I don't care," Charlie said. "He's going to pay for fucking up my life, and if this is the last time I get to play, I'm going to enjoy it and make it last as long as I can. You'll be begging me to kill you. But I won't. Not right away. We're going to play a long game. You, me, and Fuckface."

"I won't give you the satisfaction of begging," Sara said, still trying to sound confident and failing.

That hollow laugh again. "Oh, you'll beg me. They all beg in the end. Sometimes I even cut out their tongues, if I get tired of listening to them whine. Will I get tired of listening to you, bitch?"

Sara shook her head, a jerking, uncoordinated movement. Her insides turned and twisted from her bowels to her throat. Her heart raced, her blood pounding in her ears. She tried to respond, to tell him that she would be good, but her mouth was dry and sticky and the words refused to climb over the lump in her throat.

Charlie smiled. "Good." He stepped toward her and stuffed her T-shirt in her mouth. "We won't need this after Fuckface gets here," he said, tying the gag behind her head. "But we wouldn't want you giving away the surprise, now would we?" He stood in front of her, caressing her cheek with his finger, following the line of her jaw to her neck.

Sara flinched as his finger reached the hollow below her neck. *The suprasternal notch,* she thought wildly, remembering a line from a romance film she once saw with Ken.

The knife was in Charlie's hand again, the hideous grin on his face widening. He touched the tip of the blade to her shoulder, causing her muscle to twitch under her skin. He dragged the blade down her arm, cutting just deep enough to leave a raised, red welt. His breath quickened as he slid the blade under her bra strap, cutting it with a flick of his wrist. Sara turned her head and closed her eyes so she wouldn't have to look at his lecherous face.

"Uh, uh," he breathed. "Keep your eyes open or I'll cut off your eyelids. You understand?" He placed the tip of the knife on her cheek to emphasize his point.

Sara nodded faintly, trying not to look at Charlie, but not look away either.

Charlie resumed his grotesque grin, baring his yellowed teeth this time. He let the tip of the knife fall from her cheek to her shoulder where he used it to play with her other bra strap before cutting it. His tongue slithered out of his mouth and licked his lips, sending new waves of nausea through her.

As if sensing the twisting knot in her gut, Charlie moved the knife blade to her bare stomach. Her twitching caused the point of the knife to dig into her skin. Slowly, so she could feel every slight tug, he drew the blade up to her chest. Sara began sobbing as he cut the front of her bra, no longer able to control herself. Blood oozed from the trail the knife had left from her belly button to the center of her chest. The sight of her blood and the stinging heat from the cut caused more tears to fill her eyes, blurring her vision. Charlie pulled off her bra, then stepped back and licked her blood off the blade.

"Unit twenty-three, Dispatch." The tinny sound of the radio made Sara jump.

"Duty calls," Charlie said, still smiling. "Now don't you go nowhere while I'm gone." He laughed, then turned and walked out to the deck. As soon as the door was closed, Sara broke down crying, whether from fear or pain or anger, she didn't know.

*

Ken and Allen were driving east on Route 39 toward Murphy Creek in Allen's rental car. Neither said anything. By unspoken agreement, they were headed to the Simmons' house. In spite of the deputy stationed there, Ken had a hollow, anxious feeling in his gut that Sara was in trouble. It wasn't that they hadn't been able to reach her. Cell phones were useless inside the Radio Quiet Zone anyway. It wasn't really even that the deputy at the house hadn't seen her. It was more like a sense of fear, but not his own.

He had tried to explain it to Allen when they left the sheriff's office, but he had only managed to come up with, "Sara's in trouble." To his credit, Allen didn't look at him like he was a lunatic. Probably because of all the bullshit with Charlie over the last few months.

The wipers were flying across the windshield in a useless attempt to clear off the rain so they could see the road. The downpour meant the forty-five-minute drive to Ken's house would take closer to an hour and a half unless the rain let up. Allen seemed to be determined to push the limits of safety to cut that down as much as possible. Ken, normally not a risk taker, fully supported that approach, even though his stomach turned every time he looked out the windshield and couldn't see ten feet in front of the car.

Instead, he stared out of the passenger window at the guardrail that separated the roadway from the gulley holding Knapp Creek. Occasionally the rain would slow enough that he managed a glimpse of the creek itself, already swollen with runoff from the surrounding hills.

"Everything's going to be okay," Allen said, breaking the silence.

Ken just continued to stare out the window.

"Ken, listen to me. Sara's going to be okay. Charlie doesn't want her. He wants you. Even if he managed to find her, and I'm not saying he did, but even if he did, he knows that if he hurts her, he'll never get to you."

Ken turned to look at Allen. "I don't believe that, and neither do you." He turned back to watch the guardrail flash by through the rain.

"I do believe that. In fact, I know it. I've interrogated this guy. He's arrogant, but he's also cautious and meticulous. How do you think he's gotten away with killing all those people for so long?"

Ken noticed that Allen didn't say *women*.

"And part of that is not taking any chances," Ken replied, still staring out the window. "Leaving her alive would be risking a witness."

"Yeah, but he'll plan on keeping her alive until he can get you."

Ken grunted in reply.

"But he's not counting on me. He wouldn't expect me to come all this way, even if he suspects that I figured out where he was going. Besides, if he had Sara, don't you think he would try to...you know, contact you?"

"He doesn't need to contact me. He knows where I'm going. So did Sara. She would have gone straight to the house from her parents' place, which is exactly where Charlie would have gone. He's there, and he has her."

"Come on, Ken. There's a deputy sheriff up there checking in every ten minutes. If Sara had shown up there, we'd know."

"He's already killed one deputy. Two, if you count yours. What's one more?"

Allen fell silent for a while. Ken knew bringing up Renee's death would hit a sore spot. He didn't care. He was tired of Allen trying to convince him that he was wrong.

After a while, Allen continued, but his voice was subdued. "Renee was home alone getting ready for bed. He caught her off guard. As for Deputy Armstrong... Well, Sheriff Moore didn't take me seriously. He thought I was being paranoid about Charlie coming here, so I don't think he sent Armstrong out with the full picture. I put Armstrong's death on Moore. He screwed the pooch on that one. I think he knows it too."

The rain started to slow about the time Allen turned onto Route 28, easing their progress. Neither of them said anything more until they reached Murphy Creek a few minutes later.

"Mrs. Harper makes the best pies in the county," Ken said absently as they passed Billy's.

"Huh?"

"Marianne Harper. Her husband owns that store," Ken said, pointing to the general store. "She has a little bakery in the back. She makes fresh doughnuts every morning. And her pies are legendary. Remember the apple pie you had when you were here a few weeks ago? Marianne made that. Sara tried to pass it off like she made it, but Sara couldn't make a pie from scratch if her life depended on it. Besides, I know Marianne's apple pie anywhere." Ken turned away to stare out the window again. "I never told her I knew," he said, almost to himself.

Up ahead, flashing lights from two sheriff's cruisers cut through the gloom. They were parked in front of the barn where the flea market was held on the weekends. Yellow police tape closed off the parking lot.

"That must be where they found Frank."

"Who?"

"Frank Shaw. He owns the diner we just passed. Charlie killed him."

"How do you know that?"

"Who else would do it? Charlie must have tortured him to find out where our house is."

"Listen, Ken. You'll get your chance to tell Sara about the pie. I promise you that." Allen was trying to sound convincing, but Ken didn't buy it.

He knew in his heart that Sara was already dead.

CHAPTER NINETEEN

ALLEN PULLED THE car up to the house and parked next to the deputy's cruiser. Ken's truck was parked where the deputy had left it the night before, next to Sara's. Denise Hiele's Camry wasn't there. Maybe Sara hadn't made it home yet. But then where was she? Maybe the deputy watching the house had sent her to the sheriff's station.

Allen turned off the engine. "Where's the deputy?"

Ken looked around. The deputy wasn't in his cruiser and he wasn't standing in the shelter of the covered front porch.

"Maybe he's out back taking a leak?" Ken said. Wishful thinking, he knew.

"Maybe, but let's be careful." Allen pulled out his cell phone, saw he had no signal, then put it back. "Dammit. You don't have a landline either, do you?"

"I like my quiet," Ken responded. "Maybe I should get one of those Internet phone services." In hindsight, the decision to not have a telephone didn't seem like a good idea.

"Stay here," Allen said, opening the car door.

"I'm coming with you," Ken answered, opening his own door.

"Dammit, Ken, listen to me. Stay here until I can find the deputy. Then we can all go inside and figure out what to do."

Ken's heart was racing. He was afraid. He was afraid of Charlie. He was afraid of the things Charlie would do to him if he caught him. He was afraid of dying. But mostly, he was afraid of what Charlie would do to Sara, if he hadn't killed her already. That fear overrode the others. If Sara was inside and still alive, he wasn't going to sit in the car while Charlie butchered her.

This was his fault, his responsibility. He couldn't be the spectator this time, reporting the story to his fans. This time he had to be the hero of the story. Even if the hero was destined to die.

Ken got out of the car and closed the door. Allen turned around and looked like he was going to say something, then decided better of it.

"At least stay behind me," he said. He turned back toward the house and drew his gun. Holding it in front of him with both hands, pointed toward the ground, Allen walked toward the front door. Ken absurdly thought how unlike Dirty Harry Allen looked as he followed.

Allen tried the front door, but it was locked. He held out his hand and motioned to Ken for the key. After unlocking the door, he pulled Ken to one side.

"Let me check the hallway before you come in," Allen whispered to Ken.

"Okay," he answered and huddled next to the door.

Allen swung the door open and snapped his gun up, moving it left to right, then disappeared into the doorway. Ken waited for what seemed like an eternity. He felt ridiculous, cowering on the porch next to his own front door.

This was his home. Why should he be afraid to go in? Why should Charlie be in control of his actions?

Ken strained to hear anything coming from inside. The wet air muffled the sounds of the woods around the house. The only noise was the water dripping from the trees. He shivered in the dampness.

He had just decided he wasn't going to wait any longer when Allen emerged from the house.

"The hallway's clear and so is the front room," Allen said in a low voice. "There's blood on the floor, but it looks like it's been there for a while. Probably from Deputy Armstrong. Stay behind me, and stay quiet."

Allen slipped back through the opening. Ken took a deep breath,

DARK TIES

trying to calm his nerves, then swung around the doorframe and into the hallway.

The gray daylight filtering in through the windows at the other end of the hallway was too dim for them to see anything at this end. Only the open door behind him provided any light at all, though it was enough to highlight a dark brown trail of dried blood leading from the front room to the entryway door.

Ken tried the light switch, jumping at the sound. The click sounded like a hammer in the stifling silence of the hallway. No light.

Allen looked back at the noise. "Already tried that," he said, his voice barely louder than a whisper. He shrugged, then continued down the hallway, stepping quietly and staying close to the wall. Ken followed, trying to be just as quiet. His stomach was in knots. He paused at the doorway to the front room.

The room appeared to be undisturbed, except for the area just inside the door. The blood trail led to a roughly circular reddish-brown spot on the floor. A memorial to where Mitch Armstrong had taken his last breath. A kid who had looked up to Ken, wanted to help him write his make-believe stories. Another fan Ken blew off. Another victim of his failure.

A rubber glove was lying on the back of a chair nearby. Probably left by one of the forensic technicians. Ken thought the room looked surprisingly clean for having been the scene of a murder. Other than the dried blood and a forgotten glove, it looked just like it had when he and Sara left the night before.

Then he remembered the pictures Detective Chet had shown him. Those had been in his garage. He shuddered. At some point, he would have to go to the garage. It wouldn't be as clean as his front room.

Ken turned his attention back to the hallway. Allen was shining a flashlight into the next room, a guest bedroom suite with its own full bath and outside door to the deck. Ken and Sara hardly ever went in there. Since they moved in, his mother was the only one to ever use it. She had trouble with stairs because of a bad hip. Sara's parents preferred the upstairs guest suite.

He wondered if they would ever speak to him again, even if Sara turned out to be okay.

Ken stopped next to Allen just as he was closing the door to the guest room. He looked behind him for the dozenth time since walking through the front door. Between the ticking of the grandfather clock and the pounding of his heart, Ken wasn't sure he would be able to hear a herd of elephants coming up behind him.

But then Allen whispered to him and he realized he could hear just fine.

"You okay?" Allen asked.

Ken nodded. He didn't even try to speak for fear of something more than words coming out. Allen looked at him for a minute, then turned and moved on to the next door, the kitchen. Ken followed, his heart rate increasing with each step. By the time they reached the kitchen door, he could barely hear the clock over the blood pounding in his ears. The pressure in his head and chest was making his breathing difficult. He swallowed hard, trying to calm himself with little success.

Allen was standing against the wall next to the doorway to the kitchen, his gun pointed up in front of him. He looked at Ken, then nodded toward the wall. Ken took the hint and moved closer to the wall. Allen took a couple of deep breaths, then peeked his head around the doorway. Apparently not seeing anything, he turned on his flashlight again and scanned the room, his gun hand resting on the wrist of the hand with the flashlight so he could simultaneously sweep the room with both. His first scan complete, Allen stepped into the kitchen for a better look.

Ken heard the click of the front door closing and spun around, expecting to see Charlie Reese rushing down the hallway toward him.

The hallway was empty. With the front door closed, the front half of the hallway was too dark to make out details, but there was no one standing there.

Allen came back out of the kitchen, looking toward the front door. "What is it?"

"Must have been the wind," Ken replied, his voice dry and hoarse.

"Okay. Kitchen's empty. Let's check out your office."

Ken stepped back to let Allen take the lead. Allen paused to run his flashlight over the bathroom, the last room on the left side of the hallway, then they moved to the door to Ken's office.

The door used to be the back door to the cabin before Ken had the addition put on. He had kept the heavy oak door, reversing its frame so it swung into the new office instead of into the hallway, and removing the weather-tight threshold. The finish was new too, the door having weathered decades of sun, rain, and wind. Ken had always liked the hefty piece of wood. He had felt it set the stage for the magnificence that a visitor was about to experience behind the door.

As he stood in front of it now, all of that seemed like pompous bullshit. How he had ever gotten so pretentious?

Ken found himself wishing that he had never bought the house out in the middle of nowhere. His desire for solitude had probably cost Sara her life. He swore if she was still alive, he would sell the damn house and move back to Pittsburgh like she wanted. He would deal with the occasional overeager fan with tall fences, or guard dogs, or something else less extreme than moving to the middle of nowhere. Even hiring a private security service would be more practical.

And if she wasn't alive...

He couldn't bring himself to think about that.

An odd thought occurred to him as he stood in the hall, looking at the door to his office. He had most enjoyed writing when they had lived in the small apartment in Garfield and his office had been a desk in the corner of the living room. He would write when Sara was at work or asleep instead of shutting himself off in some fancy throne room dedicated to his own self-worship.

"I'm so sorry," Ken whispered, surprising himself. He hadn't intended to say it out loud.

"What was that?" Allen whispered back.

"Nothing. Let's go." Ken put his back to the wall next to the door and Allen positioned himself on the other side. He nodded to Ken, who nodded back. Allen turned the doorknob and pushed the door open. He brought up his gun and pointed it through the doorway.

"Oh, shit!" Allen said and ran into the room. Ken was startled by the loudness of his voice after so much quiet. He tried to follow, but couldn't get his feet to move. He stood with his back against the wall, frozen with dread. In his mind, he screamed for his legs to move. Finally, he pulled his left foot off the ground and took a step toward the door. His feet felt disconnected and heavy, like they were asleep and tied to cinderblocks. Slowly, each step a herculean effort, he managed to move to the doorway and look in.

Allen was kneeling next to a chair that was covered by a red and white blanket. Only it wasn't a blanket. It was a large pillow. Confused, Ken stared at the chair. He dragged his numb, weighted feet forward another step.

No, it wasn't a blanket and it wasn't a pillow.

It was the torso of a naked woman, covered in blood.

Ken stood still, his mind racing, trying to grab on to a thought or a feeling. Anything at all. For the second time that day, he felt the world swimming around him, his eyesight growing dim.

"Sara? Can you hear me?" It was Allen's voice.

Ken's mind finally cleared. The spinning ground to a stop, and his eyes focused on the chair. It was Sara. She was tied to the chair by her hands and feet, her head slumped down on her chest. She had cuts on her arms and legs, on her stomach, and on her breasts. Between her legs, the blade of a large Bowie knife was stuck into the chair.

Ken's paralysis broke and he ran to her. He tried calling her name, but only managed a hoarse cough. The chair had been placed in the exact center of the room, a mere twenty feet from the door, a few steps away. Ken ran and ran, one long stride after another. The trek was long enough for Ken to have a debate with himself about whether she was dead or alive. Finally, reaching the chair, he fell to his knees in front of her and found his voice.

"Sara? Sara!" Ken reached out to touch her cheek. It was cool and covered with sticky blood. He ignored the sensation and raised her head in his hands.

"Sara, wake up!"

Allen pressed two fingers to the side of her neck.

"She's alive," Allen said. "We need to get her help. These cuts don't look that deep, but there's a lot of them. It looks like she's lost a lot of blood."

Allen pulled the knife out of the chair and cut away the rope from her left arm.

"Please wake up." Ken kneeled down in front of Sara and grabbed her freed hand while Allen started on the rope securing her left leg.

A crashing bang echoed through the room. Ken felt a sharp pain in his ears and immediately his head filled with a loud ringing. He sat back on his heels, his head spinning again, but this time from the concussive noise that had exploded around him.

He looked to Allen, to ask him what happened. Allen's face was blank. There was a wet spot on the side of his head that he hadn't noticed before. As Ken watched, the spot grew wetter. Then Allen slumped over, his head landing in Sara's lap. Red liquid began to drip from the spot on his head onto Sara's leg.

From behind him, Ken thought he heard someone laughing, but all he could really hear was the ringing. He was trying to comprehend the image his eyes were sending to his brain, but his mind wouldn't focus.

Why did Allen have his head on his wife's lap? He was supposed to be cutting the ropes off. And why was his head ringing? It was like he was inside a church bell after a wedding. Ken brought his hands up to his ears and pressed them into his head trying to make the pain and noise go away.

Something pressed into his back. A voice made its way through the ringing in his ears.

"Stand up, Fuckface!"

In spite of his impaired hearing, Ken recognized the voice and suddenly understood. Charlie. Now he had the gun in Ken's back.

Ken had used the phrase "his heart sank" in his stories many times over the years, but he had never understood how real the feeling was. He actually felt the sinking feeling in his chest as he came to understand that he had failed.

He had failed to save Sara. And because of his failure, Allen was dead too. And Mitch Armstrong and Renee Watts. And whatever deputy had been here to watch the house this morning. Soon he would be dead and Sara too. And who knows how many more people Charlie Reese would go on to kill because of him.

"I said stand up!"

Ken managed to get to his feet, his eyes never leaving the limp figure of his wife, covered in tortured slashes inflicted by the monster that was standing behind him. The body of his friend was slumped over her lap, a bullet hole in his head, one hand still holding the knife he had been using to try to free Sara. A pointless thought formed in his head—it was probably the same knife that had inflicted the wounds on Sara's body.

Anger rose up inside him, almost volcanic. Charlie Reese wouldn't get away with this. Not as long as he was still alive.

Ken took a deep breath and dropped his hands to his sides. He had never been much of a fighter, but he had read enough to know if he could get around fast enough, surprise Charlie, he might be able to knock the gun away from him and get the upper hand. Charlie was a predator, but he wasn't a lion or a bear. He was more like a house cat, relying on surprise to render his victims powerless, then taking his time to kill. He wouldn't be ready for an aggressive attack. As long as Ken could move quick enough to catch him off guard, there was a chance.

Ken took another deep breath and clenched his fists. Gathering all of his strength he spun around—

Ken's head exploded with white light as something hard smashed into the side of his skull. He collapsed to the floor, unable to move. Charlie was standing over him, grinning. He was wearing a deputy sheriff's uniform and holding a gun. There were dark stains on the blue shirt. Sara's blood.

"Did you really think I wouldn't expect that, Fuckface?"

Charlie holstered the gun. Still grinning like a schoolboy on prom night, he bent down and grabbed Ken's wrists and pulled him a few feet away to another chair that was set up facing Sara. Ken had been so focused on her, he hadn't noticed the other chair. Another failure.

Handcuffs were attached to the back legs of the chair and zip ties attached to the front. Ken tried to clear his head. If Charlie managed to handcuff him, it was over. He was still weak, the blow to the head accentuating the nausea he had been feeling all morning. He tried in vain to get his feet under him so he could stand, maybe spring up into Charlie's face, knocking him backward and off balance. He managed to bend his knees, but when Charlie dropped his wrist, he was left lying on the floor like a newborn baby unable to move on his own.

Charlie grabbed Ken under the arms and dragged him into the chair. Ken knew his last chance was about to slip away, so he tried to fling himself forward, only to have Charlie's forearm smash into his throat. He collapsed into the chair, his breath hitching from the blow to the neck. By the time he could breathe again, Charlie had cuffed his wrists to the rear legs of the chair and zip-tied his ankles to the front legs.

The police radio on Charlie's hip sparked to life. "Unit twenty-three, Dispatch."

Charlie grinned at Ken and walked out of the room, closing the door behind him. Still dazed, Ken tried to focus on Sara. He thought he could see her chest rising and falling. She was still alive. He felt a mixture of relief and fear. If she was dead so she wouldn't have to endure any more of Charlie's torture. Which led to the thought that if it hadn't been for him, she wouldn't have had to endure any of it.

"Sara?" Ken tried to keep his voice low enough so Charlie couldn't hear him. "Sara, I don't know if you can hear me or not, but I want you to know I'm sorry. I'm sorry I got you into this mess. I want you to know that. If there was anything I could do to take it back I would. I love you. Seeing you like this, knowing what that monster did to you…" His voice cracked and he couldn't get any more words to come out. His vision blurred as tears filled his eyes and began running down his cheeks. He tried to talk to Sara some more. Even though she couldn't hear him, he needed to tell her, needed her to know he was sorry.

Charlie came back into the room before Ken could speak again.

"Sorry, old buddy. That was the office. They wanted to know if you and Sheriff Shitforbrains had showed up. I told them you was here drinking coffee and hooting it up with your bitch over there. Then they gave me the good news: they aren't sending any more doughnut eaters up here. They said since everyone was accounted for, and you aren't a suspect in the little piggy's death, there was no reason to waste any more resources watching your house."

Charlie's excitement rose as Ken's hope fell.

"Oh, and they wanted me to tell you to follow your original plan to get out of town and let the professionals handle it." Charlie laughed, a sound that even Ken couldn't describe. A hollow warbling sound that made his skin crawl.

"I was debating whether to kill you quick or to take you somewhere else so we could have a few days of fun, but now we can just stay here!" Charlie seemed almost giddy. "Oh, we won't have days here. Eventually they'll figure out that the other fucker they had watching the place never came back and they'll come looking for him. But until then, we can play all we want."

Charlie took off the deputy's duty belt and pulled out the stun gun. He dropped the belt on the couch.

"They left me some new toys to play with," Charlie said. Ken wasn't sure if Charlie was talking to him or to himself. "This one is really fun. Your bitch got to play with it a little bit. I think she liked it, but she's just another fucking whore anyway, so of course she liked it. I should let you play with it. See what you think." He dropped the stun gun next to the duty belt.

"I guess it doesn't matter what you think. I like it. It makes the catch so much easier. I don't have to waste time coming up with a way to catch them from behind and covering their mouths until they pass out. One little click and *BAM*, they're ready to be secured. It leaves more time for the fun part. I hope it's more reliable than their ankle monitors. Those things are worthless. A strip of aluminum on the contacts, and a coat hanger for the latch." He laughed. "What a joke."

He bent down and pulled out a collapsible baton from the discarded duty belt. He turned it over in his hands, admiring it. He looked up at Ken and smiled, then swung his arm down, flicking his wrist to open the baton.

"They call this one an ASP-21. Do you think they called it that to make it sound scary?" He chuckled, admiring the baton again. "You're the writer. Is that what you would do?"

Charlie walked back across the room toward Ken, tapping the baton on the palm of his hand.

"You know, your little cunt is a bonus. I figured you'd leave her behind, but I never expected her to come after you. You don't know how happy I was to see her. Saved me a lot of work chasing her down."

"It's me you want," Ken said. "Leave her alone."

Charlie looked at Ken with mock sympathy. "Aw, you care about your little cunt bitch, don't you?" His face melted into a snarl. "Too fucking bad. I had a good thing going until you came along and fucked it up. You and your piece of shit book. But you got the story wrong, Fuckface. I'm the hero of this story! The sheriff doesn't bust in to save the day this time!"

Charlie's grin returned.

"And that's not the only thing you got wrong. You thought it all started with Sandy. Oh, she was my first project, but she wasn't my first ride. That trophy goes to Gracie. She wasn't planned, I just found her at a bar and did her that night. Turned out she was some cop's girlfriend. Who knew? I call her January."

His grin faded.

"I almost had my full calendar, but you fucked that up. I'm going to make you suffer long and slow for that."

He sneered at Ken and poked him in the chest with the baton.

"Besides, I promised you I would let you watch. I got started without you, though. Sorry, but I couldn't help myself. Your bitch was begging for it anyway, so I had to give it to her. Hope you don't mind. There's lots more, though, so don't feel bad. There's just one thing: we don't want you trying to go nowhere while we play, so—"

Charlie swung the baton in a full arc down onto Ken's knee. He felt the crunch as his kneecap shattered and a blast of pain shot up and down his leg. He screamed.

"Hmph," Charlie grunted. "I've always been partial to knives, but that was kind of fun. Maybe I should look into expanding my horizons." He swung again, breaking Ken's other kneecap and causing another explosive scream. "Yep, I think I like that. It would probably work good on noses and mouths too, don't you think?"

Charlie stood back and looked at Ken like he was admiring his work. "That'll keep you in your seat. You don't want to miss any of the show."

Ken tried to focus through the pain. Charlie's laugh echoed through the ringing in his ears. Another wave of nausea rolled over him.

"I'll play with you some more later. Right now, it's time to play with your little whore, and we wouldn't want you passing out during the fun, now would we." He grinned again, then turned to look at Sara, his back to Ken.

"We can use this to play in other ways too." He tightened his fists around the baton's rubber grip. "How about I fuck your bitch with it? You wanna see that, Fuckface?"

Ken tried to move, to throw himself at Charlie, anything to at least try to stop him from hurting Sara any more, but he was paralyzed by the shooting pain in his knees and the throbbing ache on the back of his head.

"No," he managed to say. "It's my fault. Take it out on me. Let Sara go."

"It is your fucking fault." Charlie looked back at Ken. "That's why you get to watch while I play with your precious little whore monkey."

"You won't get away with this," Ken said, his voice cracking through his pain. "They'll know it was you."

"Who gives a fuck? They won't catch me. They're too fucking stupid." He snarled at Ken. "You know what I figured out while I was driving here? I figured out that I'm a fucking god! I've been giving the pigs too much credit. Since I stopped worrying about them, I've had the best fucking two days of my life! And once you're gone, nobody will know where I am."

Ken's mind raced, trying to find something to say or do to keep Charlie away from Sara. His eyes still burned with tears, only now they were as much from anger and frustration as they were from grief.

"Please," Ken said. "Let Sara go. She didn't do anything."

Charlie let loose his hideous laugh again. He looked down at Sara. She was still sitting unconscious, her head slumped to her chest.

"Her death is on you, Fuckface," he said. "If you had just left me alone, I wouldn't have to be here." He licked his lips, still looking at Sara. "But in a way, I'm glad. She's going to be a lot of fun. Besides, you did show me that I was being too careful, so I guess I have to thank you for that."

"I didn't know," Ken pleaded.

"Keep on begging, Fuckface." Charlie laughed again as he walked over to Sara.

"No!"

"Look at this," Charlie mocked, ignoring Ken's cries. "I think the sheriff's trying to make a move on your bitch, Fuckface. Well, there'll be enough of her to go around. Especially when I get done carving her up. Everybody can have a piece or two!"

Charlie reached down and grabbed the neck of Allen's shirt and lifted him off Sara's lap. "Sorry, Shitforbrains, your turn is up. It's my turn now!" He threw Allen's lifeless body aside and kneeled down in front of Sara.

Ken tried to turn his head away, but he couldn't. He didn't want to watch her being butchered, didn't want to see his wife pay for his failure, her blood spilling out on the floor and her life draining away while he sat helpless. He tried again to throw himself forward. All he managed to do was rock his chair, sending another bolt of pain up from his shattered knees.

"Don't you touch her!"

Charlie ignored him, leering at Sara's limp body, his tongue shooting out of his mouth to moisten his lips. He grabbed her hair and pulled he head up.

"Sara!"

"Now where were we—"

A flash of steel flew up into Charlie's throat, cutting off his words in mid-sentence. His hands shot up as he pulled away, trying to stand. Staggering back, he turned toward Ken, his eyes wide in fear and surprise.

Ken stared, unbelievingly, at the monster staggering toward him. Charlie's mouth opened and closed, wordlessly, his hands on his throat. Blood oozed from between his fingers.

Then Ken saw Sara. She was glaring at Charlie, her face scowling with hatred of the man who had hurt her. In her hand, the Bowie knife dripped with blood.

Charlie fell to his knees in front of Ken. His mouth was still moving, like he was trying to speak. The only sound that came out was a wet gurgle, then blood started to bubble out from his lips. He fell forward, one hand grabbing Ken's leg, leaving a trail of blood on his pants. Charlie rolled over as he hit the floor at Ken's feet. He stared at Ken, still trying to speak. A final gurgling gasp escaped from his lips. Charlie's cold, dead eyes stared up at Ken.

"Fuck you, you piece of shit!" Sara shouted, then she burst into tears.

*

Ken and Sara sat in the kitchen with Detective Parker answering questions while the paramedics tended to their injuries. With two dead deputies, the detective wouldn't let the paramedics take them until they had each given a statement. He promised to be quick and to follow up with them after they had been treated at the hospital.

After she killed Charlie, Sara had managed to get herself free, and then free Ken. He had used the police radio to call for help. They had helped each other to the kitchen, neither of them wanting to be in the same room with Charlie, even if he was dead. Sara was weak, but in better shape than Ken with his shattered kneecaps and probable concussion. Ken had wrapped Sara in a coat she kept by the back door, then they had waited for help to arrive, sitting on the kitchen floor, holding each other without talking.

Detective Parker had arrived before the ambulance with two deputy sheriffs. After confirming that Allen and Charlie were both dead, he had sent the deputies to look for their missing man before coming back to the kitchen. He had helped Ken and Sara into chairs and asked them to go over everything they could recall.

Sara had recounted what had happened to her since she arrived at the house that morning. Then Ken had related what happened to him and Allen. While they were talking, the paramedics had arrived.

In spite of the tear-streaked blood on her cheeks, she had never looked so beautiful to him. He wondered if she would ever forgive him for the pain he had caused her. How could she? How could anybody? He was the one who had insisted they move to the middle of nowhere. He had brought Charlie into their lives. He hadn't been there for her when Charlie attacked her, which he had only done to get to Ken.

His heart ached, another phenomenon he had written about numerous times without ever truly understanding. All the people who had died because of him. Allen, Frank Shaw, Mitch and the other deputy, Allen's deputy. But as hard as it would be to live with their deaths on his hands, their families would be the ones to truly suffer. At least Sara was alive.

Ken was determined to do something to help all those families. Especially Allen's wife and kids. If not for Allen, he and Sara would probably be dead, too. Now his wife was without her husband and his kids without their father. He would have to find some way to help them, even though Allen's wife probably wouldn't even talk to him. He would find a way.

One of the deputies came in looking like he had just lost his breakfast. He pulled Detective Parker aside to talk to him. Ken's ears were still ringing, but he managed to catch the gist of the conversation. They had found Deputy Jacob's body in the garage. Apparently, Charlie had taken out some of his frustrations on him while waiting for Ken.

While Detective Chet was talking to the deputy, Ken turned to Sara. "I love you. I'm so sorry. I'm going to quit writing. I don't want to put you through anything like this again."

Sara gave him a weak smile. "If you quit writing I'll kick your rear end, Simmons. You do that and Charlie wins. I didn't go through all this so he could win."

Ken put his arms around her and held her close. He didn't know what to say to her. All he knew for sure was that he was the luckiest man alive.

EPILOGUE

CHARLES FRANKLIN REESE, resident of Ashford, South Dakota, was killed yesterday in the home of bestselling author K. Elliot Simmons. Reese, suspected in the murders of eight women in and around Woodford County, South Dakota over the last ten years, was killed by Simmons' wife, Sara, in a struggle that left Mr. and Mrs. Simmons suffering from multiple injuries. They are both recovering at Pocahontas Memorial Hospital in Buckeye, West Virginia. Reese is also suspected of killing two Pocahontas County deputies, Mitchell Armstrong and Austin Jacobs, as well as Woodford County, South Dakota Sheriff Allen James and Deputy Renee Watts.

Authorities have released very little information regarding why Mr. Reese was at the Simmons' home outside of Murphy Creek, West Virginia, saying only that Mrs. Simmons killed Reese in self-defense and no charges will be filed against her.

Drina Burton, better known as Madam Drina, set down the newspaper and smiled.

"We got him, Lexi. Rest in peace."

Her plan worked in the end. Maybe not the way she had initially hoped, but the bastard got what was coming to him.

She was actually amazed at how it had turned out. Her curse had gotten him arrested, but somehow the cops had never put together that he was the one who had killed all those girls.

And then the writer just happened to show up at her tent.
Well, luck was as good a tool as any other.
"Hey, Drina! You ready? Gates open in five!"
"I'm coming!"

ACKNOWLEDGEMENTS

I've had a lot of help putting this novel together, and there's no way I can mention everybody by name; I'd have to write another book just to thank everyone individually. There are, however, a few I would like to mention.

First of all, my wife. Writing a piece of work like this is tough on the psyche, but it was probably worse for her. She had to put up with all my requests to read particularly disturbing passages to see if I've gone too far or not far enough or if the character reactions felt realistic. And then somehow manage to go to sleep in the same bed without keeping a knife under the pillow. At least, I don't think she put a knife under her pillow…

Then, of course, all of my beta readers. Anndee, Anne, Chris, Dan, Laura, Michelle, Pam, and others. I really appreciate their feedback, the good and the bad. I particularly want to thank Detective Matt: his feedback on the law enforcement aspects was incredibly helpful, even when I didn't take his advice because I felt the story needed to diverge from reality (that means mistakes regarding law enforcement procedures and equipment are mine, not Matt's).

And special thanks to my editor, Holly Atkinson (http://evileyeediting.com/). Her advice and feedback have been invaluable. Thanks for making me work harder than I wanted to!

I also want to mention Jaye Wells (http://jayewells.com/). Her help with streamlining the opening, navigating the publishing world, and general feedback has been incredible. I really appreciate it. If you like urban fantasy or dystopian vampire stories, check out her books!

And finally, for all my readers, thanks for reading. I hope you enjoyed this little story. If you were entertained, then I've done my job. If you were disturbed, then I've done my job well. Sleep tight!

Made in the USA
Middletown, DE
19 May 2022